BREANNA'S SURRENDER

GUARDIANS OF ALBA
BOOK THREE

JAYNE CASTEL

WINTER MIST PRESS

All characters and situations in this publication are fictitious, and any resemblance to living persons is purely coincidental.

Breanna's Surrender, by Jayne Castel

Published by Winter Mist Press

ISBN: 978-0-473-59268-4 (paperback)

Edited by Tim Burton
Cover design by Winter Mist Press
Cover photography courtesy of www.shutterstock.com
Dagger vector image courtesy of www.pixabay.com

Visit Jayne's website: www.jaynecastel.com

***

For Marita and Quinn

***

Historical Romances by Jayne Castel

DARK AGES BRITAIN

The Kingdom of the East Angles series
Night Shadows (prequel novella)
Dark Under the Cover of Night (Book One)
Nightfall till Daybreak (Book Two)
The Deepening Night (Book Three)
The Kingdom of the East Angles: The Complete Series

The Kingdom of Mercia series
The Breaking Dawn (Book One)
Darkest before Dawn (Book Two)
Dawn of Wolves (Book Three)
The Kingdom of Mercia: The Complete Series

The Kingdom of Northumbria series
The Whispering Wind (Book One)
Wind Song (Book Two)
Lord of the North Wind (Book Three)
The Kingdom of Northumbria: The Complete Series

DARK AGES SCOTLAND

The Warrior Brothers of Skye series
Blood Feud (Book One)
Barbarian Slave (Book Two)
Battle Eagle (Book Three)
The Warrior Brothers of Skye: The Complete Series

The Pict Wars series
Warrior's Heart (Book One)
Warrior's Secret (Book Two)
Warrior's Wrath (Book Three)

The Pict Wars: The Complete Series

Novellas
Winter's Promise

MEDIEVAL SCOTLAND

The Brides of Skye series
The Beast's Bride (Book One)
The Outlaw's Bride (Book Two)
The Rogue's Bride (Book Three)
The Brides of Skye: The Complete Series

The Sisters of Kilbride series
Unforgotten (Book One)
Awoken (Book Two)
Fallen (Book Three)
Claimed (Epilogue novella)

The Immortal Highland Centurions series
Maximus (Book One)
Cassian (Book Two)
Draco (Book Three)
The Laird's Return (Epilogue festive novella)

Stolen Highland Hearts series
Highlander Deceived (Book One)
Highlander Entangled (Book Two)
Highlander Forbidden (Book Three)

Guardians of Alba series
Nessa's Seduction (Book One)
Fyfa's Sacrifice (Book Two)
Breanna's Surrender (Book Three)

Epic Fantasy Romances
by Jayne Castel

Light and Darkness series
Ruled by Shadows (Book One)
The Lost Swallow (Book Two)
Path of the Dark (Book Three)
Light and Darkness: The Complete Series

"You will never know love unless you surrender to it."
—Katherine Reback

1

WHOLLY DISREPUTABLE

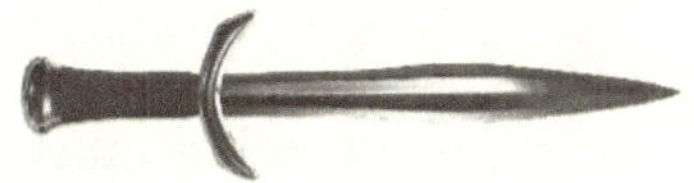

Perth, Scotland

December, 1306

SHE COULD HEAR the brawling from outside in the street. Shouts and curses echoed through the thick stone and timber walls, followed by the crash of crockery.

Halting, Breanna pulled her cloak close about her. It was a freezing, sunless day, and she longed to huddle next to a roaring fire. Instead, she had an important task she could no longer put off.

Breanna peered up at the run-down façade of the alehouse and frowned. This was where the mercenary she was looking for was supposed to be drinking. However, she didn't feel like fighting her way through a brawl to reach him. Remaining where she was, Breanna considered her next move. *Maybe it would be wise to wait?*

A cart trundled by then, laden with turnips and kale bound for market, drawn by a stocky garron. As it passed, the pony lifted its tail and left a steaming line of manure behind it.

Breanna's mouth pursed as she glanced around her. The alehouse was on one of Perth's shabbiest streets—a fetid alleyway that stank of piss and now horse shit. A brothel sat opposite, and one of the whores who stood on the steps in the hope of beckoning men in was giving Breanna an assessing look.

Breanna raised an eyebrow, returning the woman's bold stare. Aye, her blue cloak and kirtle made folk curious. There were rumors all over the Highlands—some of which had reached Lowland towns like Perth—of the mysterious blue-robed women who brought news of rebellion and hope.

Breanna was one of them: a Guardian of Alba. For centuries now, her order had protected Scotland from invaders, although, of late, they'd met their greatest challenge.

The English and the hated Edward Longshanks.

Breanna's smile faded. *Curse the bastard.* He was getting on in years now—why couldn't he just die?

She was considering this, and wondering if his son would cause the Scots as much trouble when he took the throne, when the door to the alehouse flew open, and a man hurtled out onto the street.

He sprawled facedown in one of the piles of fresh dung the pony had left in its wake.

A group of men crowded out onto the street behind him.

"Had enough, Stewart?" One of them, a huge man with a bald head and high-colored face, drawled. "Or do ye want to come back inside for another thrashing?"

Breanna, who'd moved back against the wall at the men's arrival, tensed, apprehension tightening her belly. *Stewart? Surely not?*

Her gaze shifted to where the man rolled into a sitting position and wiped the dung off his face. He then spat out a curse. "I'm always ready to give ye a fat lip, Ross Duncan," he slurred.

Breanna grimaced, her hands clenching at her sides. The man was rotten drunk.

This comment drew a few guffaws of laughter. And then Duncan sneered, rolled up the sleeves of his lèine, and approached the man, his meaty fists flexing.

His opponent rolled to his feet and staggered. He then shook his head as if trying to clear it.

Breanna studied him, misgiving wreathing up within her like wood smoke. She really hoped this man wasn't

Cameron Stewart—former captain of the Stirling Guard turned mercenary, and the warrior she'd been sent to find.

The individual before her looked wholly disreputable. Tall and lean—he had wild black hair, a stubbled jaw, and wore leathers coated with grime. Breanna's face twisted once more. Despite the reek in this alleyway, even from a few feet distant, she could smell him.

Whoops went up as Stewart launched himself at Duncan, his fists flying. He actually managed to land a heavy punch to the man's belly before the bigger man retaliated with a blow of his own to Stewart's jaw.

Stewart staggered and then went down like a sack of oats, sprawling across the cobbles.

There he lay, unmoving.

"Christ, Ross," one of the onlookers muttered. "Have ye gone and killed him?"

The big man approached his fallen opponent and nudged him in the ribs with the toe of his boot. Stewart groaned, and Duncan's mouth twisted. "No … it seems not."

Breanna's gaze narrowed. Here they were, suffering English overlords, and her fellow Scots were busy fighting each other.

No wonder the English had gotten such a foothold here.

As if sensing her glare, Ross Duncan glanced up, his gaze settling upon Breanna. "It's a rough street this, lass," he said with a leer. "I'd move on if I were ye."

The shock of ice-cold water hitting his face yanked Cameron Stewart sharply into consciousness.

"What the devil!" Spluttering, he sat up and blinked the water out of his eyes.

Glancing around, he saw that he lay sprawled in the stable yard behind his favorite alehouse, right next to the water trough.

A statuesque figure, holding an empty wooden pail, stood beside the trough. The woman wasn't a beauty; her features were too strong for that. Yet her long peat-dark

hair, the exact same hue as her narrowed eyes, and full
sensual lips drew his eye.

Even drunk—body aching from the beating he'd just
taken, and now soaked through with icy water—Cameron
could appreciate a comely woman.

"Hello there," he murmured. "Have we met before?"

That luscious mouth thinned, and the dark brows that
winged over those penetrating eyes drew together.

"No," she said curtly. "And ye could do with another
one of these ... ye stink like rotting cabbage."

Cameron frowned at the insult. No lass had ever
made such a comment. Yet when he lifted his arm and
sniffed cautiously under it, his face screwed up.

Aye, maybe she had a point.

It had been a few days since he'd seen any soap and
water. After his last job, flush with silver, he'd headed
straight to Perth for some ale and gambling. However,
somehow he'd lost track of time.

The woman scooped up another pail of water and
took a menacing step toward him.

Cameron forestalled her with a raised hand. "No, ye
don't!"

She cocked her head. "Ye reek ... believe me, I'm
doing ye ... and anyone five feet from ye ... a favor."

"Enough, woman," he growled, rolling to his feet. The
ground shifted beneath him, and he staggered. Suddenly,
it felt as if the sky were rotating around him.

Perhaps I overdid it on the ale today.

Aye, he likely had. He'd been drinking heavily ever
since his arrival in Perth. Maybe he needed to get sober.
Once he did, he'd give Ross Duncan the beating he
deserved.

"Why were ye fighting?" the woman asked, still
glaring at him. She was tall. She only had to raise her
face a little to meet his eye. Cameron noted that she had
a slight cleft to her chin, a detail that only added to her
allure. He'd also marked the strong, curvaceous body
under her blue kirtle.

"A disagreement over a game of dice," Cameron
replied, taking the pail off her and emptying it back into

the trough. "Someone accused me of cheating ... and I had to defend my honor."

Her mouth twisted at this, making it clear what she thought of his honor.

Irritation spiked within Cameron. He didn't know this woman and didn't appreciate her censure.

"Ye are Cameron Stewart, I presume?" she asked, her tone clipped now.

He arched an eyebrow. "Aye ... why?"

Her expression hardened as if she'd hoped he might tell her otherwise. "Ye once captained the garrison at Stirling, is that right?"

Cameron nodded. He had once—although, despite that only two and a half years had passed since Stirling had fallen to the English, it seemed like a lifetime ago now. "And ye are?"

"My name is Breanna."

Breanna. The name suited her. Although Cameron's head ached and his mouth tasted like old leather, he wasn't drunk or injured enough not to feel the stirrings of interest within him.

"And what can I do for ye, *Breanna*?"

The charm he'd just smoothed into his voice didn't have the effect he'd expected. Instead of softening toward him, Breanna merely folded her arms across her impressive bosom and looked down her nose at him. "I've been looking for ye, Stewart," she said after a pause.

"Ye have?" Cameron flashed her a cocky smile. Perhaps his day was about to get brighter after all.

However, the woman's expression merely darkened at his flirting, her strong jaw tensing. "Aye," she replied. "I need ye as my husband."

2

NEGOTIATION

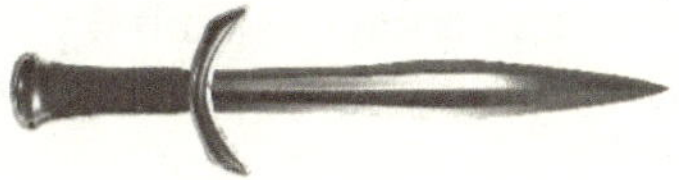

THE MAN'S FACE went slack for a moment, even as his eyes snapped wide.

If Breanna hadn't been seething with irritation, she might have found Cameron Stewart's reaction to her words amusing.

As it was, she clenched her jaw, impatience thrumming through her.

Hume got it wrong, she thought bitterly. *This drunkard can't help us.*

Crone's tears, it was barely after midday and the man could hardly stand. This couldn't be the brave captain of the Stirling Guard, the warrior who'd helped keep the castle from falling to the English for many long months. Hume Comyn—the only male member of the Guardians of Alba—had assured her that Stewart was the right man to accompany her on this mission.

"He's a bit rough around the edges ... and thinks he's God's gift to women ... but ye want someone like him at yer side in a scrap," Hume had informed her with a wry smile. "If ye wish to protect the Bruce, ye need to bring a man like him along."

Breanna's teeth started to ache, and she realized she was still clenching her jaw. She hated the thought that she couldn't do this alone. And yet, she knew Hume had spoken true.

Warriors from all over the Highlands had flocked to Robert the Bruce, but a woman arriving on her own would attract too much attention.

Hume had also warned her not to mention him and Fyfa. He believed Stewart would be more cooperative if he didn't know about their involvement. And if the mercenary accepted the mission, he'd meet them soon enough.

"Fear not," she ground out, her gaze never leaving his face. "I don't want an *actual* husband. I plan to join the Bruce in his fight for our freedom … and need a warrior to *pose* as my man."

The surprise ebbed from Cameron Stewart's face. She wasn't sure whether it was the icy water or her utterance, but he appeared to have sobered up somewhat. His eyes gleamed—whether in amusement or incredulity, it was hard to tell.

"Ah, so ye are a freedom fighter, lass?"

Breanna heaved in a deep breath, struggling against her quickening temper. She didn't like the way he'd drawled those words and the thinly veiled disdain in his voice. Crone's tears, the man was a Scot too. He should be clamoring to join the Bruce—not brawling in alehouses. Reining in her ire, she answered calmly, "Aye, and so will ye be, if ye agree to join me."

Stewart eyed her for a moment longer before he turned, leaned over the water trough, and scooped water into his face. Lumps of ice floated in the trough, for there had been a hard frost that morning and the stable yard still lay in shadow. The air was so cold that their breaths steamed.

Yet apart from a sharply indrawn breath, the mercenary braved the freezing water better than he had moments earlier when she'd emptied that bucket over him.

The Goddesses forgive her, but she'd enjoyed doing that.

Straightening up, Stewart wiped the water out of his eyes, flicked his mane of tangled blue-black hair off his face, and turned to her once more.

His expression was shuttered, his gaze shrewd. If Breanna hadn't seen him stagger around moments earlier, she'd have thought he was stone-cold sober. "And what's in it for me?"

Breanna's mouth thinned. She shouldn't have been surprised at the question, and yet she was. This man was, indeed, a mercenary. However, she would first try to appeal to his sense of patriotism, his love for Scotland. Surely, under that jaded veneer, he wished to fight to liberate his home from the English?

"Ye get to be part of something greater than yerself, Stewart," she replied, her tone even.

The mercenary's mouth quirked. "And what if I have no wish to do so?"

Irritation spiked within Breanna, yet she swallowed it down. "Don't ye wish to aid the man who will one day rule Scotland?"

He snorted. "So, ye can see into the future can ye?"

Aye, she *could* actually. Breanna was highly skilled in casting the bones and reading their divinations—even if it was the leader of her order, Colina, who'd seen the Bruce's future in a dream, and not her. If this wastrel actually agreed to join her—she was starting to hope he wouldn't—she'd likely have to reveal a few details about her identity and purpose. But not yet. She didn't trust this man in the slightest.

Apart from Hume Comyn, who'd wed her sister Fyfa, she trusted few men.

It galled her that she had to involve a male in her plans.

"I don't need to know what fate holds," she said after a pause, her voice hardening. "The Wallace is dead, and The Bruce has risen in his place. As we speak, he calls fighters to his side. We can help him beat the English back, help him reclaim our lands."

Stewart snorted, his eyes narrowing. "Yer devotion to the cause is admirable, lass," he said in a tone that revealed he thought the opposite. "However, I lost my thirst for freedom years ago." His mouth curved into a hard smile. "Silver is my mistress these days ... if ye want my assistance, ye are going to have to pay for it."

Breanna drew herself up, her jaw clenching once more. Hume had warned her it might come to this. Nevertheless, it disappointed her that this man was so grasping.

"So, ye'd never lend yer sword for the love of yer country?" she asked coldly.

He laughed. "No. Not these days."

Silence fell between them. A biting wind whipped through the yard, digging its fingers through the thick layers of Breanna's cloak and woolen kirtle. She longed to return to the inn where Hume and Fyfa were waiting and warm her hands around a cup of warmed wine.

Instead, she was standing here, about to negotiate with a man she now wished to spit at.

"I've heard tales about secretive women clad in blue," Stewart broke the silence, his gaze never leaving her face. "They appear and disappear like wraiths throughout Scotland ... rallying folk to the Bruce's cause." He raised a dark eyebrow then. "I take it ye are one of them?"

Breanna didn't break his stare. "I might be." She wasn't giving this man anything else, not unless he agreed to help her. "What's yer rate then ... as a hired sword?"

Stewart's mouth lifted at the corners before he raised a hand and rubbed his knuckles over his stubbled jaw. "It depends."

"On what?" Breanna fought the urge to scowl. She was rapidly losing her patience.

"On how long the job will take ... and the level of personal peril required."

"I'll require ye for six months, at least," she replied, biting out the words between clenched teeth. "And the mission is likely to be highly dangerous."

"Well, in that case." He cast her a careless smile. "I don't come cheap ... one hundred silver pennies ... paid in advance."

Breanna sucked in a sharp breath. *Greedy bastard.* It was an eye-wateringly high sum. However, Colina had instructed her that she was to pay whatever was required to get the assistance she needed. The Guardians of Alba lived simply, yet they held large reserves of coin, gathered over the centuries to aid them in times of need.

Even so, Breanna fought the urge to tell Cameron Stewart to go to the devil. It was only her bull-headed stubbornness—and the knowledge that it would take her days, possibly weeks, to find someone else—that prevented her from doing so.

"Half now … and half when the job's done," she replied after a pause. She was surprised how calm her voice sounded, even if she was simmering inside.

Stewart cocked his head, his smile fading. "Eighty now … the rest when I'm done."

The simmering came to a boil within Breanna. She was now finding it difficult to keep control of her temper.

"Sixty now, and forty later," she growled. "And that's my final offer."

Their gazes dueled, and Breanna's body quivered with tension. She had to bite her tongue to prevent herself from snarling at him. She'd had enough of Cameron Stewart. Aye, it would take her time to find someone else suitable, but she suddenly didn't care.

However, when he replied, her belly twisted in disappointment.

"Very well," Stewart murmured, flashing her a disarming smile. "I agree to yer terms." He thrust out a hand. "Shall we shake on it?"

Breanna swallowed. She'd rather shake hands with a leper. Nonetheless, she had to overlook her dislike of this man and keep her focus on what he would give her: safe passage into Robert the Bruce's inner circle. Aye, the Bruce was on course to fulfill the destiny the High Bandruì had foreseen. But Colina had also warned them that forces would move against him. Robert Bruce needed a Guardian at his side—and Breanna had volunteered to be the one to protect him.

But she needed this man in order to do so.

Reluctantly, she unfolded her arms and took his hand. Stewart's grasp was firm and warm, and it sent an uncomfortable jolt of awareness up Breanna's arm.

Scowling, she wrenched her hand free and stepped back from him. "Where are ye lodged?"

Stewart motioned to the building behind her. "At this fine establishment, of course."

Breanna sucked in another calming breath. How was she supposed to travel with this irksome man? Drawing her cloak about her as another gust of wind buffeted the stable yard, she dragged her gaze over his disheveled form. "Get yerself cleaned up, and meet me at dusk, at the Kirkside Inn, where I shall pay ye the first part of yer fee. We'll be staying at the inn overnight before setting off tomorrow ... in search of Robert the Bruce."

He held Breanna's gaze a moment before casting her another smile, a goading one that made her hackles raise. "And shall we be sharing a room, *wife*? After all ... it is our wedding night."

Breanna's scowl returned, and she moved forward, crowding his space. To her fury, the man merely grinned back at her. "Let's make something clear from the start, Stewart," she growled. "Ye and I will merely *pretend* to be husband and wife." She then shoved back her cloak, to reveal the dirk sheathed at her hip. "Touch me, and ye shall taste this."

Cameron Stewart watched the woman in blue stalk from the stable yard without a backward glance.

Breanna's shoulders were rigid, giving her ire away.

Cameron's gaze lingered on her, admiring the way her peat-dark hair tumbled down her back. Some women were truly lovely when vexed, and this Breanna certainly was one. Her high cheekbones had flushed, her large brown eyes deepening to black. She'd looked like she wanted to draw that dirk and stab him with it. There was something about her stance that warned him she knew how to use the weapon too.

He really shouldn't have goaded her, but he hadn't been able to resist.

She'd been so painfully earnest, and she'd prattled on about the cause and helping Robert the Bruce.

Cameron didn't want to hear about how important her mission was, or how he owed it to his countrymen. All he cared about was knowing that he'd be well paid for lending her his blade.

Breanna disappeared from sight, and a shadow fell over the grey, windy December day. Cameron stifled a groan. He was suddenly aware of his burning jaw, from where Ross Duncan had slugged him. His head throbbed, not from the beating, but from the jugs of ale he'd consumed, and his mouth tasted sour.

Running a hand over his face, he muttered a curse. Aye, the lass would pay him well—he'd deliberately tossed a high figure at her, yet she hadn't flinched—but that didn't mean taking this job was wise.

Cameron usually worked alone. And he wasn't in the habit of pretending to be any woman's husband. A queasy sensation stole over him then, and he silently vowed to stay away from the ale for a while.

One hundred silver pennies. He'd be set up for the year. He could even hang up his sword for a while if he wished.

And what would ye do with yer time then? Drink?

Mouth thinning, Cameron pushed his damp hair off his face and headed toward the alehouse. He needed to bathe, change clothing, and ready himself to meet the fiery Breanna once more.

But before he did, he had to give Ross Duncan a lesson he wouldn't easily forget.

3

THE LURE OF COIN

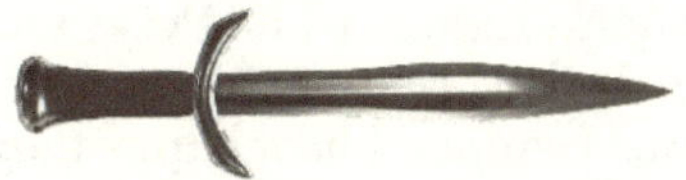

"HE'S LATE," FYFA Comyn murmured, leaning against the back of the booth and placing a hand over her swollen belly. "Perhaps he's not coming."

"He'll come," Breanna replied, even as she glanced toward the door for what felt the hundredth time since she'd taken a seat in the common room of the Kirkside Inn. "He won't want to give up all that silver."

Across from Breanna, Hume Comyn huffed a soft laugh. "I take it Cameron Stewart didn't make a good impression on ye?"

Breanna shifted her attention back to the warrior who waited with her and Fyfa in the shadowy booth at the back of the inn's busy common room, her brow furrowing. "No."

Hume favored her with a lop-sided smile. "He's not that bad ... surely?"

Breanna snorted. Of course, Hume had once worked with the former captain of the Stirling Guard. Hume had been steward of the castle at the same time.

She liked and trusted Hume. He was steadfast in his dedication to their cause, and she thought him a good judge of character. However, he'd erred in suggesting Stewart to her.

"He has the manners of a goat," she muttered.

"It's disappointing that ye found him drunk and brawling," Fyfa spoke up once more. A groove had formed between her sister's brows. "Perhaps the defeat at Stirling has turned him bitter?"

"It might have," Hume replied, his smile fading. "But he's still one of the bravest men I ever met."

Fyfa nodded. She sat nestled against Hume's side while he looped a protective arm over her shoulders.

Breanna viewed them a moment. They made quite a couple. They were both red-heads, although Hume's short hair was dark-auburn while Fyfa's wild mane was a more fiery hue. And every time Breanna saw them together, she was reminded how happy they were.

Even so, she didn't envy them. At thirty-two winters, she was used to being on her own, used to watching her own back. She couldn't see that ever changing.

Of course, Breanna wasn't truly alone. She'd grown up surrounded by love. Her sisters, Fyfa and Nessa especially, were all she needed. Even if Nessa no longer lived amongst them. The three of them, all foundlings, had been raised together in the order. They weren't related by blood, yet Breanna saw them as kin.

Nessa now lived at Grosmont Castle on the Welsh Borders with her English husband, Hugh de Burgh. Three years earlier, Nessa had been sent to seduce one of The Hammer's knights, in order to gain details of where and when the English would strike next. 'The Hammer' was the name her order had given Edward of England, 'The Hammer of the Scots'. She had succeeded in her mission—but she'd also fallen in love with the man she'd seduced. In the last missive that Nessa had sent them, she'd written that she was with bairn again. She and Hugh already had one daughter, and their second child was due in the spring.

Breanna's chest tightened then. How she missed Nessa.

The three of them had once been inseparable. But with Nessa and Fyfa wed, things had changed. Breanna knew her sisters loved her as much as they ever had—yet their focus was on their husbands now, and on the families they were building together.

Life moved on—something Breanna sometimes had trouble accepting.

An icy draft gusted through the inn then. Breanna's attention snapped to the doorway, where she spied a tall, lean black-haired figure clad in leather.

"I told ye he'd come," Breanna murmured to her companions. "The lure of coin is too great."

Hume gave another laugh before replying, "Put away yer claws, Bree ... remember, ye are supposed to pose as his loving wife once ye leave Perth."

The reminder made her belly clench. Aye, she remembered the bargain she'd struck with the man who had just spied her and was now weaving his way through the tightly-packed tables toward their corner.

Supper was approaching, and a cold, grey day had turned even chillier as the sun went down. As such, merchants, laborers, and fishermen packed the common room. A huge hearth burned up one end, throwing out an orange glow that illuminated the faces of the men as they huddled over tankards of ale.

A serving lass approached Cameron Stewart and greeted him. He said something to the young woman before pressing a coin into her hand. He then favored her with a grin and a wink.

The serving lass, lithe and fair-haired, smiled up at the mercenary under lowered lashes before going to fetch him his order.

Breanna's lips thinned. She continued to observe Stewart as he approached their booth. At least he'd tidied himself up. He'd looked a right mess that afternoon. Stewart had changed into fresh clothes, and his washed hair hung in damp waves around his shoulders. He'd even shaved off the stubble on his jaw. Breanna saw that a faint bruise had come up there, where that man at the alehouse had slugged him. Over one shoulder, Stewart carried a leather bag—presumably, this man traveled light—and a dirk hung from one hip, while he'd strapped another knife to his opposite thigh.

Breanna's first impressions of Cameron Stewart hadn't been positive, but she had to admit, as her gaze tracked his approach, that he was a rakishly attractive man.

He knows it too.

His attention shifted to Hume and Fyfa then, and his gaze widened, his expression sobering. Breanna marked his reaction and realized that Hume's advice not to reveal their involvement in this mission to Stewart initially had probably been wise. He wore a guarded expression now, although she decided not to remark upon it.

"Ye shall have to stop making eyes at every woman who crosses yer path," Breanna greeted him coolly. "If we are to convince others we are a wedded couple."

Stewart's mouth curved, even if his gaze remained wary. "Fear not, mo leannan," he replied. "I promise *only* to have eyes for ye."

Breanna resisted the urge to sneer. *My lover.* Crone's tears, would she have to suffer more of this nonsense?

Before she could come up with a suitably cutting response, Stewart dropped into the booth, next to her, and slid close, dumping his bag under the table. He then nodded to the couple opposite.

"Hume and Fyfa Comyn," he drawled. "I should have known ye two were behind this."

"Who do ye think recommended ye to Bree for this mission?" Hume leaned forward, and the two men clasped arms in greeting.

"Aye, she seems to think ye a scoundrel … yet I'm sure ye shall put her right," Fyfa chimed in.

Stewart's mouth kicked into a proper smile. "But ye know I *am* a scoundrel, Fyfa." He then shifted his attention to Hume. "How did ye know where to find me?"

"Yer fame as a hired blade goes before ye," Hume replied. "It only required a few well-placed questions." Hume paused then, his moss-green eyes narrowing. "I hear ye are expensive these days?"

"Aye … the more dangerous the job, the higher the fee." Stewart reclined in his seat, and to Breanna's irritation, he flung his arm over the back, behind her shoulders. His gesture mirrored that of the couple opposite, yet their relationship couldn't have been more different.

Breanna clenched her jaw. She didn't like him sitting so close and was aware of the heat of his thigh just inches from hers. She noted then that—unlike earlier—the mercenary didn't stink. The scent of soap, leather, and warm, clean male enveloped her.

Cameron Stewart's gaze moved to Fyfa, and to the swell of her belly, just visible over the edge of the table. "Congratulations to ye both," he said, his tone shifting from teasing to sincere.

Fyfa smiled back. "Thank ye … it's our first."

Stewart nodded, a thoughtful expression settling upon his handsome face. "Ye two left Stirling in a hurry … although I heard what ye did at Edward's victory banquet." He flashed Fyfa a grin. "I wish I could have seen Longshanks's face."

Breanna allowed herself a small smile in agreement. She too wished she could have witnessed the scene that had occurred two and a half years earlier after the fall of Stirling Castle to the English. To prevent Robert Bruce from drinking from a poisoned goblet, Fyfa had leaped to her feet and caused a scene. She accused Bruce of allowing himself to be shamed, bullied, by the English king. She'd then knocked the goblet from his hand.

Longshanks had been incensed. But most folk, including the English king and the mercenary seated beside Breanna, didn't know that Fyfa had actually prevented the Bruce from being poisoned. They all thought her act was one of patriotic defiance.

"Fyfa was magnificent." There was no mistaking the pride in Hume's voice.

"We had to flee the camp after that," Fyfa admitted, her smile turning rueful. "Hume traveled north with me … to the Highlands … and joined our cause."

Stewart's gaze widened at this revelation. "And what *cause* is this exactly?" He paused then, his attention swiveling to Breanna and the blue robes she wore. She was the only one at the table who was dressed thus. "As I told ye earlier ... I've heard a few rumors about the 'women in blue' of late."

"Aye?" Breanna met his gaze, unflinching. "And what do they say?"

"That ye have been rallying support for the Bruce ... and that ye dabble in sorcery." His reply was calm, almost drawled. It was as if he'd been discussing something as innocuous as the weather.

Breanna stilled. The mercenary's reaction wasn't what she'd expected. She'd spoken with Fyfa at length on how to broach the subject of their order with Stewart. They'd decided that it was best he didn't know they were bandruìd—druidesses—for the moment. Once they were on the road, Breanna would likely need to reveal her true identity.

The idea of 'witchery' tended to make a man's balls shrivel. But it appeared that the mercenary didn't care.

Breanna decided to test him. "Aye, both of those rumors are true ... although we are bandruìd, not sorcerers," she replied. "Does that bother ye?"

He inclined his head. "Not really."

"Our order is cloaked in secrecy," Fyfa interrupted then, her voice carrying a warning note. "As such, ye must promise never to share anything we reveal to ye about us."

"Agreed ... although ye aren't *that* secretive," Stewart replied, a note of derision creeping into his voice. "Or inconspicuous either." His gaze was still fixed upon Breanna. "And what's the significance of the blue?"

"It's the color of loyalty," Breanna replied. "It reminds us what we're fighting for."

A hush fell over the booth then. Breanna became aware of the rise and fall of voices around them, punctuated with bursts of laughter.

"So, what now?" she asked finally. "Will ye still take the job?"

Stewart's mouth lifted at the corners in a half-smile. "Aye ... but the price might go up."

Heat arrowed through Breanna. *Bastard.* "We already agreed on a fee ... and shook on it," she reminded him, her tone cooling.

His smile widened. "Aye, but a man can change his mind."

Hume cleared his throat then. "Careful, Stewart."

At that moment, the serving lass brought Stewart's tankard of ale to the table. She favored him with an appreciative look as he smiled his thanks. The lass then shifted her attention to the other occupants of the booth. "Will ye be ordering supper?"

"Aye," Hume replied. He dug into his vest and produced a coin before passing it to her. "Bread, cheese, and blood sausage for all of us." He then motioned to his empty tankard. "And another round of ales."

When the serving lass had gone, Stewart lifted his tankard to his lips and took a sip. He then grimaced and set his drink back down on the table.

"The ale's not to yer liking?" Hume asked.

"It's good enough," Stewart replied. "I'm just still nursing a sore head from earlier in the day."

Breanna snorted.

The mercenary ignored her. Instead, he held Hume's eye, a challenge in his gaze. "And what part do *ye* play in all of this, Comyn?"

4

WE LIVE IN A MAN'S WORLD

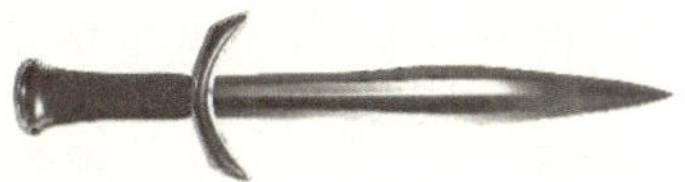

HUME FROWNED. "I assist the bandruìd in their work."

"Even when we were in Stirling?"

Hume's green eyes shadowed, while next to him, Fyfa tensed. Of course, she'd hidden her identity from her husband for years before he'd stumbled on the truth. It had been a difficult time for them—one that had nearly torn them apart.

Breanna's fingers clenched into fists under the table. She didn't want Stewart raking all that up. It was none of his business anyway.

"I discovered who Fyfa really was shortly before the fall of Stirling," Hume admitted after a pause. He then cut his wife a look, their gazes fusing. "I'll admit it came as a shock at first, but I soon accepted her true identity ... and I now wouldn't have Fyfa any other way."

"Admirable," the mercenary murmured. "Ye are a loyal man, indeed, Comyn."

Somehow, the comment didn't sound like a compliment.

Hume's expression darkened.

"He is," Fyfa cut in, her gaze flashing. "Although that's just one of his many attributes."

The atmosphere at the table had changed; tension crackled in the air as if a storm hung overhead. Breanna wondered then just how well Fyfa and Hume had gotten on with this man. Hume had spoken of Cameron Stewart's valor and skills as a warrior and leader of men, but that didn't mean they'd been friends.

Pushing aside her cloak, she reached down and unfastened the heavy leather pouch attached to her belt. A moment later, she thumped it down on the table before the mercenary.

She didn't have the time or patience for all this word-play. "Sixty silver pennies … as agreed," she said, not bothering to hide the disdain in her voice. "And another forty when we're done. Take it or leave it. If ye no longer wish to help us, tell me now, and we'll stop wasting each other's time."

Stewart met her eye, his expression shuttered.

Breanna desperately hoped he would renege. Aye, she needed a warrior to accompany her on this mission, but Stewart was a poor choice.

As such, disappointment sank like a heavy stone in her belly when the mercenary replied, "I take it, *mo leannan*" —his mouth curved then as his hand closed over the pouch of coins— "that ye know where to find the Bruce?"

"Aye," she snapped.

"We've discovered he's taken refuge with his men at Dunaverty Castle upon the Kintyre peninsula," Hume cut in, his tone cool. "If ye ride hard, ye should reach him before Yule."

"The Three give me strength, we've made a mistake hiring him." Breanna paced the floor of Fyfa and Hume's bed-chamber. She then whirled around and fixed her sister with a gimlet stare. "The man would sell his own mother!"

Seated upon the bed, Fyfa spread her hands in a placating gesture. "Don't over-react, Bree," she said. "I know he's a bit rough around the edges … but he's trustworthy."

Breanna resumed her pacing. "He'd better be," she growled.

It was getting late in the evening. The women had retired upstairs while Hume and Cameron Stewart lingered over the last of their ale in the common room. Hume was giving the mercenary details about the movement of English patrols to the west, where they were to be traveling.

Breanna hoped that Hume was also issuing the man a stern warning about what would happen if he let them down.

Frustration churned through her. She wished to set out in search of the Bruce tonight. Yet it wasn't an eve for traveling. Outdoors, the wind had sprung up. It rattled the wooden shutters and made the fire that burned in the hearth in the corner of the room gutter. Breanna and the mercenary would depart at dawn the following morning, and with the weather having taken a turn for the worse, it would be a frosty journey west.

Muttering a curse, Breanna went to the chair next to the hearth and threw herself down upon it. "I won't have Stewart jeopardize this mission," she muttered. "I'll take a knife to his throat first."

"There's no reason why he'd do that," Fyfa replied, her tone pained now. "I know it didn't seem so tonight ... but the man is as loyal to Scotland as we are. Ye should have seen him during the Siege of Stirling. He did all he could to keep the castle from falling to the English."

Breanna pulled a face. "A man can change in two and a half years. What if he no longer cares about such things?"

Fyfa's expression shadowed, her heart-shaped face taut. "If I weren't with bairn, Hume and I would have joined the Bruce," she murmured. "Saving ye Stewart's company."

The sisters' gazes met and held before Breanna shook her head. Fyfa now looked so worried that she was starting to feel bad about her outburst. This wasn't Fyfa's fault. Her sister and Hume had done their best to help her. However, she worried that they had erred in their judgment of Cameron Stewart's character.

"No ... it's my turn," she replied. "Ye and Hume have exhausted yerselves since Stirling furthering the cause." She paused then, her expression softening. "It's time ye stayed at home and focused yer energies on the family ye are starting together."

She thought then of the cottage Hume had repaired. It was indeed a welcoming spot. Sitting on the edge of Loch na Gainmhich, under the shadow of Glas Bheinn, the cottage had been in a poor state of repair when the couple moved in. But these days, a verdant garden surrounded it and Hume had built on a wing for guests at the back. Whenever she visited them and took a cup of wine by the fire, Breanna always felt at ease. During those relaxed evenings, she could almost forget about the cause that drove her.

"I'm looking forward to that," Fyfa admitted with a sigh. "I was beginning to think my womb would never quicken." She paused then before gently patting her rounded belly. "Hume has always wanted bairns."

There was no mistaking the regret that tinged her sister's voice. Fyfa was referring to the fact that up until Hume had discovered her true identity, she'd taken a herbal draft every morning to prevent herself from falling pregnant. Breanna understood why her sister had taken such precautions: a Guardian of Alba's first loyalty was to keep Scotland safe from invaders. Fyfa hadn't wanted to be waylaid. But her decision had come at a price, for Hume had been incensed when he'd discovered what she'd done. Breanna was relieved that her sister and Hume would have the family they now both wanted so much.

"And ye will have them," she murmured. "Worry not, there are plenty of us ready and willing to carry the torch in the meantime."

"Aye." Fyfa flashed Breanna a brittle smile. "Ye are right, Bree. This is yer mission ... one ye were made for. The Bruce will likely restart his campaign in the spring ... and when he does, his enemies will close in once more."

Fyfa's features tightened then. "I don't think we've seen the last of Lamia Delamare either."

Breanna nodded. She held the same view. A chill trailed down her spine at the thought of the witch who'd traveled with the English. She'd been at Stirling and was behind the failed attempt to poison Robert the Bruce and Fyfa. They hadn't seen or heard anything of the woman since, although Breanna often found herself wondering what had become of her. She hadn't yet mentioned Lamia to the man she'd just hired and hoped she wouldn't need to.

Pushing aside worries about the witch, Breanna clenched her jaw, stubbornness rising within her. "Well then, Stewart and I had better do our best to win his trust." She paused then, irritation flaring. "Although I really don't see why I need the mercenary at all."

Fyfa huffed a sigh. This was a discussion they'd had numerous times before. Breanna had wanted to seek out Robert Bruce on her own and pledge her loyalty to him. A small number of bandruìd, Breanna among them, had spent years training in physical combat. She could use her fists and wield a dirk, sword, longbow, and quarter-staff better than most men.

"Ye know why, Bree," Fyfa said after a pause. "We can't achieve everything on our own, dear sister. Sometimes, we need to reach out and accept help from others." She shook her head then. "As capable as ye are, the Bruce is unlikely to accept a lone female into his inner circle of warriors. Aye, it isn't fair ... but we live in a man's world nonetheless. If ye wish to get close to the Bruce, ye need to use a man to do so."

Breanna pulled a face yet didn't argue. It galled her, but Fyfa was right. Even so, she still found herself rebelling against the situation.

Fyfa rose from the bed then and walked over to where her cloak hung near the door. Reaching into a slit in the lining, she drew something from it. Her sister turned and approached Breanna before holding a small stone out on her outstretched palm.

It was a lump of smoky quartz.

Breanna stilled, her impatience and frustration momentarily forgotten. "Ye found me another cairn stone?" she whispered.

"Aye," Fyfa replied. "I know ye lost yer old one ... but we can't have ye going into battle without carrying one of these. Every bandruì needs a stone of protection and persuasion within easy reach."

Cameron shifted against the back of the booth and raised the tankard of ale to his lips. Yet his attention never left the man opposite. The two of them, who'd once worked so closely, hadn't seen each other for years.

But even when they'd both resided at Stirling Castle, their relationship had been uneasy, strained. Back then, Hume Comyn had been dogged by insecurity. He'd doubted himself as a man and mistrusted his beautiful wife.

Cameron would never forget the day he'd stopped Fyfa in a hallway within the castle. He'd pushed the boundaries by crowding her space and flirting with her. Fyfa hadn't responded to him, but that didn't stop Hume from flying into a rage when he appeared to find the captain of the guard looming over his wife.

If Cameron were honest with himself, he felt bad about the incident. He'd sensed the rapport between husband and wife was strained. They certainly hadn't needed him making things worse. But at the time, he hadn't cared.

And despite that he was possibly even more cynical these days than he had been then, he was pleased to see that Hume and Fyfa had mended things. He had no wish to be encumbered by a wife or bairns, but Hume was a different sort of man.

A much better one.

Viewing Hume under hooded lids, Cameron cleared his throat. "I'm surprised ye would fight to further the Bruce's cause," he said, breaking the silence between them. "After Dumfries."

Hume met his eye, his expression shuttering.

News of what had happened upon that fateful day the previous February had traveled to every corner of Scotland. John Comyn, Hume's cousin, had died at the hands of Robert Bruce. Various rumors were circulating about what actually had transpired.

Some folk believed that the Bruce had murdered Comyn in cold blood because he was a political rival, while others whispered that Comyn had actually betrayed Bruce to the English. Some said that the murder had been planned, while others said it was an accident. To make matters worse, Bruce had killed his rival at Greyfriars, on holy ground, and in doing so had committed sacrilege.

Cameron didn't pay any of the rumors much mind. He was more interested in knowing why John Comyn's cousin still followed Robert the Bruce.

"I loved my cousin and would never have wished him dead," Hume replied after a pause. A shadow moved in his eyes as he spoke. Indeed, Cameron remembered how much time Hume and 'The Red' had spent together in the past, for the man had resided at Stirling Castle for a spell as Guardian of Scotland. "But he should have never moved against the Bruce as he did." He paused then, sucking in a deep breath. "The Bruce requested to meet him within the church of Greyfriars because it was neutral ground ... he wished to mend things between them and unite against Longshanks." Hume's mouth twisted. "But our contacts at Dumfries tell us that things didn't go as he'd hoped. My cousin always had a blistering temper, and he let it get the best of him that day."

Cameron raised an eyebrow. "So, ye're saying that the Bruce stuck him with his dirk in self-defense?"

Hume shook his head, his mouth thinning. "I wouldn't know ... for no one actually witnessed their struggle. But what I *am* saying is that I'd be a fool to let a longstanding feud between two men shadow my better judgment. Robert the Bruce is our only hope, Stewart … and I'm sorry my cousin failed to see that." Hume paused there, his expression growing severe. "Instead of worrying about the Bruce, John should have been focused on the *real* enemy. The English must be driven from Scotland, Stewart … or all will be lost."

5

ON THE ROAD

"THERE THEY ARE," Cameron announced, raising his voice to be heard over the whine of the wind. "The English await."

Up ahead, a company of two dozen soldiers gathered around a roadblock on the highway. Stern-faced men clad in hauberks and plate armor, they watched Cameron and Breanna approach with narrowed gazes.

The English army had camped in Argyll for the winter. They might not have been campaigning this time of year, yet they didn't intend to let the Scots forget they were present either. Aymer de Valence, the commander Longshanks had sent to oversee this campaign, was continuing to patrol his conquered territory.

It was mid-morning, and this was the first English patrol Cameron and Breanna had encountered. Above them stretched a windswept sky, and wooded hills flanked the road. They'd taken the highway directly west—their horses' hooves beating out a tattoo on the dirt, passing a trickle of merchants and travelers along the way—until Cameron had spied something in the distance.

He slowed his mount to a walk and allowed Breanna to approach alongside. It had been too dark earlier to notice her clothing, yet he was pleased to see that she'd cast aside her blue robes in favor of a dark green kirtle and matching cloak. She'd also braided her long dark hair and wrapped it around the crown of her head. At first glance, she looked like a merchant's respectable wife—until one observed her stony expression.

Cameron had never met such a charmless woman.

Pretending to be Breanna's loving husband would be a challenge, even for him. Aye, she was comely, but he wasn't fond of lasses with sharp tongues—women who spoke and behaved like men.

"Try not to look so fierce, wife," Cameron chided her as she drew level with him. "Ye don't want to slay the English with yer glare."

Breanna didn't reply, although the glance she now bestowed upon him wasn't friendly either.

Unbothered, Cameron continued, "Remember ye are my dutiful wife. Let me do the talking."

She visibly bristled at that, and Cameron readied himself for an argument. Yet, after a moment, she managed a curt nod.

Reassured that she'd let him handle the situation, Cameron turned his attention to the nearing roadblock. He had a story ready if they were questioned.

Even so, he wondered—not for the first time—at the wisdom of taking this job. Aye, they were paying him well—and the silver was the only reason he'd accepted— but misgiving had stirred in his belly after he'd bid Hume good eve and retired to his own bed-chamber the night before.

The mercenary liked straightforward missions—and this one looked as if it would be anything but.

Cameron had been in a dour mood ever since leaving Perth. He'd met Breanna in the stables just before dawn. Likewise, she hadn't been talkative. Apart from checking on practicalities such as supplies and weapons, they'd barely spoken as they saddled their horses deftly.

"Fine mounts you've got there," one of the men called out in French as they clip-clopped past.

Cameron dipped his head in thanks yet continued on. They both rode coursers, athletically-built mounts that would carry them to their destination quickly. Dunaverty was quite a distance, for the castle sat on the southernmost edge of the Kintyre peninsula. Even with fast horses, it would take around four days to reach it.

"What's your business on this road?" Another soldier asked, stepping out to block their path.

Cameron schooled his features into a neutral expression. "I'm a wool merchant from Kilberry," he answered in the same tongue. "We've just visited my wife's kin in Perth and are now heading home."

The second soldier frowned. "Kilberry ... never heard of it."

"I'm not surprised. It's a tiny village on the Kintyre peninsula. Nothing but a few sod-huts ... and lots of sheep."

The soldier snorted, his gaze shifting to Breanna. Cameron saw interest flare in the man's pale blue eyes as he took his time viewing her, dragging his gaze down the length of her body. He then murmured something in English.

Cameron frowned. He didn't speak that tongue, yet the words and the lecherous tone they'd been spoken in needed no translation. He was concerned that his companion might do something rash if the soldier continued to insult her.

But Breanna's gaze was currently downcast. The only sign of her annoyance was the whiteness of her knuckles that grasped the reins.

"Are you content now?" Cameron asked in French after a pause. "Can we move on?"

The soldier lazily dragged his gaze away from Breanna. Instead, he now focused on Cameron. "You don't have the look of a wool merchant," he replied. "At first glance, I'd say you're a fighting man."

Cameron arched an eyebrow, his lips lifting at the corners. "No ... as I said, I'm just a humble merchant."

The soldier frowned. He approached Cameron then, his gaze raking over him. Reaching out, he pushed the mercenary's cloak back to reveal the dirk sheathed at his waist. "And you carry steel too, I see."

"The roads are dangerous at present," Cameron replied, his voice calm. "And I like to take care ... especially when traveling with my wife."

His gaze met the soldier's cool stare and held.

Despite his unruffled exterior, tension coiled in Cameron's gut. His right hand itched to draw his dirk. He could feel the soldier's aggression and see the naked challenge in his eye. The bastard wanted him to react.

Cameron inhaled slowly. He'd been ready for trouble yet hadn't thought they'd encounter hostility so soon. However, it wouldn't help them if he got into a knife fight at this roadblock. He needed to keep his own aggression leashed.

Moments passed, and Cameron waited for the soldier to question him further. If he carried out a thorough search, he'd find more blades, and that would turn curiosity into open suspicion. What would Cameron do if that happened?

However, to his surprise, the soldier eventually smirked. "Aye, well ... a woman that striking draws a man's eye. I wouldn't mind giving her a swiving. You're wise to be prudent." He stepped to one side and favored Cameron with a nod. "Go on then."

Cameron nodded back, careful to keep his expression shuttered before urging his gelding on. Breanna followed suit.

They rode in silence away from the roadblock, the wind catching at their cloaks. It was an effort not to urge his courser into a fast canter, yet Cameron resisted the impulse. It wouldn't do to look as if they were fleeing.

Likewise, Breanna rode sedately beside him. Only when they were out of earshot of the guards did she mutter a curse under her breath. It was a salty one—not an imprecation Cameron usually heard women utter, and he cast her a veiled glance. Her shoulders had relaxed, and she'd eased her grip upon the reins.

"That was a close thing," he admitted with a tight smile.

"Aye, ye kept yer cool admirably." Did he imagine it, or was there was a reluctant note of respect in her voice?

"Ye also did well back there," he replied.

Breanna pulled a face. "Did I? All I wanted to do was kick that bastard in the teeth."

Cameron snorted. "Well, I'm glad ye didn't give in to the impulse. Now, let's put some distance between us and them."

They quickened their pace then, moving away from the roadblock and into a shallow wooded valley. Copses of skeleton trees spread out either side of the road; it was a wintry scene, a reminder that they still had months of bitter weather to endure before spring brought the world to life once more.

An icy wind blew in from the north, drilling through the layers of wool and leather that swathed the travelers.

Cameron bowed his head against the wind, his thoughts turning inward.

No, he shouldn't have accepted this mission, but he'd backed himself into a corner. The night before, when he'd glanced across the table at where Fyfa and Hume had watched him with a mixture of disappointment and hope in their eyes, he'd known he couldn't decline. He wasn't close to either of them, and yet for the first time in years, he found himself caring what folk thought of him.

Hume and his wife remembered him as stalwart Captain Stewart. That man no longer existed, and Cameron wanted to tell them so. But he hadn't. Instead, he'd taken their money.

The gelid air stung Cameron's cheeks and numbed his nose and the tips of his ears. It wasn't yet noon, and he already felt half frozen. A roaring fire and a hot meal at the end of the day would be welcome indeed.

Weariness descended upon him then. A sellsword's life was an exciting one, but after a busy year, he'd been looking forward to spending the winter in Perth, sheltering from the cold. Yet now he was off in search of the outlaw king. Robert the Bruce was a wanted man and a dangerous one to be near at present.

Glancing once more at where Breanna rode beside him, Cameron took in her proud profile and the stubborn set of her jaw. This woman didn't seem to care about the danger. There was a wildness to her, a barely leashed energy, that concerned him. Aye, she'd held her tongue at the roadblock, yet only just.

Cameron's mouth pursed. Breanna needed a firm hand, or she'd likely land them both in trouble.

Dusk came early this time of year, and darkness was settling in a heavy curtain over the wooded hillsides and craggy peaks beyond, when they arrived at the village of Ardvorlich upon the shores of Loch Earn.

Breanna peered up at the shadowy outlines of the great mountains to the north. They were skirting the edge of the Highlands now, although their journey would take them southwest soon.

The wind, which had blown steadily all day, settled to a whisper with the sunset, bringing a reprieve from the numbing chill.

All the same, Breanna was relieved to arrive at their destination. Anticipation also smoldered in her belly— for, with each furlong, they were drawing closer to the Bruce.

Inside the stables, out the back of a small roadside inn, she unsaddled her horse and rubbed it down. She then checked the other stalls. Her breathing had quickened, her pulse thumping against her ribs, when she returned to her companion's side.

"We've got company," she informed Stewart, her voice tight.

The mercenary turned from where he'd been hanging his saddle up over the partition between the stalls. His brow furrowed at her tone. "What?"

"There are four horses stabled in here ... leggy, expensive-looking beasts too."

His frown deepened.

"There'll be English soldiers staying here," she continued, trying not to let her worry show. After their encounter at the roadblock, she had no wish to deal with more of the enemy today.

Stewart gave a curt nod. Even so, when he replied, she marked the weariness in his tone. He likely felt the same way. "Ye go on indoors then, and I'll scout around … and make sure they don't have friends camped nearby."

Breanna snorted. "*I'll* do the scouting."

"No, ye won't," he snapped. "Secure us a room, and order us some supper. I'll join ye shortly."

Breanna met his eye. She then folded her arms across her breasts, her chin kicking up. "This is my mission, Stewart, not yers. Don't order me around."

To her ire, the man held her gaze boldly. He then stepped forward, crowding her. "Aye, but ye hired me to pose as yer husband," he replied, his expression surly. "And that means ye must heed me, woman." Gone was the flirtatious, careless individual she'd met in Perth. Ever since their departure, Stewart had grown increasingly quiet and watchful. Now that he'd accepted this job, he'd indeed assumed the role of mercenary.

Breanna should have been relieved about that—for she'd paid the man to take this seriously. However, his abruptness and high-handed manner now infuriated her.

They continued to stare each other down.

"I can wait ye out all night, Breanna," he growled, his gaze never wavering. "Do ye have the same patience?"

Fury now pulsed like a hot coal in her gut. Nonetheless, she could see the man wasn't going to back down—and she was too tired and hungry to lock horns with him over this.

Instead, she growled an insult under her breath, twisted on her heel, and stalked, stiff-backed, out of the stables.

Stewart has won this round, she seethed inwardly. *But not the fight.*

6

A HEAD START

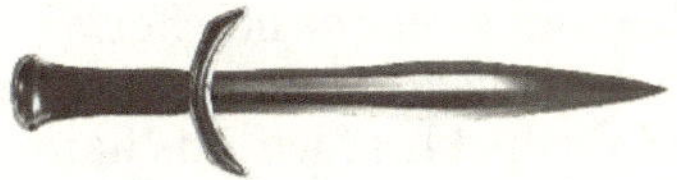

STEPPING INSIDE THE inn, Breanna inhaled the scent of wood smoke, sawdust, and roasting mutton. She did as bid, securing a room and supper for them from the innkeeper's wife while she scanned the common room.

It wasn't difficult to spot the English soldiers for, save two elderly men tucking into their supper in one corner, they were the only patrons in here this eve.

The English, big men wearing hauberks with their coifs lowered, sat around a table by the fire.

Breanna's mouth thinned when she saw that they'd hogged the best table in the establishment. They talked and laughed loudly as they diced and drank from tall tankards.

She didn't wish to eat in the same space as these men, but there was little she could do about it.

Crossing to a table in a shadowed corner, her boots sinking into the fragrant sawdust, Breanna sat down. Of course, the soldiers noticed her. Ignoring their wolfish looks and murmurs of appreciation, she waited for Stewart to join her.

When he eventually did, she was sipping from a cup of warmed wine and pretending to ignore the rowdy Englishmen a few yards away. They were paying far too much attention to her now. One of them had been halfway out of his seat, his gaze riveted upon her, when Cameron Stewart appeared. At the sight of her companion, the soldier's face had twisted. However, instead of challenging Stewart, he sank back down into his seat and muttered something to his companions.

Stewart was a lone man, yet there was a coiled energy to him, an arrogance to his stride, that carried a silent warning.

"Any others lurking nearby?" she whispered when the mercenary pulled out a seat beside her.

Stewart shook his head. Coming in from the cold to the warmth had flushed his face. His hair—as black as crow feathers—had been mussed by the wind. The firelight gilded his handsome features, turning his iron-grey eyes a smoky shade. "They're traveling alone."

Breanna nodded, glancing away from him as the inn-keeper approached bearing dishes of roast mutton, onions, and oaten bread. Her belly growled at the sight. Goddesses, she was hungry. "Good," she replied when they were alone once more. "I suggest we eat quickly and retire for the eve. Once those bastards get drunk, they'll start looking for trouble."

As if overhearing her comment, the four soldiers erupted into harsh laughter. The noise caused Breanna to scowl.

"I agree," Stewart grunted, reaching for a chunk of bread. "I'm too tired for another brawl ... not while I still nurse the bruises from the last one."

Breanna eyed him. Indeed, that bruise on his jaw was now a fine shade of purple under the darkness of new stubble. The man's expression was difficult to read, yet she sensed his fatigue, as she had in the stables. Her instincts warned that it was a weariness that had little to do with a long day's journey. Cameron Stewart hid it well, yet a shadow lay over him.

Mulling this observation, Breanna shifted her attention from her companion and, instead, concentrated upon her supper. She ate hungrily. The mutton was delicious, tender and slow-roasted, and the wine warmed her belly.

The pair ate in silence for a while before Stewart eventually broke it. "Hume warned me that there would be English patrols." Despite that there was little risk of

them being overheard, for they spoke Gaelic, the
mercenary still kept his voice low, his tone matter-of-
fact. "But there were too many of them on the road today
for my liking." He'd just finished his plate of food and
had leaned back in his chair cradling his cup of wine. "I
wonder if they suspect the outlaw king is hiding nearby."

Breanna frowned. The heavy English presence
bothered her as well. They'd only encountered one
roadblock, but there had been plenty of mounted
soldiers traveling both east and west, as well as these
men staying at the backroad inn. "All the more reason to
make haste for Dunaverty then," she murmured. "We
need to find him before the English do."

She took another gulp of wine before noticing that
Stewart was still observing her. The glint in his eye made
her tense. "What?" she asked warily.

"I hope ye have taken just one room for the night,
rather than two?" he asked, favoring her with a cool
smile. "If we're going to pose as a wedded couple, we
need to start now."

Breanna stiffened, irritation surging through her. She
didn't need him to keep reminding her of that. "Don't
take me for a half-wit, Stewart," she muttered. "Of
course, I have."

Preparing for bed was a trifle awkward.

It had been a long while since Breanna had shared a
room with a man—or anyone for that matter. Even back
at the Wailing Widow Falls, she was used to having her
own alcove. As a lass, she'd shared with her sisters, yet
being a senior member of the order brought certain
privileges.

She was on edge as she undressed behind a screen in
the corner of the room and hastily washed. All the while,

she was aware of Cameron Stewart's presence on the other side of the screen as he moved about the room.

"Christ's bones, it's freezing in here," he complained. She heard the thud and clang of the poker in the hearth as he attempted to rouse the embers.

"Aye," Breanna agreed as she reached for a drying cloth. "We'd be warmer in the stables."

Indeed, although a fire burned in the small hearth opposite the bed, the night's chill still managed to drive into the chamber through the damp stone walls. Goose-flesh rose on her skin, and by the time she'd pulled on the lèine she'd sleep in tonight, Breanna's teeth were chattering.

Emerging from behind the screen, she padded barefoot across the icy floorboards and dove into the bed before pulling up the covers high under her chin.

Across the room, Stewart had just pulled off his boots and gambeson—a long-sleeved, quilted tunic. Underneath, he wore a loose lèine, open at the throat. A scattering of crisp dark hair was visible there.

Stewart shrugged of the lèine and moved toward the screen. Breanna noted he had a lithe torso. Although tall, the mercenary's body wasn't bulky and broad. Instead, he was all lean, corded muscle and virile strength. The firelight played across his skin, highlighting several silvered scars.

This warrior bore the signs of a violent life.

Realizing that she was staring, Breanna averted her gaze.

Impatience spiked through her. She'd hired this sellsword to pose as her husband—but that didn't give her the right to gawk at him. Aye, he was attractive, but then so were a number of men.

Rolling over onto her back and moving as far as she could toward her edge of the bed, Breanna stared up at the crisscrossing beams overhead. She frowned as she reflected on the journey before them. She wished the Bruce weren't still so far away. Urgency tugged at her gut. She had to reach him. "We should leave early tomorrow," she announced then. "Before dawn."

"Aye." Stewart emerged from behind the screen, clad in nothing more than a pair of woolen leggings. He crossed to the bed and threw back the covers. "I want to get a headstart," he continued, his tone businesslike. "Just in case those soldiers are heading in the same direction as us."

Breanna tensed at these words. Crone's tears, she hoped they weren't.

"There it is," Cameron announced, raising his voice to be heard over the wind. "Dunaverty Castle ... I can see the 'rock' in the distance." A sigh of relief gusted out of him as he reined in his gelding, allowing Breanna to draw alongside. Finally, after four cold, tiring days, they'd reached their destination.

Next to him, Breanna peered west. "I spy the castle," she replied, her voice catching. "At last, we've reached the Bruce."

Cameron's lips pursed. He didn't reply, even if he noted Breanna's excitement. The woman was obsessed with meeting the outlaw king—he was her hero. Her fervor irritated the mercenary a little. After all, Robert the Bruce was just a man, not a god.

However, he decided against pointing out such to his companion.

Instead, he urged his mount along the narrow track toward the castle. This was the farthest point of the headland. It was a wild, treeless landscape that offered no protection from the salt-laced wind that gusted in from the sea. Cameron had never been to this remote corner of the Kintyre peninsula before—for unless one was visiting the MacDonald stronghold, one didn't have a reason to venture here.

However, he had to admit that the castle, perched high upon a great rock overlooking the sea, was a fine sight. As they approached it, he made out high ramparts surrounding a lofty stone tower. A narrow, fortified path led down the steep rock from the drawbridge, and a high wall surrounded a tightly-packed collection of thatch-roofed dwellings. Cameron inhaled the tang of peat smoke, blended with the nutty aroma of baking bread.

A little of his travel fatigue lifted. He was looking forward to spending a few days out of the biting wind.

Yule was just three days away now, and they'd hopefully be able to join in the festivities at the castle. Angus MacDonald, a staunch ally of the Bruce, ruled here, and although Cameron had never met the man, he'd heard that he was hospitable to travelers.

Cameron's senses sharpened then, his relief at their arrival at Dunaverty dimming just a little. He turned his attention to Breanna. The cold had turned her cheeks pink, and dark strands had come free of her braided hair, whipping around her face. Her peat-brown eyes gleamed with anticipation, and her full lips were parted slightly. She was a vibrant and sensual sight—one Cameron found a little distracting.

The mercenary frowned. "We need to be alert here ... what with the English so close."

Breanna nodded, her expression sobering. They'd both expected the numbers of English patrols to lessen as they made their way along the Kintyre peninsula, but they hadn't. It didn't bode well for the Bruce. He wouldn't be able to remain on the mainland for much longer.

They would need to warn him.

Approaching the gates to Dunaverty, Cameron noted that the guards waiting there wore tight expressions beneath their iron domed helmets.

"Good day," Cameron greeted them with a smile, even if he marked the tense set of the men's shoulders. It wasn't that surprising—this peninsula was crawling with the enemy. "Is the MacDonald in residence?"

"Aye." One of the guards stepped forward, his brow creasing. "And ye are?"

"The name's Cameron Stewart. I have business with the laird."

The guard's frown deepened. "At Yuletide?"

Cameron's smile widened to a grin. "Aye ... what better time to avail oneself of fine MacDonald hospitality."

"We are kin to the laird's wife," Breanna said, her voice uncharacteristically sweet and demure.

Cameron had to admit the woman was adept at mummery when she wished to be. Over the past few days, she'd alternated between briskness and aloofness whenever they were alone. Likewise, he'd been distant. Unless they were putting up a front for the proprietors of the inns they stayed at en route or discussing practicalities, they spoke little. That suited Cameron, although it dawned on him they would have to show a bit more warmth toward each other at Dunaverty, or they wouldn't convince folk for long.

The guard grimaced. "Well, kin or not, ye should have sent word ahead."

Cameron's grin faded. "Why's that?"

"The castle's full of English guests at present ... ye'll have to bed down in the stables."

Cameron stiffened. It was an effort not to let his alarm show.

"Since when?" Breanna asked, her tone sharpening.

"A month now," the guard replied, his gaze flicking between the two of them. "The laird's been asked to billet English soldiers over the winter."

Tension rippled down Cameron's spine. *Has he?*

Where the devil was Robert Bruce then? He burned to ask the question but restrained himself.

The guard stepped back and waved them through. "Go on ... get out of this wind. No doubt we'll find space for ye somewhere."

Nodding his thanks, Cameron gathered the reins and urged his horse through the gate. Breanna silently followed.

They rode into a small village—a collection of tightly-packed homes encircling a muddy clearing—and drew their horses up before what appeared to be an alehouse. The raucous sound of laughter and drunken singing drifted out from the establishment. A moment later, a soldier clad in a hauberk lurched through the doorway, fell to his knees, and threw up the contents of his belly.

Cameron screwed up his face. "There must be stables around here, somewhere," he muttered.

Swinging down from the saddle, his boots sinking into the mud, Cameron craned his neck up then, taking in the steep row of steps, protected on the seaward side by high ramparts, that led up to the lowered drawbridge of the castle itself.

"I don't like this." Breanna had also dismounted and moved close to him. Her face was pinched, her gaze wary. "The English shouldn't be here … not yet."

Cameron gave a brusque nod. "MacDonald will have the answers we need," he murmured. "And once we see to our horses, we'll pay him a visit."

7

BITTER AS WORMWOOD

"YE ARE A moon too late," Angus MacDonald said, eyeing the couple who had joined him for a cup of wine in his solar after supper. "Bruce had to flee in November ... when the English started sniffing around here."

Breanna's mouth thinned. Curse it. The information she had was old. She should have traveled here sooner.

"Do they know ye harbored him within yer walls?" Stewart asked.

Angus MacDonald raised a sandy brow. A tall, rawboned man with flaxen hair and heavy features, the laird had welcomed them into his keep without hesitation. They hadn't said a word to him about their real intentions, yet MacDonald had played along. He'd told the English captain and soldiers who'd dined with them that eve that Stewart was indeed his wife's cousin.

Even without a word from Breanna and Stewart, MacDonald had known why they were here. Wisely, he'd waited until they were alone before saying anything.

"They have their suspicions," he admitted. "However, they've never been able to prove anything." He scowled then. "Instead, I have to host the bastards until spring."

"They're keeping an eye on ye then?" Stewart said. He leaned a shoulder against the mantelpiece, availing himself of the fire's warmth, his fingers wrapped around a cup of wine.

MacDonald snorted. "Aye ... although they'll get nothing from me." His gaze narrowed then, as it swept from Stewart's face to Breanna's. "I'm sorry, but ye can't linger here. I don't like the way Captain Marshall kept eyeing ye over supper. He's a sharp man … and I'd wager he suspects something."

Tension rippled through Breanna at the warning before she dipped her head. "We won't stay beyond tonight," she assured him. "Just as soon as ye tell us where Robert Bruce is now, we'll trouble ye no more."

Angus MacDonald's blue eyes glinted as he held Breanna's gaze. "So ye *both* wish to join the cause?"

"Aye," Stewart answered smoothly. "I led the Stirling defense against the English two and a half years ago, and my wife also knows how to handle herself with a blade. We have skills that will serve Scotland … and we want to make ourselves useful."

An unexpected warmth suffused Breanna at Stewart's words. Although she'd initially chafed at his insistence on taking the lead since they'd left Perth, she'd started to get used to him. She was accustomed to fighting her own corner. It felt odd, and disarmingly pleasant, to have a man support her in this fashion.

Careful, she warned herself. She might actually grow to like the mercenary. *Remember why Stewart took on this job. It's silver he cares about. Nothing more.*

The reminder was a sobering one. Although he hadn't wasted many words on her during their journey to Dunaverty, Stewart had a way with them. She noted how MacDonald's expression softened when the mercenary spoke, respect glinting in his eyes. "Aye, well," he replied, clearing his throat. "I wish Rob had more staunch allies like ye two. Only then will we be able to drive the English from this land."

"He will," Breanna replied firmly. "Come spring, more Scots will rally to his side."

MacDonald's mouth curved in a wry smile. "I hope so, lass."

"I can't believe he's been forced to take refuge beyond Scotland," Breanna muttered as she lay out a blanket over a thick layer of straw. "The king shouldn't be forced to flee his own lands!"

They were bedding down for the evening in an empty stall. The stables weren't the most comfortable of lodgings—but since it was that or bed down on the floor of the great hall with a host of English soldiers, they'd decided to sleep with the horses instead.

"No, he shouldn't," Stewart agreed. "But Rathlin Island is a safer haven than Dunaverty. At least there he's beyond the enemy's reach."

Breanna straightened up, still frowning. It had taken Angus MacDonald a while before he'd eventually admitted where the Bruce was hiding. She didn't blame him for being cautious though—such knowledge had to be guarded carefully.

Rathlin Island wasn't distant—located across the water, just off the coast of Ulster. But despite that she now knew where to find the outlaw king, disappointment soured Breanna's mouth.

"I feel like a fool," she admitted. Exhaustion pressed down upon her this evening. "I thought the information I received was fresh ... yet it wasn't."

Stewart shrugged. "Don't be too hard on yerself." He took off his cloak and stretched out his long body on the blanket. A lantern hanging from the wall—a guttering candle in a metal frame—cast a golden light over the stall. Stewart then rolled up his cloak as a pillow and placed it under his head. "Rathlin Island is but a short journey from the Mull of Kintyre ... and tomorrow we'll seek out a fisherman willing to take us there."

MacDonald had told them to travel up to the Mull the next day to find passage across the water. The laird had his own birlinn, but it would arouse suspicion if they departed on it.

Breanna grimaced. "I just hope our presence here hasn't made that English captain suspicious. Did ye notice how Marshall kept glancing at me over supper?"

Stewart's mouth curved. "Aye ... but I don't think those were suspicious looks he was giving ye, but appreciative ones."

Tension rippled through Breanna. Stewart was likely right. Captain Marshall *had* been overly attentive, and he'd tried to catch her eye numerous times throughout supper, despite that her husband sat at her side.

"Cursed English," she muttered, taking off her own cloak and rolling it up into a ball as her companion had. "They're the scourge of our times." She lay down upon the blanket and pulled the dusty sheepskin one of the castle's servants had given her over them.

"Indeed." His tone was dry. "A bane that shows no sign of receding."

"They will one day," she replied firmly. "The Bruce will see it done."

Silence followed, and when Stewart eventually broke it, there was no mistaking the tone of chagrin in his voice. "Ye seem very sure of yerself, lass?"

Breanna rolled to face him, meeting his gaze. "I am."

The mercenary raised an eyebrow. "And why's that?"

"The head of my order ... the High Bandruì ... had a vision," she told him, her gaze never leaving his. "And in it, she saw the Bruce's banner flying victorious over a battlefield. He *will* defeat the English, Stewart. And I will stay by his side to ensure he fulfills his destiny."

A vaguely amused expression played across her companion's face now. "So, ye intend to become the man's personal guardian?"

Quashing the irritation that simmered in her belly, Breanna drew in a deep breath before answering. "Aye ... for our divinations also warn that his life is in danger." She paused then. "That incident in Stirling ... when Fyfa knocked the goblet of wine from the Bruce's hand ... was a ruse rather than an insult. She did it because someone had poisoned his wine and her own. A witch-woman named Lamia Delamare ... who traveled with the English."

That wiped the amusement from Cameron Stewart's face. His gaze widened. "Longshanks has a *witch*?"

Breanna nodded. "And she may not be the only threat to his life. The incident with John Comyn proves that it isn't only the English we need to be wary of."

Stewart stared back at her, his grey eyes gleaming in the lantern light. His mouth then lifted at the corners. "And ye shall single-handedly shield the Bruce from harm?"

"No," she replied, her tone cooling. His cynicism was chafing her sorely this evening. "I brought ye along to help me."

His lips twitched as if he was swallowing a laugh. "A necessity that vexes ye greatly."

"All the same," Breanna replied, ignoring the barb. "Ye are to keep a close eye on the Bruce's men once we reach Rathlin. There may be an assassin hiding among them. We must trust no one."

Stewart's expression sobered, his gaze veiling. "Ye need not worry about that ... I'm not the gullible sort."

Breanna inclined her head. "Aye, I'd noticed." She paused then, observing him. "Can I ask ... why are ye so bitter?"

His mouth twisted into a humorless smile. "Bitter?"

"Aye ... as wormwood."

He snorted before rolling over onto his back and looking up at the shadowy, cobweb-festooned ceiling of the stables. "Life has taught me some harsh lessons, Breanna," he replied, his voice flattening. "These days, I prefer to look out for myself before others."

Breanna marked the heaviness upon him—one she'd caught glimpses of a few times since they'd left Perth. Her comment had scored a direct hit. Despite his best efforts to appear unbothered, something in this man's past weighed him down. "Stirling left its mark upon ye then?" she asked, her tone gentling.

He didn't answer.

Moments passed, and then Breanna pulled the sheepskin up around her chin. She wouldn't question the mercenary further, even if the cynicism he wore like a shield intrigued her. She knew what it was to be guarded, but at least Breanna's devotion to the Guardians of Alba was her North Star, holding her steady. What did the mercenary believe in?

Breathing in the oily scent of lanolin, Breanna mulled over the enigma that was Cameron Stewart. He shouldn't have fascinated her—yet he did.

Breanna awoke to a sensation of warmth and comfort before rising slowly from the fog of deep sleep.

She became aware then of the slow, steady rhythm of a heartbeat against her ear.

Confused, her eyes flickered open, and as the lingering remnants of sleep drew back, Breanna realized the warmth and comfort came from sleeping in a man's arms.

Cameron Stewart held her close.

She was nestled against his chest, her ear resting over his heart. And, judging from his slow, even breathing, her companion was still asleep.

Breanna tensed. Maiden's blood, how had this happened?

Sleep hadn't come easily the night before. Her mind had been too anxious, busy with thoughts of what the next day would bring. Eventually, she'd drifted off—but she had no memory of rolling toward Stewart, or of him wrapping his arms about her.

Heat washed over her. This was awkward indeed.

Ironically, she felt more rested than she had in a long while. The warmth of Stewart's body wrapped her in a protective cocoon, the scent of leather and warm male invading her senses.

Yet she couldn't remain in such a position. She had to disentangle herself before Stewart awoke and realized that they'd been sleeping curled up together. The man would likely believe he'd made a conquest.

Breanna's mouth thinned. He most definitely hadn't.

Drawing in a deep breath, she attempted to push herself up. However, the cage of Stewart's arm held her fast. Embarrassment prickled Breanna's skin now. There was nothing for it—she wouldn't be able to disentangle herself without waking him.

She reached down, took hold of his wrist, and drew his arm off her. She then pushed herself up.

Cameron Stewart's eyes flickered open.

Staring down at him, Breanna noted the rare unguarded look upon his face. The mercenary's black hair was mussed, his features relaxed with sleep, and a dark shadow of stubble covered his jaw. His smoky eyes, hooded with sleep, stared up at her for a moment before realization dawned.

Her body chilled when his mouth quirked. He then gave a long, languid stretch, his lean, hard body sliding against hers. This was too close—too intimate. She needed to get away from him.

"Mother Mary, I slept well," he announced. "Did ye?"

"Fine," Breanna bit out. Jaw clenched, she scrambled to her feet and dusted straw off her clothing.

"Were ye warm enough?" he asked.

"Aye."

Ignoring his grin, she turned and stalked out into the aisle that ran between the stalls. The snorts and whickers of the stables' inhabitants greeted her, yet Breanna didn't stop to greet her mount as she usually did in the mornings.

Instead, she kept going. A frigid gust of air engulfed her as she pushed open the heavy doors to the stables and stepped out into the narrow yard beyond. Her breath steamed like smoke, and icy cold stung her eyes.

It was still early, although the sky was lightening to the east. They needed to depart shortly, before the English delayed them. MacDonald had assured her that he'd come up with a plausible excuse as to why they hadn't remained for the Yule celebrations as they'd planned. Something about not wishing to break bread with his English guests would be truthful enough without arousing suspicions.

Teeth chattering, Breanna went to draw her cloak around her. However, she then realized that, in her haste to escape Stewart's presence, she'd left it behind.

8

THE MULL OF KINTYRE

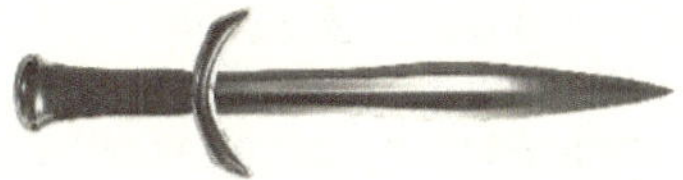

CAMERON FOLLOWED BREANNA along a narrow, rock-strewn track. He leaned forward, allowing his gelding to pick its way up the stony slope. Although their destination wasn't that far, as the crow flew, this path took them over a craggy, windswept landscape to the Mull of Kintyre—the southwestern-most tip of the peninsula. It was the point closest to Ulster, across the water, and Rathlin Island.

Angus MacDonald had assured them that a number of fishermen sailed from the Mull, even in winter, and with the right amount of silver, they might be able to persuade someone to take them across to the island.

Around the two travelers, the headland sparkled as the first rays of sun bathed the frosted landscape. There hadn't been a breath of wind as dawn broke, yet as Cameron and Breanna continued their journey, a biting breeze sprang up, and the formerly clear sky darkened.

Cameron's mouth thinned. He wasn't much of a sailor at the best times—for sea-sickness always assailed him— but he would like it even less if the weather turned against them.

When Breanna had decided to embark on this mission, she'd chosen a poor time of year for it. Winters were long, bitter, and harsh. He'd planned to wait it out in Perth, yet here he was freezing his bollocks off as they tracked down the elusive Bruce.

The things ye'll do for coin, he thought wryly.

The land continued to rise steeply before they reached the peak of the rocky hills around noon and descended the other side, toward the sea. Apart from a hasty piece of bread in the stables, neither Cameron nor Breanna had eaten much that morning. And Breanna didn't seem inclined to rest.

They'd barely spoken since dawn.

Cameron shifted his gaze ahead once more, to where his companion rode—taking in the way Breanna's hair hung in a heavy braid down the long curve of her back. The woman had an unconscious sensuality about her, despite her frosty attitude toward him most of the time.

She certainly hadn't been pleased to discover that she'd inadvertently rolled into his arms during the night. Cameron didn't recall her doing so, yet he had no complaints. Awaking to find her warm, yielding body pressed against his had been a welcome surprise. They'd shared a bed for a few days now, and despite that Breanna was still standoffish toward him when she was awake, her instincts had overruled while she slept.

Cameron's mouth curved. Perhaps she'd forget herself again in the coming days. Maybe under that icy veneer, she had a need to be bedded. *If that's the case, I'll be happy to give her a tumble.*

His gelding stumbled then, nearly unseating him. Cameron pushed aside thoughts of what Breanna would look like naked and focused on navigating the rough path instead.

Best to keep his mind on the job.

Going downhill was harder-going than the first part of their journey. The track, which was already rough, turned even narrower and more rutted, and they were forced to slow their mounts. It was so exposed that the wind gusted against them, pushing back their hoods and making their horses flatten their ears back and pin their tails between their hind legs.

Ahead, the sea was a rough expanse of grey, churning whitecaps.

Cameron's belly clenched at the sight. He didn't want to set sail in this weather.

The two horses wound their way down the hillside, following the track down to the rocks. Before them stretched a stony beach, while to the south loomed craggy cliffs. The clouds had lowered now, the smoke-grey of the sky layered against the iron hue of the sea. Cameron had heard that on a clear day one could see the coast of Ulster from this spot, although this wasn't one such occasion.

A cluster of cottages perched above the shore, smoke drifting horizontally from their chimneys, and Cameron spied a row of fishing boats—long, low timber craft— sitting up on the beach.

There was no sign of anyone out fishing this afternoon.

Cameron's belly growled when they drew up their horses. He swung down from his gelding and dug into his saddlebag, withdrawing a half loaf of bread and some hard cheese. Breaking off some of each for Breanna, he passed the food to her. "We should both eat something," he said, breaking the long silence between them.

Cameron didn't bring up the crossing—surely, with the sea so choppy, they could delay it.

Breanna took the food with a brusque nod. She then shifted her attention to the churning sea, her dark gaze narrowing. "Curse the weather," she muttered. "How are we going to convince someone to take us across the water in this?"

"It won't be easy," Cameron answered. Secretly, he hoped they'd be refused. Far better to wait until the weather calmed. However, he could see from the determined set of his companion's jaw that she didn't want to wait.

Finishing their light meal, they approached the nearest of the cottages.

Breanna withdrew an object from a pouch at her waist then, a small lump of what appeared to be smoky quartz.

Cameron's brow furrowed. "What's that for?"

She shot him an impatient look. "It's a cairn stone ... and should help if anyone needs a little extra *persuasion*."

Cameron scowled. Persuading someone to take them across the water against their will wasn't a clever idea in his opinion. And he was about to tell Breanna so—and remind her to let him take the lead—when a grizzled-looking older man emerged from the cottage.

Before Cameron could speak, Breanna stepped forward and greeted the fisherman. She then inquired whether he'd be willing to take them to Rathlin Island that very afternoon.

The fisherman's leathery face twisted into a grimace. "Only a fool would go out in weather like this," he muttered.

"But it's not far," Breanna replied.

The man eyed her. "Far enough to drown ye, lass." He shook his head then. "Many a sailor has come to grief in this channel."

"We'll pay well," Breanna pressed on, undaunted by his words. "Twenty silver pennies ... and both our horses."

Cameron stiffened. Damn her, Breanna should have left him to do the negotiating. Twenty silver pennies was a ridiculous amount to pay for such a short passage—and he'd hoped to sell their horses for a decent price before crossing the water.

"Breanna." He injected a warning note into his voice. "I don't—"

"Will ye take us?" Breanna cut him off, her gaze focused upon the fisherman.

Glancing down, Cameron saw that her fist that held the cairn stone had clenched.

Misgiving slithered down his spine. He was a man who took much in his stride. He'd heard of the mysterious blue-robed women who were helping rally warriors to the Bruce's cause, and the whispers of old magic that followed them, and it hadn't bothered him. He didn't care that Breanna was a druidess, only that she paid well. He'd even accepted her tale the night before—

of how a witch had tried to poison the Bruce, and of her order's foretelling that the Scottish king was in danger.

But seeing her at work was another matter.

It reminded him that this wasn't a woman who knew her place. He'd thought they'd established an understanding, but it seemed that Breanna had merely been biding her time.

Now that the Bruce was close, she intended to push Cameron aside.

The fisherman stared back at her, his gaze narrowed now. Misgiving shifted to uneasiness within Cameron. Instead of persuading the fisherman, she was making him suspicious. It seemed the order she belonged to had deep coffers—but that didn't mean she had to throw coin around like this.

This man had the face of someone who'd had a hard life. It was likely he'd never be able to afford *one* of their coursers, let alone a pair of them.

"Ye must be desperate indeed to reach Rathlin, to offer me so much," he murmured, still eyeing Breanna. There was a canny edge to the man's voice, and Cameron wondered if he knew that the Bruce was hiding upon the isle. Folk in this area likely would. "But I wonder if ye have wool in yer ears, lass. Did ye not hear what I said about it being too dangerous?"

"I heard ye," Cameron snapped. "Ten silver pennies if ye take us across tomorrow ... once the sea settles."

The fisherman's expression changed, and Cameron's belly sank as he saw greed glint in the man's eyes. He didn't appreciate the lower offer—especially when he knew what Cameron's companion was prepared to pay.

The devil's cods, why couldn't the woman let me negotiate with him?

Breanna cleared her throat "Don't listen to my husband," she said, her voice ringing across the windy shore. There was a resonance to her tone now, a power, and Cameron felt a strange pull. Whatever she was doing was starting to affect him as well. "My offer still stands ... if ye take us across *today.*"

Silence followed, broken only by the whistling of the wind and the roar of the waves behind them. Cameron's belly twisted then, as his temper quickened.

He wasn't easily moved to anger these days. Ever since Stirling, he'd swallowed his ire. Anger meant he cared about things, and he didn't. That was why he'd become a mercenary. He hired out his blade, his skills, but didn't invest his hopes in the outcome.

But Breanna was starting to vex him. Aye, he could be rash at times, yet her imprudence was foolhardy.

The fisherman should know better than to negotiate with someone who was so obviously desperate, someone who didn't heed his warnings about the perils of taking the boat out in this weather.

The man's gaze darted to where the horses stood behind them, their manes and forelocks fluttering in the wind, and when he shifted his attention back to Breanna, a grim smile stretched his mouth. "Agreed."

9

INTO THE STORM

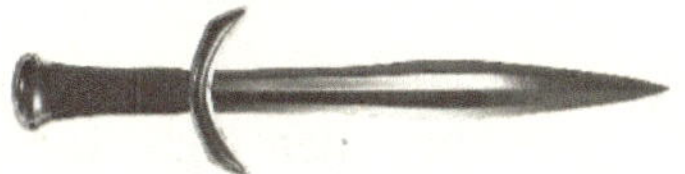

"THIS IS UTTER folly, Breanna." Stewart's voice was clipped and cold when he drew her to one side on the beach. "The Bruce isn't worth drowning for."

Breanna met his gaze. She could see anger burning in his eyes, yet she didn't care. If it were up to him, they'd wait days here. Who knew when the sea would settle? Impatience thrummed through her. She didn't trust Captain Marshall either. MacDonald would provide a solid excuse for their departure, but she wouldn't be surprised if the English captain had them followed nonetheless.

It was imperative they went today—she had to reach Robert the Bruce. The sooner they found him, the sooner they could provide the protection he needed.

"Aye, he is," she replied through clenched teeth. Meanwhile, the fisherman had gone back inside to fetch his oilskins. "Although I think ye are being overly cautious. The man has agreed to take us, hasn't he?"

"Only because ye turned him witless with yer witchery." Stewart then motioned to the horses. "There's a market nearby at Ceann Locha. I was going to sell the coursers there ... we could do with the coin in the months to come."

Breanna snorted. "We'd waste precious time doing that." She paused then before patting the heavy purse attached to the belt cinched about her waist. "I've got enough silver to see us through."

"All the same, it's clearly perilous to take a boat out in this weather ... ye don't have to be a sea dog to understand that." Stewart's glare was unwavering, and a muscle bunched in his jaw. For the first time since they'd met in Perth, she'd succeeded in truly vexing him.

Breanna scowled. "I didn't take ye for a fazart, Stewart."

His grey eyes narrowed. "Maybe I am," he drawled. "If ye call good sense cowardice ... but at least I'm not daft enough to sail out into a storm. This is what happens when a woman takes charge."

Breanna drew herself up. *Thrice-cursed condescending bastard.* She was tempted to tell him that he needn't bother coming with her. How she wished she didn't require his help. But Bruce wouldn't welcome her into his band of freedom fighters without a male protector in tow.

As much as she wished it weren't necessary, she *had* to take the mercenary with her.

The fisherman emerged from his cottage then, swathed in heavy oilskins. He gestured behind him. "Ye can tie the horses up under the lean-to at the back," he instructed, raising his gravelly voice to be heard over the wind. "I'll get the boat ready." He paused then and held out a large hand. "But first, I'll have those twenty silver pennies."

Breanna gave the man a reluctant nod. Aye, her cairn stone had done a fine job of persuading this man—but then so had the generous sum of silver she'd offered him. She didn't like the avaricious look in his eye, but it couldn't be helped. Digging into the pouch at her waist, she started to count out the coins.

All the while, she did her best to dismiss the worry that had suddenly started ringing like a storm-bell in her head. It really wasn't a long journey across the water to Rathlin Island. They'd reach their destination before they knew it.

The small boat bucked, flying high in the air before it hit the water with a 'slap'.

Breanna's belly dropped, and she gripped the wooden side of the fishing vessel. Saltwater stung her face, and the wind tore at her skin.

Around her, the waves looked as big as mountains: huge, dark, glassy peaks.

The sight of the one they now climbed made her bowels turn to water.

Perhaps this crossing wasn't a good idea after all.

It was too late for regrets now though, for they were out at sea—and the headland was lost from sight.

Breanna's attention shifted then to the fisherman. When they'd joined him on the pebbly beach, he'd informed them his name was Ewan. He was seated before her, his leathery face contorted as he rowed up the wave. Water dripped off his oilskins.

Hunching down as more seawater sprayed over her, Breanna forced herself to glance left, at where she knew Stewart was also clinging on like grim death.

Face pale, eyes wide, the man's throat worked as his gaze remained fixed upon the bow of the boat. He looked as if he was going to be violently ill.

The mercenary wasn't much good to her in this state—not that there was anything he could do.

As the storm howled and the sky above turned purple, Breanna whispered to The Three.

Maiden, Mother, Crone ... please spare us.

She dug then into one of the many pouches upon her belt and grasped her cairn stone once more. The smoky quartz provided protection as well as persuasion. Thank the Goddesses that Fyfa had gifted her a new one of these. She'd been right: a bandruì shouldn't travel without one.

Whispering a protection sain, Breanna tightened her grip on the cairn stone. The wind gusted harder still, and amongst the brine scent of the sea, she caught the smell of pine and freshly turned earth: the scent of witching. A moment later, the cairn stone warmed against her palm, as it had when she'd convinced the fisherman to take them across the water.

And all the while, the boat climbed, up and up, until it reached the crest of the great wave—and there it hung, for a breathless moment, before the craft dropped into the hollow between this wave and the next.

Breanna's belly lurched up into her throat before slamming downward as the boat hit the water with another resounding 'slap'.

Fear soured Breanna's mouth, even as her grip on the cairn stone tightened. At this rate, this small boat would break up.

She should have heeded the fisherman before her witching had clouded his judgment. This was not a day for travel.

Ye should have listened to Stewart.

Aye, she should have. What good was she to the Bruce if she drowned in this channel? And if they managed to get to safety, she'd let that bastard crow.

At present though, she had to focus. She couldn't access her witch-will with fear clouding her thoughts.

Murmuring the sain with renewed vigor, she closed her eyes.

"I'm not taking ye any farther!"

Breanna's eyes snapped open, and she looked upon the fisherman, horror hollowing out her belly. "What?"

"Ye heard me!" Ewan bellowed to be heard over the storm that roared around them. "Rathlin is right in front of us now, but if I attempt to row in, my boat will be dashed on the rocks. Ye will have to swim for it."

Breanna gaped at him.

Swim for it? She thought the persuasion charm she'd used on him back on the shore should have lasted longer than this. However, it seemed the man's fear had overridden her witching.

He glared at her. "Ye *can* swim, woman?"

Numbly, she nodded before casting her attention in Stewart's direction. "Can ye swim, Stewart?" she gasped out the words.

The mercenary's face now held a greenish hue. His mouth clamped into a thin line as he gave a jerky nod.

Breanna's belly clenched. Tearing her attention from Stewart, she took in the churning water around them. Aye, she could swim—Colina had made a point of teaching them all as bairns—but that didn't mean she was a *strong* swimmer.

The fisherman said the island was in front of them, but what if he was lying? What if he simply didn't want to row any farther?

As if sensing this, Cameron Stewart lurched toward him and gripped the man's collar, hauling his face close. "Ye'd better not be lying to us," he growled.

"I'm not," Ewan gasped back. "I know this channel well ... the coast is only a short swim ... but I'll wreck my boat if I go any farther."

"If I go overboard and discover otherwise, I'll find a way back to the mainland," Stewart snarled back. "And when I do, I'll come for ye."

Ewan's eyes bulged. "I'm telling ye the truth." His voice was strangled now. "It's safer for us all if ye swim the rest of the way."

"Ye better be."

Stewart let the fisherman go then and shifted back to beside Breanna. With shaking hands, she'd put her cairn stone away in its pouch. It hadn't proved much help so far, and she was too scared to focus on the sain.

Stewart's gaze fused with hers. "Can ye do this, Breanna?" he asked roughly.

A heartbeat followed, and then she nodded.

"Over ye go!" Ewan shouted as a wave hit the boat, spraying them all with icy water. He'd now stopped rowing and was viewing her with panic glinting in his dark eyes. "I can't wait any longer!"

Cursing, Breanna looked over at where their two satchels—containing clothing, provisions, and other essential items—sat. They couldn't take those.

"Take off yer cloak and yer boots." Stewart's hoarse voice reached her then. "They'll only drag ye down."

With numb fingers, Breanna struggled to comply. She couldn't believe this was happening. It was as if she were observing events unfold from afar.

But it was real, and when she stripped off her boots, her body started to tremble.

She didn't want to go into that churning sea.

As if sensing her reluctance, Stewart grabbed hold of her hands and pulled Breanna to her feet. Then, wrapping an arm around her waist, he launched himself off the boat, taking her with him.

Breanna sucked in a deep breath—just as she hit the freezing water.

A wave sucked them under, swallowing them into its maw like a great kraken. Terror clutched at Breanna, especially when the force of the wave ripped her from Stewart's grip.

Desperate for air, she clawed her way upward. Her long skirts pulled her down and tangled in her legs, yet she was able to kick them aside and use her bare feet to propel herself upward. Lungs burning, she broke through the waves. An instant later, Cameron Stewart appeared. Gasping for air, he trod water, glancing around him. His hair was plastered to his skull, and his eyes appeared huge on his taut face.

He then choked out a curse.

Breanna didn't answer. Frankly, she was too busy treading water and praying to the Goddesses for assistance.

The fishing boat bobbed a few yards distant, rolling dangerously in the waves as Ewan struggled to turn it around.

Stewart's gaze shifted back to Breanna. "Come on," he gasped. "We have to swim for it."

Drawing in a deep breath, Breanna then struck out, doing her best to swim to safety.

After taking a few strokes, she glanced over her shoulder, to make sure the mercenary was following her. He was, although Stewart had waited till she drew ahead before he started swimming.

He's watching out for me.

If Breanna's belly hadn't been lodged in her throat, if her heart hadn't been galloping like a bolting horse, she might have been warmed by his protectiveness. But as it was, she wasn't sure either of them would manage to get safely to shore.

10

FANNING THE FLAMES

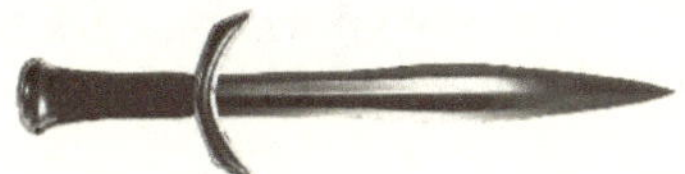

SHEETS OF RAIN sluiced across Breanna's face as she dragged herself out of the foaming surf and staggered toward the pebbly beach. Her wet skirts tangled in her legs then, and she tripped, sprawling face-first into the water once more.

Strong hands gripped her around the waist and hauled her upright.

Stewart, who'd swum behind her during the terrifying last stretch between the boat and shore, had caught up with her.

The stones dug into her bare feet, and her breathing came in gasps as she struggled to remain upright. Fortunately, Stewart's iron grip held her up, and together they staggered the last few yards up the slope of dark grey stones before collapsing upon the shore.

And all the while, the wind and rain lashed them and the waves boomed as loud as thunder.

A sob ripped from Breanna as she struggled to catch her breath.

The Three strike her down, she'd never been so scared. Pure terror had pulsed through her as she'd swum into the darkness. Part of her had been sure the fisherman had lied to them, as Stewart had suspected. She'd been certain they'd swim until exhaustion dragged them down into the sea's cold embrace.

But then, when she'd crested that last big wave, she'd caught sight of a dark headland, and hope had flowered in her breast.

They would survive this after all.

Rolling onto her back, she let the rain pepper her face. She didn't care that she was wet and cold and would likely catch a deathly chill out here.

All that mattered was that she hadn't drowned.

Above her, the sky was a wild tangle of slate-grey and purple clouds, turning the afternoon dark, and bringing the dusk—which always came too early this time of year—with it.

Her breast still rose and fell sharply, but as the relief drew back, she glanced over at the man who lay sprawled upon the rocky shore next to her.

Cameron Stewart's clothing was plastered to his tall, lean frame, and she could see that he too struggled to regain his breath. And as she observed him, the mercenary rolled up into a sitting position and pushed his wet hair off his face.

And then, he turned his attention upon her.

Breanna's breathing caught. She wasn't sure what she'd expected to see in Cameron Stewart's eyes: relief, concern, or fear. But none of those emotions were evident. Instead, his eyes—the same hue as the clouds that roiled overhead—burned with rage.

His handsome face was pinched and white, his skin drawn tightly over his cheekbones.

And he was glaring at her as if he wished to throttle her.

"Clod-headed, goose-witted, daft woman," he choked out. "I should have left ye out there to drown!" Fury had nearly rendered the man incoherent, she noted. Warning prickled over Breanna. She hadn't expected his wrath— not yet anyway—although she knew she deserved it.

Her rashness had nearly gotten them both killed.

"I misjudged the weather," she admitted, her tone uncharacteristically meek. "And ... I'm sorry for it."

"*Misjudged?*" A muscle worked in his jaw. He shifted closer. "Ye willfully ignored that fisherman's warning ... and mine. Yer arrogance, yer obstinacy, nearly ended with us having a watery end."

"Aye, but we didn't." Struggling to keep her voice even, Breanna shifted around to face him fully. After their narrow escape, she felt fragile. Nonetheless, she didn't appreciate the way her companion was railing at her. They'd survived, hadn't they?

"Only by a miracle," he growled, his chest rising and falling fast now—not from exhaustion but rage. He drew closer still to her on his knees, so their faces were just inches apart. "From now on, things are going to change, Breanna. I'll not indulge yer whims any longer."

Breanna's heart started to kick against her ribs. *My whims? How dare he?*

"From this moment forth, ye are going to mind yerself and let me take charge," he went on, heedless of the storm brewing within her. "And ye are going to keep a leash on that shrew's tongue!"

Heat ignited in the pit of Breanna's belly, even though her limbs were numb and her body trembled from the cold. "Wh—"

"Enough, woman!" he snarled. "I'm not finished speaking!"

"Aye, ye are. I didn't hire ye to berate me, or lord over me, Stewart."

His hands clamped down on her shoulders then, his fingers biting through her wet clothing into her flesh. "I might be yer hired blade, but I'll not suffer the directions of a foolish woman." He forced out the words through clamped teeth, fury rolling off him in waves now. He looked like he wanted to shake her until her teeth rattled, yet he didn't. "From this moment on, ye are to act the obedient wife ... especially when we go before the Bruce. Ye are to watch and listen for once. Ye never know ... ye might actually learn something."

His scorn only served to fan the flames of Breanna's own anger. "Brute!" she snarled. "Ye have nothing to teach me!" She reached up then, her fingers locking around his wrists. "Now get yer filthy hands off me!"

Stewart cursed, and instead of heeding her, he hauled her against him, his mouth crashing down on hers.

The kiss was hard, searing, and dominant.

A heartbeat passed, and then Breanna reeled back.

The crack of her open palm striking him across the face cut through the howling wind and roaring sea. She'd hit him hard, the mark of her fingers making red welts appear on his cheek—yet Cameron Stewart didn't even flinch.

Their gazes fused, tension pulsing between them. And then Breanna grabbed him by the collar of his soaked gambeson and yanked him toward her, kissing him back with a violence that equaled his own.

Stewart's arms went around her, and suddenly they were devouring each other.

All thought, all reason, fled from Breanna's mind. Raw need obliterated everything else. The heat of Stewart's mouth, the strength of his grip, the hardness of his wet body pressed against hers, caused something to give way inside her.

Aye, he was handsome, but she hadn't even realized she was attracted to this rogue—not until they kissed.

He gave her no quarter, pushing her back over the iron barrier of his arm, as his tongue tangled with hers, as he tasted her lips and grazed them with his teeth.

Breanna's body turned molten under the onslaught.

She'd had a few kisses in her thirty-two winters. Yet never one like this. She'd never known what it was to be utterly transported—to lose control.

She kissed him back, one arm linking around his neck to pull him closer, with her free hand tangled in his wet hair.

Hunger twisted her belly, and a throbbing ache began between her thighs. Goddesses, how she wanted him to take her right here, right now—upon this windswept, rocky shore. She wanted their passion to burn as bright as their anger, to be consumed by it until everything else burned to ash.

She felt sick with need.

"Ho, there!"

A rough male voice intruded, ripping through the haze of lust that wrapped around them.

Breanna and Stewart sprang apart, and the mercenary rolled to his feet, his hand straying to the hilt of the dirk at his hip. Breanna scrambled up, trying to ignore the weakness in her legs, and followed suit, her fingers wrapping around the bone-hilt of the dagger she carried strapped to her waist.

Tall shadows surrounded them, and Breanna's heart leaped into her throat.

They'd been so taken up by each other, by that fiery kiss, that they hadn't even noticed the approach of this band of men.

"Sorry, if we're intruding." The same voice continued, laced with amusement now. "But from a distance, it looked as if ye were in trouble." The man stepped forward then. He was tall and strongly built with shoulder-length brown hair. A stern, strong-featured face and light-brown eyes the color of walnut regarded them.

Breanna's skin prickled, even as her hand relaxed its hold on her dirk hilt. The bur of the man's voice told her this was one of her countrymen, yet there was something else about him—something that made her already racing pulse quicken further.

"Ye weren't intruding," she replied, cursing the huskiness of her voice that betrayed her. "My husband and I just narrowly escaped drowning." Her face heated as the man's mouth curved, amusement glinting in his formerly serious eyes.

"Ye didn't try to cross from the Scottish mainland, did ye?" One of the other men asked, incredulous. "Not in this weather?"

"Aye," Stewart spoke up. "Although the boatman refused to take us into shore, so we had to swim."

Muttered oaths followed this statement, and Breanna's cheeks started to burn. It seemed that Stewart wasn't the only one who thought such a trip was foolhardy.

However, the man who was clearly the leader of this band didn't join them. Instead, he fixed Stewart with an appraising look. "I know yer face," he murmured. "Have we met before?"

For the first time since they'd been interrupted, Breanna looked at the mercenary's face. Stewart's cheekbones were stained with a faint blush, and to her chagrin, she could still see the red mark where she'd struck him, yet his gaze didn't waver from the stranger's. "We might have," he replied, a wary edge to his voice now. "Although I couldn't say where."

"Stirling," the man replied after a pause. "Ye were with those defending the castle. I saw ye after the surrender."

Stewart's gaze widened. "Aye ... I'm Cameron Stewart ... and I was once captain of the Stirling Guard." He paused then, his face tensing. "And ye are?"

The man stared back at him before a real smile stretched across his face. "I am Robert Bruce."

11

RESTLESS

The English Camp
Argyll, Scotland

LAMIA DE EYNSFORD lay awake, listening to the rain lash the sides of the pavilion. It wasn't late, yet she and her husband had retired to bed early, and Philip was already in a deep sleep.

Glancing her husband's way, Lamia's mouth thinned. Sleep always came so easily to Philip. He slumbered like a man with an easy conscience. But Lamia's active mind and the icy cold kept her awake. Despite the layers of blankets and sheepskins covering them, and the large brazier that still burned in the center of the tent, the chill still managed to find its way in. If it wasn't for Philip's warmth, she'd have been frozen to the marrow.

Philip de Eynsford's face was gentle in repose—and even more handsome. Even so, Lamia felt a stab of irritation as she gazed upon him.

She'd let attraction cloud her good sense when it had come to Sir Philip.

He wasn't the catch she'd been hoping for. Lamia had wished for a powerful husband—a man who led armies and had the king's ear—but Sir Philip's holdings near London were humble, and he commanded a small company of men-at-arms.

But right from the beginning, when Philip had joined Edward's army at Stirling, during the latter part of the siege, the attraction between him and Lady Lamia

Delamare—the queen consort's favorite—had been palpable.

And soon after the fall of Stirling, they'd become lovers. Six months after that, Sir Philip had proposed.

Lamia hadn't accepted immediately. Initially, she'd been vexed that he'd asked at all. However, when the irritation passed, she realized that Philip was her only way to ensure she remained in Scotland.

If she hadn't wed him, she'd be back at Westminster right now with the other ladies-in-waiting, simpering and scheming.

Huffing out an annoyed sigh, Lamia cast aside the covers and slipped out of bed. The loss of her husband's warmth made her shiver, and she threw on a heavy woolen shawl, wrapping it about her shoulders. She then went to the basket upon a nearby table, where a small white grass snake curled.

Lamia reached out, trailing her fingertips lovingly along the snake's scaly skin. "What are we to do, Fantôme?" she whispered. "All this waiting is stretching my nerves to the limit."

The snake awoke, its small, flat dark eyes fixing upon her. An instant later, a tiny forked tongue darted out.

Lamia's mouth quirked. As always, her familiar counseled her to remain patient.

In the bed, Philip murmured in his sleep and turned over, his dark hair fanning out over the pillow. Glancing over at him, Lamia's features softened. There were worse husbands than Philip de Eynsford. He'd never tried to temper her sharp tongue or at times caustic observations. And he'd accepted the fact that his wife had a pet snake.

The fleeting moment of tenderness passed then, and Lamia frowned.

Of course, Philip had no idea of who she really was.

He didn't know she was a witch—a woman with ambitions, and one driven by the need to make her mark on the world.

Lamia shifted her attention from her sleeping husband and gave Fantôme another stroke. "And I will," she murmured.

Aye, she'd been thwarted thus far, and been required to exercise far more patience than she thought herself capable of, but she hadn't given up.

If anything, her defeats had strengthened her resolve.

She would help see England rule Scotland.

She would prevent Robert the Bruce from rallying his countrymen to his side.

And she wouldn't permit that meddling coven of Scottish witches to thwart her.

Lamia's belly started to ache then—as it often did when she dwelled too long on thoughts that vexed her. Reaching down, she rubbed it, even as she relived the disappointments of the past.

Firstly, one member of that coven, a druidess named Nessa, had prevented her from pursuing Hugh de Burgh, the powerful knight who'd once been Edward's right-hand; and then Fyfa, another of the mysterious order, had thwarted her attempt at poisoning the Bruce. The failed assassination attempt had happened just after the fall of Stirling, and Fyfa and her husband had fled the English camp before Edward could arrest them. He'd sent a cutthroat after them—a Saracen—who'd somehow failed in his mission.

The ache in her belly started to burn then, and Lamia shifted over to where a jug of milk sat nearby.

She was pouring herself a cup when a sleepy male voice intruded. "Is all well, love?"

Warmth rippled over her, and the burning in her belly ebbed just a little. Yet Lamia took a gulp of milk and let it wash down before she turned back to her husband.

Philip had propped himself up on an elbow, his oak-brown eyes dark in the half-light inside the tent.

"Aye," she murmured. "Just thirsty."

His brow furrowed. "Is your belly troubling you again?"

Lamia made an irritated sound in the back of her throat. She hated it when Philip fussed over her. She knew why her stomach bothered her.

Anger and frustration—it was eating her up inside.

Years were passing, and she was no closer to her goals.

Lamia took another sip of milk, sighing as it settled her churning stomach.

At least there were some things to be thankful for. Edward had had the sense to send Aymer de Valence to Scotland to crush the Scottish rebellion. As soon as she'd heard of the planned campaign, Lamia had ensured her husband went with him.

And it hadn't been a good year for Robert the Bruce. The Scottish outlaw king was hiding away somewhere now, no doubt licking his wounds. He'd murdered one of his countrymen, John Comyn, in February and had been declared a fugitive for both his sacrilege and breach of fealty afterward. Then, at the beginning of June, De Valence had taken Bruce completely by surprise in an early morning sneak attack at Methven. In the months following, the Bruce's brother Neil had fallen into English hands and been hanged, drawn, and quartered; and his wife, daughter, and sisters were all currently English prisoners.

"Come back to bed, Lamia," Philip said, intruding on her brooding once more. "It's freezing in here."

Lamia set down the cup and turned back to her husband before padding across the mat that had been laid down over the frozen ground. Wordlessly, she then slid into bed next to Philip.

His arm snaked out and looped around her waist, drawing her close as she snuggled under the heavy covers. With a sigh, Lamia sank into his warmth. Philip placed a kiss upon the crown of her head before his hand stroked her back. "You haven't been yourself of late," he murmured. "Does something worry you?"

Lamia tensed. Of course, she'd done a poor job of hiding her impatience recently. She'd spent enough winters in Scotland to know that the months in which

their armies waited out the bitter weather seemed
endless. The English preferred to wage their campaigns
in summer. Once winter came, they hunkered down and
waited out the cold, only to sweep back like a springtide
once the last of the snow passed.

The custom annoyed Lamia. These English and their
irritating habit of calling a truce in the winter months.
Meanwhile, who knew what those devious Scots were up
to?

"I'm just frustrated," she admitted, deciding that she
could be honest about that at least. "The Bruce still
eludes us."

"He does," Philip replied, "but not for much longer.
We've got the bastard on the run now."

"I'm sure he *was* hiding out at Dunaverty Castle," she
said, her tone hardening. "And if we'd gotten there
earlier, we'd have caught him."

Silence followed, and Lamia felt her husband's long
body tense against hers. They'd already argued about
this, for Lamia hadn't been able to contain her
disappointment when he'd returned from the Kintyre
peninsula with news that the Bruce had eluded them—
again.

"Aye, but we didn't ... and MacDonald gave us
nothing."

Lamia's jaw clenched, her belly gurgling in response.
"You should have tortured him ... he would have talked
then."

Philip laughed, although the sound was a trifle brittle.
"*You* should have been born a man, my love," he chided
her. "You'd have made a formidable interrogator."

Lamia tensed against him. Aye, she should have been.
But instead, she'd been forced to live out her life in this
weak woman's body, forced to put up with bungling men.
Ire pulsed within her then. "Luckily for you, I wasn't,"
she replied, not bothering to hide the tart edge to her
voice.

Philip huffed another laugh, this one warmer. "Aye."
His hand stroked her back once more before it cupped

the curve of her bottom. He then pulled her against him. Lamia felt the hardness of his arousal.

Her breathing caught, irritation warring with desire.

Damn him, but Philip de Eynsford knew just how to scatter her wits. She wouldn't be distracted though. Waiting here in this camp for another two months, while the Bruce plotted against them, would drive her mad.

Philip wouldn't like it—but it was time for her to take action.

Resolve tightened within Lamia, even as the feel of Philip's hand upon her naked thigh did its best to distract her.

Upon the dawn, she would find a way to leave the camp and strike out on her own. Philip had a council with Sir Aymer and the other knights at first light. She would slip away then and wouldn't be missed till much later.

The town of Dunoon was half a morning's walk away—so she'd begin her search for Robert the Bruce there.

Although she was neither English nor a Scot—having been born and brought up in France—Lamia knew how to blend in with her surroundings. She was adept at using misdirection and glamor charms so that folk wouldn't think they were speaking to an exotic-looking lady with a French accent. Instead, they'd believe she was just a curious local lass.

With her familiar's assistance, she'd surely be able to discover what these incompetent knights couldn't.

Decision made, Lamia let out a sigh, the tension melting from her. A fluttering excitement filled her then, one that was amplified by her husband's sensual caresses. Raising her face to him for a kiss, Lamia's mouth curved into a smile.

Indeed, Philip would never sanction her going off on her own. He'd be livid when he discovered her gone, but she wasn't going to let him keep her here.

All the same, she'd miss the man's company, both in and out of bed. It sometimes caught her by surprise how much she liked Philip—a sentiment she tried hard to quash. Such feelings would distract her from her purpose, would cause her ambitions to wane.

She didn't want to become like her best friend, Margaret, the queen consort of England. The two women had always been close, but these days all Margaret cared about was having her husband's babies. She'd turned boring of late.

Lamia had no patience for such women.

She reached out then, her fingers trailing a path down Philip's chest and belly before they curled around the hardness of his shaft. He groaned before deepening their kiss.

Lamia melted into him. She wouldn't lie with her husband for a while after tonight—and so she would make sure she had her fill of him.

12

THE OUTLAW KING

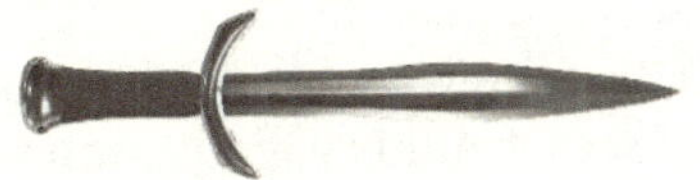

Rathlin Castle
Rathlin Island—Off the Coast of Ulster

The same evening …

"I WILL GLADLY accept yer fealty, Stewart." Robert Bruce's voice rumbled across the solar. He then glanced over at where Breanna sat meekly by the fire. "As well as that of yer wife."

Cameron favored him with a smile. It was difficult to rouse the energy even for that, for fatigue pressed down on him like a boulder upon his back. His eyes were gritty, and his head ached. It was late, and most of the inhabitants of the castle were abed—but after a lengthy supper in the great hall with the Bruce and his men, Cameron and Breanna had been summoned to the solar for a private conversation. This was the space of Hugh Bissett, lord of this castle and island, and of the Glens of Antrim in Ulster. However, Hugh had graciously let them speak here—for the castle had few places where one wouldn't be overheard.

After Bruce had met them upon the beach, he took his two castaways back to Rathlin Castle. Darkness had been settling over the world as Cameron climbed the path to the castle, stones biting into his bare feet. Perched on a rocky headland, the castle looked northeast, toward Scotland.

"I am relieved to hear it," Cameron admitted after a pause. "For my wife and I are keen to do what we can to aid ye."

Robert Bruce's mouth curved. "Aye ... ye almost drowned yerselves in yer eagerness to do so."

Cameron kept his own smile fixed upon his face, even if inwardly he still smoldered.

He was no lover of the water at the best of times, but it had taken every inch of his will to climb aboard that fishing boat and let Ewan row them away into the choppy waves.

And no sooner had they lost sight of shore when the weather took a turn for the worse.

Cameron didn't know how he'd managed to stop himself from heaving his guts out over the side of the boat. Cold sweat had bathed him, and his stomach lurched with every roll, every dip, of the small vessel.

And when the waves rose like vast peaks around him, he'd been sure that it would be his last afternoon alive.

Initially, he'd been too scared, too sick, to be angry—but once they'd reached shore, the strength of his rage had awed even him.

He'd shocked himself too when he'd grabbed Breanna and kissed her. The move hadn't been planned. Just moments earlier, he'd envisaged himself choking the life out of the infuriating woman.

It was her arrogance, her recklessness, that had nearly gotten them killed—and although her wan face and frightened eyes told him that she was truly sorry for it, his wrath couldn't be contained.

Cameron cleared his throat. "Aye, well ... fortunately we can both swim."

He did cut his companion a look then. Breanna sat there, hands folded demurely upon her lap, a pose as innocent as the Virgin Mary herself. Yet the deep-red kirtle she wore—a loan from the lady of the castle—made her look like Mary Magdalene instead. Her usual clothes were looser, while this garment hugged her delicious body like a glove. She was a distracting sight; nonetheless, he was relieved she was behaving herself.

Her relief at finding Robert the Bruce had been obvious when the king introduced himself on the shore. Cameron had marked the way her eyes shone and the wide smile that had flowered across her face. He hadn't seen Breanna look at anyone that way. Especially him.

The first part of their mission—finding the Bruce—had been completed. Now they just had to ensure he remained alive to fulfill his destiny as the savior of Scotland. Cameron was one step closer to receiving his final payment and taking a well-earned rest.

His gaze fell upon Breanna and the rapt look upon her face as she observed the Bruce. Perhaps now they'd found Scotland's outlaw king, she'd let Cameron take the lead without fighting him every inch of the way.

His cheek still stung from the blow she'd landed, even if he'd expected her to retaliate. However, he *hadn't* expected her to launch herself at him a moment later. He hadn't been gentle and had noted during supper that her lips were swollen in the aftermath. Yet her fierceness had matched his.

If the Bruce and his men hadn't interrupted him, he'd surely have taken her.

Cameron's belly tightened. How he'd like to bed Breanna, to feel the softness of that lush body pressed up against his again. He wanted her to bite him, to sink her nails into his back as he rode her.

Lust arrowed through his groin. Shifting in his seat, Cameron shoved the torrid thoughts from his mind and attempted to focus on the Bruce.

To his consternation, the man was watching him with a veiled expression—as if he was trying to decide what to make of him.

"Ye did an admirable job at Stirling," the Bruce murmured after a pause. "Few castles have withstood such an attack for so long."

Cameron's smile turned strained, although he acknowledged Bruce's compliment with a nod. He didn't like it when folk brought up Stirling. Even now, bitterness filled his mouth when he recalled how Edward of England's Warwolf—a giant trebuchet assembled at the end of the siege—had brought down the eastern curtain wall in just one hit.

The humiliation of being marched out of the fortress afterward and taken before Longshanks himself had been worse than he'd expected. Cameron had known things were dire. Their supplies wouldn't last, and when they realized that the English were readying a new weapon, it had only been a matter of time before the castle fell. And he'd even advised Sir William Oliphant, the governor of Stirling, to negotiate with the enemy.

Even so, something had changed in him on the day Stirling fell.

Cameron Stewart had once been a proud, patriotic Scot. He'd believed in fighting back against the English.

Wrath had overtaken him that night, as he'd sat with his fellow Scots in the midst of the English camp, and he'd gone looking for a fight. A group of English soldiers had given him one—along with a battered face, two black eyes, and cracked ribs.

And afterward, cynicism had set in. He'd left Stirling and his hope behind him. It was useless anyway—Longshanks couldn't be stopped.

And yet Robert the Bruce believes he can be.

Cameron shifted uncomfortably in his chair again before glancing Breanna's way once more. She was observing his exchange with the Bruce intently. Unease rippled over the mercenary then. This woman saw too much. The night before, when they'd bedded down in the stable at Dunaverty, her questioning had gotten under his skin. He'd made a mental note afterward to be more careful about what he divulged to her.

Focusing on the Bruce once more, Cameron noted the lines of strain on the man's face. Lifting a goblet of wine to his lips, the outlaw king took a deep draft. "Defeat is difficult to stomach, Stewart," he murmured. "I see in yer eyes the lingering shadow of it." His face hardened then. "I too have known much loss of late."

Cameron stilled. Aye, he'd heard the stories too. Of the crushing defeat at Methven, of how the Bruce's wife,

Elizabeth, was now an English prisoner—as were his daughter and sister.

He'd heard too of what they'd done to Neil Bruce.

"I was sorry to hear of yer brother," Breanna spoke up then, her voice subdued. It seemed her near-death had cowed her after all. Cameron wondered how long this demure behavior would last. "I hear he defended Kildrummy bravely."

A nerve flickered on Robert Bruce's cheek. "Aye … although he was betrayed by one of his own countrymen … for gold."

Cameron stiffened. The Bruce hadn't intended them that way, yet his words were a sharp reminder of the bargain Cameron and Breanna had struck. *He* was only here because she was paying him a king's ransom in silver. Irritated that his conscience had pricked him, Cameron clenched his jaw. Aye, he was a mercenary, but despite everything, he was still a loyal Scot. He'd never betray his countrymen for coin.

"Edward the younger bribed a blacksmith at Kildrummy with 'as much gold as he could carry'," Bruce continued. "And the bastard took it before setting fire to the grain stores. With their food supply destroyed, the men of Kildrummy were forced to surrender." His eyes guttered then. "They did to my brother what they did to the Wallace … hanged, drawn, and quartered."

A shiver crawled over Cameron's skin. A cruel, brutal death indeed.

"Did ye ever manage to apprehend the blacksmith?" Breanna asked after a pause.

"Aye." Robert Bruce's face turned to stone. Hatred burned in his walnut-brown eyes. "We found him … ensured he did indeed receive his reward for betraying Neil: all the gold he could carry was melted and poured down his throat."

A brittle hush settled over the solar at these words, while Cameron silently made a note that the Bruce wasn't a man lightly crossed.

The outlaw king raised his goblet to his lips again and drained the last of his wine. He then set the pewter goblet down, his gaze traveling to Breanna once more. "Yer husband informed me earlier that ye wish to fight alongside my warriors," he said, his voice gentling. "I'm not sure that's wise."

Breanna's proud face tensed. "I know how to wield a dirk, a sword, and a quarter-staff," she replied, her voice cooling. "I can shoot a bull's-eye at forty yards with a longbow, and I'm skilled with my fists."

Cameron's jaw tingled in response to these words. Breanna knew how to use the flat of her hand too. She had a remarkably strong arm for a woman.

The Bruce's gaze widened before he huffed a laugh. "That might be so … but I'm still not sure it's a good idea to let ye fight alongside my men. They might find ye a … distraction."

Cameron fought the urge to favor Robert Bruce with a rueful smile at that.

He noted that Breanna was frowning now. Her meekness was starting to crumble. She likely sensed that the Bruce was merely humoring her. Aye, she'd cause a stir if she fought alongside his warriors, but the truth was that Bruce didn't believe she was capable of it.

Cameron shared the Bruce's skepticism. She was fierce indeed, but that didn't mean she had the stomach for battle. He'd never met a woman who did. Breanna had told him she was skilled in combat, yet he hadn't seen her tested. Secretly, he was pleased Robert Bruce was denying her. Best she let him do what she'd paid him for, while she kept safe. She'd told him that the Scottish king's life was in danger, but she was likely more use keeping an eye on the goings-on in the castle than donning chain-mail and striding into battle with the Bruce.

"Let me prove it to ye, Sire," Breanna replied. She'd drawn herself up, her hands now clenched into fists upon her lap. "Let me fight one of yer men tomorrow … and then ye can decide."

Cameron tensed. "Breanna," he growled. "I don't think—"

"At least allow me to show ye that I can wield a sword," Breanna continued, cutting him off. She ignored Cameron now, her gaze riveted upon the Bruce. "And if ye don't believe I'm strong enough, I won't ask again."

Another silence settled over the solar. The anger that still simmered in Cameron's belly glowed hot once more. God's teeth, it hadn't taken the woman long to start defying him again. No doubt, Robert Bruce would think him a weak husband who couldn't control his willful wife.

Yet the Bruce wasn't looking at him at present but at Breanna. And Cameron didn't like the glint he saw in his eyes. "Very well," he murmured after a pause. "I shall pit ye against one of my brothers … it shall be Yuletide entertainment for us all."

13

MADE OF STONE

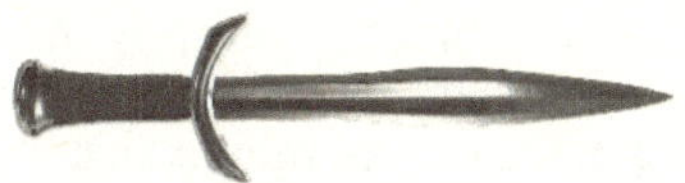

"WHY DO YE insist on undermining me?"

As soon as the pair of them were alone, the mercenary turned to Breanna. His eyes were dark with anger, his face strained.

Breanna snorted before folding her arms across her chest. They stood in the tiny bed-chamber they'd been given. The room was windowless and barely bigger than a storeroom. There was just enough space for a bed and little else. But since most folk here—except for Robert Bruce, Hugh Bissett, and his kin—slept on the floor of the great hall, they were fortunate indeed to have their own space.

As a wedded couple, Bruce had thought they'd appreciate some privacy.

Nonetheless, Breanna would have preferred to sleep in the great hall. It would prevent Stewart from questioning her, and from either of them repeating what had happened on the shore earlier in the day.

She still wasn't sure what had come over her. One moment she'd struck the mercenary across the face for the liberty he'd taken—the next she'd thrown herself at him.

Shoving aside the traitorous memory of how his mouth had felt savaging hers, the taste of him, and the coiled strength of his lean body, Breanna faced the man who was pretending to be her husband.

"I told ye from the start that I wanted to do my part ... to fight," she informed him coldly. "And I will."

"Aye, but the role ye are playing means that ye need to start acting like a wife," he replied, his voice equally cool. "Not a willful scold."

Breanna arched an eyebrow. *A scold?* "I won't be ordered around by ye, Stewart," she replied, her tone sharpening. "It matters not how I behave … just as long as we keep up some form of mummery. And once we've done our bit to help Scotland's king regain his lands and defeat the English, we can go our separate ways."

"Aye, and I heartily look forward to that day," he growled. "If I'd have known how much trouble ye were going to be, I'd have asked for twice as much silver."

Breanna scowled, her own temper quickening. "I'm sure ye would have." She pushed past him and began to unlace the bodice of her kirtle, readying herself for bed. After the day's ordeal, her body ached with exhaustion. She longed to crawl under the covers to escape the cold.

The kirtle was a pretty dark-red one, the color of plum wine. Lady Bissett had kindly loaned her clean clothing while her own was washed and dried. Breanna appreciated the gesture, even if the woman was of a slenderer build than her. This kirtle, and the lèine she wore under it, hugged her curves indecently.

Indeed, the thin undergarment—despite that it reached her ankles—felt like a second skin. Teeth gritted, she pulled off her kirtle and hung it upon a hook on the wall. She then made the mistake of looking down at herself. It was cold inside the chamber, for the room didn't have a hearth and there wasn't enough space for a brazier. As such, her nipples stood out through the fine linen of her lèine like two hard pebbles, the dark shadow of their areolae clearly visible.

Breanna's jaw tensed. *Maiden's blood, I might as well be naked.* Her attention swiveled then to Cameron Stewart—and she saw him staring.

Not at her face—but at her breasts.

And the heat that smoldered in his grey eyes had nothing to do with anger.

Breanna's belly somersaulted. She was transported then back to the storm-swept shore and the wild kiss they'd shared.

Suddenly, the bed-chamber felt even more cramped. Breanna dragged in a deep breath before immediately regretting the action that made her breasts push tightly against the linen.

Although it was cold inside the room, warmth bathed her skin. Nonetheless, she didn't move to cover herself up or shrink under the intensity of his stare. Stewart already knew she desired him, and his kisses had left her in no doubt that he'd swive her right now if she gave him the slightest encouragement.

Breanna clenched her teeth. Despite that her lower belly had just turned molten, she wouldn't succumb to this.

Relations between her and the mercenary were strained enough without them being lovers too. He'd just use the connection to try and control her. But he wouldn't get the chance.

"I didn't hire ye to question me, Stewart," she said, cursing the slight tremor in her voice.

"No, I can see ye are a woman who doesn't like to be questioned," he replied hoarsely, his gaze shifting up to her face once more. "Such arrogance will likely be yer downfall."

Breanna glared back at him. How dare this cur talk of arrogance? He was the living embodiment of it.

She wanted to strike back, to tell him so, yet her throat had gone tight and her mouth dry. Traitorously, her gaze slid down across the clothing Lady Bissett had loaned him, a dark quilted gambeson and leather trews. The latter were tight, revealing what looked like a painfully hard erection.

Swallowing, Breanna tore her gaze away from it and met his eye.

Indeed, there was a pained look on the mercenary's face now. She could almost taste his desire for her—it shimmered between them, warming the cold, damp air.

Breanna wet her suddenly parched lips. How easy it would be to succumb to this hunger—to reach for him as she had on the beach.

No! Get ahold of yerself, woman!

"What I needed from ye was to provide an excuse for me to enter our king's inner circle," she forced out. "And ye've done that. Ye've offered him yer sword ... and now it's time for me to do my part."

"Ye can protect the Bruce without becoming one of his warriors," Stewart shot back. His chest rose and fell sharply now as if he'd been running. "Drawing too much attention to yerself is foolish." He took a step toward her. "Ye'd be better to observe the comings and goings of this castle ... and the behavior of those closest to the king."

"I can do that too," she answered. Curse it, her voice had gone all breathy. What was wrong with her? "With my *husband's* protection."

"Ye want me to protect ye now, do ye?" he asked roughly. Suddenly, he was standing too close to her, the heat of his body wrapping around her, drawing her in.

"Aye," she murmured, taking a step back and finding the icy wall against her spine. "Ye might as well make yerself useful."

Stewart leaned in and placed his hands on either side of her, bracketing Breanna in. "If we're to continue pretending to be husband and wife, I need ye to start heeding me." His voice was soft, yet rough, and his eyes had gone dark in the flickering light of the single cresset burning on the wall. "Otherwise, the others will suspect the truth."

"The truth?" Breanna was finding it hard to breathe. He was too close, the virile male scent of him drowning her senses.

"Aye ... that we are deceiving them all."

"We aren't deceiving them," Breanna said weakly. "*I'm* trying to help the Bruce."

"That may be so ... but we're still weaving a lie." He leaned in, his breath feathering across her cheek and the shell of her ear. "The Bruce wouldn't be pleased to discover such." His lips grazed her jaw.

Breanna's core contracted at his touch, her sharply indrawn breath echoing through the chamber. The rogue. He shouldn't be standing so close, and he certainly shouldn't be trailing his lips along her jaw in a sensual caress. She wanted to reach up and push him away, yet her hands wouldn't comply.

Instead, they rose, unbidden, and splayed across his chest.

The Three give me strength.

Breanna liked to think she was tough—stronger than most women. She also liked to think she was immune to the likes of Cameron Stewart. But she clearly wasn't. With just one touch, this knave had disarmed her. She now struggled to form a coherent thought.

With a moan of surrender, she dipped her chin, her lips brushing his.

All the while, common sense screamed at her to push him away.

And then Stewart captured her mouth with his.

Suddenly, his hands were everywhere, and his mouth was a brand upon hers. A soft cry escaped Breanna when she parted her lips for him.

It was too late. She wasn't made of stone. She couldn't resist this.

14

A DISTRACTION

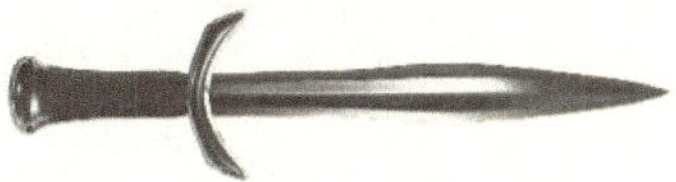

JUST LIKE UPON the shore that afternoon, the mercenary kissed her with a wildness that ignited the same abandon within her.

Breanna clawed at his clothing, desperate to touch the skin beneath the layers of fabric while she bit down on his lower lip.

His sharply indrawn breath caused the fire within her to burn brighter still, especially when he nipped at her lips in return and then soothed the sting with his tongue. And as he did so, Stewart undid the heavy braid that hung down her back. He unwound her hair, letting it cascade upon her shoulders before his fingers slid through it, to cup the back of her head.

Holding her prisoner, he deepened the kiss, his tongue dueling with hers.

Meanwhile, Breanna had pushed up his gambeson and lèine, her fingers sliding across the hard planes of his belly, down to the waistband of his trews.

Impatience thrummed through her. She wanted to see him, to touch him.

Dragging his mouth from hers, Stewart growled a curse. Then, releasing her, he stepped back and hauled off his gambeson and lèine. And as he started to unlace his trews, his gaze seared hers.

"Take off yer lèine," he commanded roughly. "Let me see ye."

Breathing hard, Breanna stared back. Then, with trembling hands, she reached down, grasped the hem of her ankle-length tunic, and drew it over her head.

She stood before him, naked. She knew it was as cold as a meat store in this chamber, yet she didn't even notice, for Stewart's gaze scorched her skin, made sweat bead upon it.

Her knees quivered under the force of that melting look.

A moment later, he divested himself of his trews and kicked them aside.

Breanna's gaze greedily took in the impressive length and girth of his shaft thrusting up between them from a nest of curly dark hair.

Wet, aching heat throbbed between her thighs. She was desperately ready for him, and he'd hardly touched her.

With another growled oath, Stewart hauled her against him, and together they fell upon the bed. And there they attacked each other: limbs tangling; mouths devouring; hands grasping, stroking, and kneading.

Breanna was lost in a storm of sensation.

This man addled her wits more potently than the strongest of wine or even those mushrooms she sometimes ate before carrying out a powerful divination. Under the onslaught of his wicked mouth and skilled hands, she risked forgetting who she was, who he was— or where they were.

Tearing his lips from hers, Stewart moved down to her breasts—suckling each one hard, till she writhed and gasped beneath him.

And then, when she lay there, a trembling wreck, her breasts swollen and tingling from his ministrations, Stewart drew away and rolled over so that he lay upon his back.

Panting from need, her skin now damp with sweat, Breanna pushed herself up and took the hand he offered.

Stewart's gaze seared hers, and her heart bucked like a wild pony against her ribs.

Wordlessly, he guided her, pulling Breanna up so that she sat astride his chest, facing away from him.

Excitement fluttered low in the cradle of her hips as she realized what he wished to do—an act she'd never experienced before. Gripping her hips, he drew her toward him, lowered her to his mouth, and began to pleasure the most intimate part of her.

Breanna's back arched, her cry echoing through the chamber. The things he was doing with his lips—the flick of his tongue—made delicious heat pulse through her loins.

Gasping as her thighs started to tremble, she leaned forward and reached for his quivering shaft. Greedily, she took him into her mouth, sucking, licking, and tasting him.

Stewart groaned against her, lifting his hips to meet her hungry mouth. And all the while, his wicked lips and tongue didn't cease their sensual torture.

The trembling in her thighs increased, and if he hadn't been holding her up, she'd have collapsed against him.

Breanna ripped her mouth from his jerking shaft. Her back snapped rigid, and she shattered against him. Her throaty cry joined his deep growl of pleasure.

She was still trembling when Stewart shifted from under Breanna and pushed her onto her back. The mercenary loomed above her, his lean body glistening with sweat, his face savage with lust. The sight of him made an ache rise under her breastbone. Goddesses, how she hungered for him.

He then parted her thighs wide and thrust into her.

It had been a long while since Breanna had welcomed a man inside her, and the shock and suddenness of it drove the air from her lungs. The feeling of fullness, of being stretched to the limit, made her whimper.

Stewart stilled, letting her adjust to him—and then he gave a slow, sensual roll of his hips, sliding deeper still.

Breanna groaned. She didn't remember coupling feeling this good. Had it really? The feel of him buried deep inside her awoke sensations she didn't even realize she was capable of.

He held himself up over her then and started to move. And all the while, Stewart's hot gaze held hers prisoner—almost as if he dared her to look away.

Breanna wasn't a coward, and so she stared up at him, letting him see every nuance of pleasure in her eyes, her face.

Stewart was relentless. He took her fast and then slow, shallow and then deep. He thrust into her until she writhed, gasped, and pleaded under him, until she shattered once more—and only then did he find his own release.

It took Breanna a long while to recover afterward, to come down to earth.

Vaguely, she was aware of Stewart drawing the blankets over them, of his arms wrapping around her, pulling her back so she spooned against him. However, such was the torpor that had spread over her body that she hardly took note.

Instead, she relaxed against her lover's body and the protectiveness of his embrace.

For a spell, her mind was a still pool, void of thought, worry, and fear.

It was a blissful state, one that made a sense of well-being seep deep into Breanna's bones. She couldn't ever remember feeling so at peace, at one with the world and everything in it.

But then, eventually, as she dozed in Cameron Stewart's arms, the torpor wore off. Ripples marred the surface of that once tranquil pool, as misgiving crept into her consciousness.

And when waves started to churn, the languid warmth seeped from her limbs.

Breanna's eyes opened, and her gaze fixed upon the shadowed wall a few feet away.

What have I done?

She was supposed to have a working relationship with the mercenary. How could she keep the upper hand now?

Ire ignited in her gut, burning like a stoked ember. However, she wasn't angry with him, but with herself. *Thrice-cursed idiot. Have ye no self-restraint?*

Clearly not—Stewart had vanquished her.

Stewart. She still used his surname when she thought of him. Even the intimacy of their coupling hadn't changed that. Good. She needed to claw back her dignity. Best if she pretended this hadn't happened.

Breanna drew in a shaky breath. Easier said than done after the things he'd done to her, and after the way she'd lost control with him.

She squeezed her eyes closed, pushing the lusty images from her mind.

I should never have hired him.

It was also imprudent to lie with a man—for here, upon Rathlin, she didn't have access to the herbs she needed to prevent her womb from quickening. She was just fortunate that it wasn't her fertile time—her moon flow was only a handful of days away.

Carrying Stewart's bairn was a complication she wouldn't welcome.

"I can hear ye thinking," a sleepy male voice intruded then, shattering her brooding. "Regretting it already?"

Stewart's flippant tone rankled, and Breanna stiffened. "Aye," she bit out.

"And why's that?" Faint amusement laced his voice now. "I liked that very much ... and I believe ye did too."

Heat washed up Breanna's chest and neck before flowering across her face. Of course, he'd watched her face as she'd unraveled in his arms. He'd heard her pleas for more. She was grateful that she was facing away from the man, for she didn't want him to see her embarrassment.

"It was an error in judgment," she muttered, "one that won't happen again."

Her response surprised him, for Stewart's body tensed against hers. A moment later, when he spoke, his voice had lost its glibness. "That's a shame."

"For ye maybe."

"For us both. The winter nights are long, Breanna. We should at least enjoy them."

Breanna dragged in another deep breath as her temper quickened. She wished the mercenary would shift back onto his side of the bed, so they were no longer touching. Yet he didn't move.

"We aren't here to enjoy ourselves," she replied, her tone sharpening, even as mortification prickled her skin. Mother's milk, this conversation was awkward. "I'm paying ye to help make sure someone doesn't make an attempt on Robert the Bruce's life, *not* to bed me."

Stewart huffed a laugh, although she noted there was little humor in it. "Ye don't need to pay me to give ye a tumble, lass," he murmured. "That's a service I won't charge ye for."

15

READY TO BE BESTED?

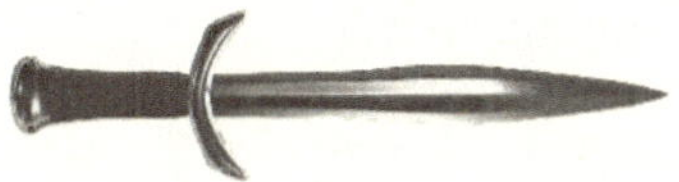

BREANNA'S CHEEKS FLUSHED hot. *Enough of this nonsense.* "I'm tired," she growled, digging her elbow into his chest. "Move over and let me sleep."

However, the mercenary didn't budge. A pause followed, and when he spoke, his voice held a questioning edge. "Ye take life very seriously, Breanna. Is carnal pleasure forbidden to those of yer order?"

"I'm a Guardian of Alba," she replied, her body now thrumming with tension. She wanted to break free of his grasp so she could rid herself of the traitorous awareness that contact with his body created. Yet his arm remained firmly wrapped around her. "Not a nun."

"A *Guardian of Alba*," he repeated the name. "So that's what ye call yerselves?"

Breanna clenched her jaw. Stewart already knew she was a druidess, yet she hadn't meant to reveal *that* to him. All the Guardians were sworn to secrecy. They weren't supposed to speak the name of their order or reveal where they resided, hidden away from the rest of the world. "Aye," she replied stiffly. "Although, I'd thank ye never to speak of us to anyone."

"I won't," he murmured. "Ye have my word."

Her mouth thinned. "And I should trust it?"

He laughed once more. "I'd say ye have little choice." He sobered then. "Ye don't trust men much, do ye?"

Breanna didn't answer immediately, even as her pulse quickened. It unnerved her that while she'd been observing the mercenary over the past days, he'd been doing the same with her.

"No ... I don't," she admitted after a lengthy pause. She drew in a deep breath then, willing her heart to calm itself. Stewart was perilously close to crossing a line. Like him, she had no wish to speak of herself, and of the events that had shaped her.

Aye, she'd allowed lust to turn her witless for a short while, but she wasn't about to confide in this wolf in her bed.

And that was what men were—wolves. Every last one of them.

She certainly wouldn't tell him of her humiliation ten years earlier. She'd been in love with a warrior named Grant MacDougal. Big and brawny with breathtaking arrogance and charm, he'd been impossible to resist. Breanna inwardly cringed at how besotted and dangerously innocent in the ways of men she'd been then. And, of course, as a result, MacDougal had torn her heart to pieces.

Breanna swallowed hard. No, Stewart most definitely wasn't going to hear any of that. If she was mistrustful, she had her reasons, but she would be keeping them to herself. When she spoke again, her voice held a brittle edge. "Tonight was a mistake, Stewart ... one that won't be repeated."

Edward Bruce faced Breanna in the inner-ward of Rathlin Castle.

A colorless sky stretched overhead, and an icy wind gusted through the large courtyard. But the two opponents didn't appear to notice the cold.

Dressed in braies and a gambeson, Breanna cut an unusual figure. And the wooden practice broad-sword she held two-handed just added to her strangeness.

Indeed, news that the wife of Robert Bruce's latest recruit wanted to prove herself had seemed to reach all corners of the keep. The castle inhabitants had gathered to watch the Yuletide spectacle. Hugh Bissett, his wife, and daughters—all swathed in thick fur cloaks—looked on from the steps below the keep's entrance. Meanwhile, Robert Bruce and his two other brothers—Thomas and Alexander—watched with the other warriors.

Cameron stood amongst them.

Arms folded across his chest, he watched Breanna as she circled Edward.

The mercenary schooled his features into a dispassionate expression, resisting the urge to frown. He was well aware that Breanna didn't care if she had his blessing or not—yet he wasn't happy about this duel.

Edward Bruce was grinning at Breanna like a wolf circling a helpless newborn lamb. Out of the four surviving Bruce brothers, Edward was reputed to be the most aggressive and hot-headed—Cameron supposed that Robert had chosen him for that very reason.

Like Robert, Edward was tall and broad-shouldered. However, his dark hair was cut in a shaggy style that framed his face. Unlike his elder brother, he was clean-shaven.

"Ready to be bested, woman?" he called out, his tone deliberately goading.

"No," Breanna called back, her own voice mirroring his. "Are ye?"

This comment brought guffaws and sniggers from the men on the sidelines. Cameron cast the warrior nearest, who'd just made a lewd comment, a dark look. The man's lecherous grin faded.

Cameron's jaw tightened. The woman was drawing far too much attention to herself—and to him. When they'd awoken at dawn, he'd warned Breanna once again that this wasn't a good idea—but she'd shrugged his comments off. And this morning, as he'd watched her warm up before the swordfight, he'd seen anticipation gleaming in her eyes.

He'd never met a woman like Breanna. She was tough, wild, and recklessly independent—and yet underneath it all, he sensed vulnerability. He'd inadvertently touched a nerve the night before when he'd questioned her. Breanna's body had frozen in his arms, and tension quivered through her.

Taking her warning, he'd wisely let the subject drop.

Thinking back on what had transpired between them, Cameron stifled a sigh.

He hadn't meant to plow her the night before. In fact, he'd been furious when they'd first entered the bed-chamber.

Until she'd started undressing for bed.

When she'd stripped off her siren's kirtle and stood there dressed only in that figure-hugging lèine, he'd forgotten what he'd been arguing with her about.

Breanna had a luscious body, and he'd been unable to prevent himself gaping at her like a moon-calf.

And when he'd touched her, he hadn't been able to stop.

Tonight was a mistake, Stewart ... one that won't be repeated.

He had to admit her words had disappointed him. One taste of Breanna had left him wanting more. Sharing a bed with the woman and not being able to touch her would no doubt frustrate him.

Cameron's mouth thinned then. Even so, he was here to do a job—and it was best he kept his mind on it.

"Come on, lass," Lord Bissett's gravelly voice carried across the inner-ward. "Show us how a woman fights."

The surrounding crowd jeered, while a smile curved Breanna's mouth. She didn't seem to mind their scorn; if anything, it appeared to feed her.

Leaping forward, she attacked.

Edward feinted easily, still grinning as he swung his blade around to counter-attack.

Clack. Clack. Clack.

Whoops and cheers went up, echoing off the surrounding stone. The fight had begun.

And as he watched Breanna handle herself with the practice sword, admiration tightened Cameron's chest.

Christ's teeth, she's good.

There was no sign now of the vulnerability he'd glimpsed the night before. There was definitely a story there, yet he hadn't pushed her, for there were details in his own past that he'd prefer not to discuss. Not every secret had to be revealed. Some were best buried deep and left to rot.

"Her footwork is excellent." A gruff voice at Cameron's side drew him from his thoughts. Cameron glanced over to see that Robert Bruce now stood before him, although the king's attention remained focused on the fight. "Did ye teach her how to handle herself like this?"

Cameron shook his head. He wasn't going to take the credit for this woman's skill. "No, her kin did ... Breanna had an unusual upbringing."

As they looked on, Edward lunged with an aggressive attack, cutting across Breanna's body. However, she danced back, avoiding the vicious jab that followed.

"Edward is the best swordsman of us brothers," the Bruce murmured then. "Although he can be rash."

"So can Breanna," Cameron replied, a rueful smile quirking his mouth.

The wooden sword blades continued to clash, the sound echoing through the now silent inner-ward. The heckling had died down when it became clear that Cameron Stewart's wife wasn't about to be trounced.

Again and again, the opponents blocked each other's attacks, as they circled, looking for a weakness in the other's guard.

Cameron noted that Edward had started to sweat, and his cocky grin had faded. While Breanna wore an expression of grim determination that Cameron had come to know well over the past days.

Edward made another vicious cut, and Breanna parried it before striking back with a speed that made gasps ripple through the watching crowd. Servants had also ventured out to watch the fight, and some of the lasses were watching Breanna with wide eyes and shocked expressions.

Few of them would have ever seen a woman dressed like a man, let alone fighting like one.

Breanna made a counter-cut then and managed to jab Edward in the arm. Her opponent cursed and lunged again. But Breanna dropped and struck once more, her blade slamming into Edward's shin.

Edward snarled another curse.

The fight turned furious then. Edward Bruce gave no quarter, and tension coiled tighter in Cameron's chest with each passing moment.

Soon, Breanna too was sweating. Her face gleamed, although her eyes never left Edward. Her long braid swung from side to side as she danced out of the reach of her opponent's blade, time after time, before swooping back in for a counter-attack.

Edward's blade caught her twice, once on the shoulder and once across the flank, yet Breanna took the blows without letting her concentration falter.

A collective gasp went up when she used a deception tactic so that Edward foolishly opened up his guard. She then kicked him in the belly and slammed the flat of her blade into the side of his head.

Edward reeled, lost his footing, and went down.

Breanna closed on him, kicked the blade from his hand, and held the point of her own sword to his throat. "Do ye yield?" she asked, breathing hard.

Glaring up at her, Edward had little choice but to nod.

A beat of silence followed before cheering erupted in the inner-ward.

A smile crept over Cameron's face. Nonetheless, he made a mental note not to vex Breanna when she had a blade in hand. The woman was lethal.

Glancing over, he caught the Bruce's gaze. "What say ye, Sire ... will ye let my wife fight with us?"

Robert Bruce's brown eyes were warm as he grinned. "Aye, Stewart. I'd be a fool not to."

16

MERRY YULETIDE

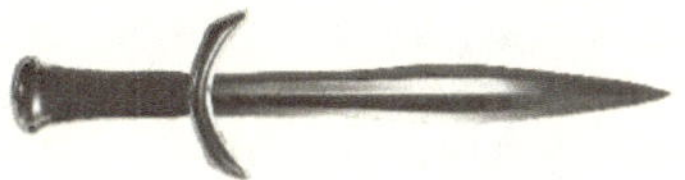

"MERRY YULETIDE TO all," Hugh Bissett boomed as he held his pewter goblet aloft. His attention shifted to where Robert Bruce sat farther down the table. "And may this coming year bring a well-deserved victory for ye, Rob."

A chorus of 'ayes' followed while everyone at the table raised their goblets.

Seated next to Stewart, Breanna took a sip of plum wine, savoring the rich, spicy flavor.

With everything that had happened of late, she'd almost forgotten it was Yuletide. However, seated in the great hall of Rathlin Castle, it was impossible to miss that the festive season was upon them: boughs of mistletoe, holly, and ivy decorated the walls and draped from the beams overhead, and rows of tallow candles burned upon the long tables.

Never had Breanna seen a hall so full—for those celebrating here today weren't just Lord Bissett's kin and retainers, but the Bruce's men as well. Extra trestle tables had been brought in, and there was barely space for the serving lasses to squeeze through bearing platters of roast venison, breads, and braised vegetables.

"That's quite a woman ye have there, Stewart," Lord Bissett spoke up once more, his voice carrying across the table. "Although I'm glad my wife doesn't know how to wield a blade ... I'd have received a knife to the gut for sure by now if she did."

The comment brought laughter, although Lady Bissett, seated next to her husband upon the dais, cast him a withering look.

When the rumble of mirth died down, Stewart raised his goblet to the Lord of Rathlin Castle and winked. "Aye … but I prefer a woman with a dangerous edge to her."

Breanna cut Stewart a look of mock censure, even if he hadn't offended her. The opposite was true, in fact. She knew he was merely acting a part, yet she welcomed the comment all the same.

Laughter rippled around the table once more. Everyone except Edward Bruce was smiling this afternoon. Instead, the king's brother hadn't stopped glowering at her since they'd all taken a seat upon the dais. Following the swordfight, Bissett had insisted that Stewart and his wife dine at their table for the Yule banquet.

"Yer husband tells me that he didn't teach ye how to fight," Robert Bruce spoke up then, his gaze meeting hers across the table. "How then did ye learn such skill?"

"My parents were not typical," Breanna replied, her mouth curving. She'd received this question a few times in the past and had a ready answer. It also pleased her that the Bruce was showing an interest in her. Being at his side was a dream come true. "I was one of many daughters with no elder brothers to protect me … so the fiercest of us were sent to a local swordmaster to learn how to defend ourselves should the need arise."

It wasn't that far from the truth. The High Bandruì had hired men from a nearby castle to teach Breanna and a few others how to wield weapons and defend themselves physically. The swordmaster had been a grueling teacher, yet he'd taught her well. Her physical skills complemented her witching and had come in handy many a time over the years.

"My wife has fought at my side on a number of occasions," Stewart added. "I wouldn't be without her in a scrap."

Then, to her consternation, he looped his arm over her shoulders.

It was a protective, possessive gesture, and one likely put on for the benefit of those surrounding them. Even so, Breanna tensed.

The contact was unnerving, for the warmth and weight of his arm about her shoulders reminded her of another, more intimate, contact the night before.

It reminded Breanna of her weakness, her serious lapse in judgment.

Cameron took a bite of venison, chewing slowly as he savored the rich, dark meat. This was a fine feast indeed, and Bissett proved a welcoming host. Serving lasses circled the table with ewers of wine, topping up any goblet that sank below half-full, and they'd just brought trays of oatcakes dripping with butter and honey to the table.

He hadn't eaten this well in a long while.

Next to him, Breanna had fallen silent. She appeared to be focusing on her meal, yet he knew better. He'd felt the way she'd tensed when he'd put his arm around her earlier.

She didn't want him touching her, yet for the sake of putting on a show for the others, he had to do so.

Cameron took another mouthful of venison.

If he were honest, he would have preferred to keep his distance as well, especially if casual touches couldn't lead anywhere. Her nearness was distracting. Breanna had changed out of her men's clothing into the becoming red kirtle Lady Bissett had loaned her—the garment that hugged her lush breasts and kept giving him tantalizing glimpses of her cleavage.

Cameron shifted on the bench seat, trying to ignore the stiffening of his groin. Inconveniently, his body was reacting like some randy sixteen-year-old lad's. He needed to rein in his response to her or it would be a long, uncomfortable winter.

His mood shadowed then, as he reflected how easily frustration could slide into longing—into obsession.

There was a reason why Cameron Stewart rarely bedded a woman more than twice.

He didn't form emotional attachments with his lovers, for he knew where they led.

To a place he'd told himself he'd never return to.

Breanna quickly shed her kirtle, and—without a glance in Stewart's direction—dove under the covers.

Despite that she'd made the situation between them clear, she wouldn't be making the same mistake as the night before. Only when she was safely tucked under the coarse blankets, her chin peeking out over the edge, did she look his way.

Stewart was disrobing at the foot of the bed. Like her, he undressed quickly, his gaze averted as he stripped off his gambeson and leather trews, leaving on the loose lèine and woolen leggings he wore underneath.

He then crawled into bed next to her.

Silence settled over the chamber, while Breanna surreptitiously wiggled her way over to the far edge of the bed, as far as possible from his warmth.

The uncomfortable hush drew out until Breanna cleared her throat.

Crone's tears, this is awkward.

The tiny chamber they shared just made the forced intimacy of their situation even more evident. There was literally nowhere to go, nowhere to escape to.

She glanced across at Stewart to see that he was lying on his back, staring up at the rafters. The single cresset burning on the wall, close to extinguishing now, outlined his profile. He appeared deep in thought.

"It was a fine Yuletide feast, was it not?" she said casually.

He glanced her way, his mouth lifting at the corners. "One of the best I've ever eaten." His smile widened then. "The only one not enjoying it was Edward Bruce."

Breanna huffed a sigh. "Aye, well ... some men are sore losers."

"They are when bested by a woman."

Their gazes met, and Breanna found herself smiling. "Are ye one such man?"

"I wouldn't know ... I've never sparred with a woman."

Her smile widened. "Well, we'll have to remedy that ... now that the Bruce has allowed me to train and fight alongside his men."

She shifted her attention away then and rolled onto her back. Like the night before, it was freezing in this chamber. Fortunately, the Lady of Rathlin Castle had provided them with multiple layers of blankets and sheepskins.

"The tale ye told during the banquet ... about how ye learned to fight ... intrigued me," Stewart said then.

She cast him a veiled glance. "I had to alter the story a little ... but most of it was the truth."

"Even the bit about yer parents and sisters?"

Breanna shook her head. "I was an orphan ... a foundling. The High Bandruì of my order brought me up." She paused then, affection stealing over her when she thought of how loved and safe Colina had made her feel growing up. "I think of the other druidesses as my sisters ... even if we aren't related by blood."

"Ye were a foundling?"

"Aye ... many of the druidesses are. Either that or we're orphans. Colina found three of us—me, Nessa, and Fyfa—during one cold spring. I'd been abandoned on a tree stump, wrapped in sheepskin, and left for the wolves to carry me off."

Stewart's eyes shadowed at this tale, despite that she had delivered it with a dispassionate tone. "Why would they do that?"

Breanna shrugged. "There are various reasons why folk believe there is something wrong with a bairn. But Colina told me that I was a strangely quiet infant. I hardly ever cried. She believes it frightened my parents into believing I was a changeling."

Stewart's brow furrowed before he muttered an oath under his breath. "They should have been strung up for such a deed."

Breanna shifted her gaze up to the rafters once more. "Aye," she agreed, "but in the end, they did me a favor." She hadn't had the best start in life, although that didn't bother her these days. "If my parents hadn't left me out in the cold to die, I wouldn't have become a Guardian of Alba."

Silence fell after this admission, and when the mercenary replied, his tone was subdued. "Ye are truly a warrior for yer cause, Breanna. I admire yer dedication."

She glanced his way once more, to see that his gaze was shuttered. Stewart was in an odd mood tonight. The candidness of his comment contrasted with his guarded expression.

Curiosity feathered up within Breanna, as did the urge to ask him about Stirling, yet she checked the impulse.

It was best she didn't question the man about his past—especially since she didn't want him delving into hers either.

17

ALL IN THE PAST

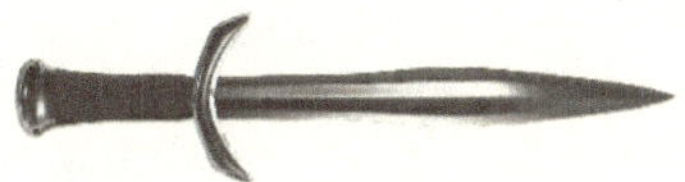

DELICATE WHITE FLAKES fluttered down, as light and perfect as apple blossom. Breanna turned her face up to them, letting the slivers of ice land upon her exposed face.

Snow had come late this year. It had been threatening for the past two days, and the sight of the crisp white flakes made her think of her sisters—and the long, bitter winters they'd spent in the cavern behind the Wailing Widow Falls as bairns. Even the four massive hearths hadn't been able to keep the chill at bay. Even so, Breanna, Nessa, and Fyfa had always been excited to see the first blizzard and had rushed outdoors to dance in it.

"Why the smile?"

Cameron Stewart's voice drew her attention from the leaden sky, and Breanna looked to where the mercenary stood at her shoulder. They were patrolling the craggy coastline northeast of the castle and had just stopped for a moment to watch the foaming surf crash against the rocks.

Like her, Stewart was swathed in fur, his dark hair mussed by the wind.

"I like the snow," she said, reaching out and catching snowflakes upon her outstretched palm. "It reminds me of when I was a bairn."

Stewart snorted. "It reminds *me* of numb fingers and toes for weeks on end."

"Aye, it's cold," Breanna admitted, "but bonny too."

Her gaze shifted then to the northeast, and she frowned. "What's that?"

The mercenary's gaze tracked hers, to where a small boat bobbed in a swell. The clouds had lowered, obscuring the dark shadow of the mainland. His brow furrowed as he studied the craft.

"It's just a fisherman," he said after a pause.

"In this weather?"

"The wind is light ... the sea was much rougher on the afternoon *we* crossed."

His reminder of her folly made Breanna tense. It also made her recall the events that unfolded afterward: that heated kiss and their torrid coupling that night. Despite the biting chill, heat flooded across Breanna's chest at the memory. In the four days that had followed, things had been awkward between the pair of them.

Fortunately, her moon flow had started that morning. That was one less thing to worry about.

During the day, they had to pretend to be a wedded couple, and as such spent much of their time in each other's company. Breanna trained with the men and took her turn at sentry duty upon the walls like all those who followed the Bruce. This morning, she and Stewart had been sent out to ensure that no one had come ashore on the northern edge of the isle.

The English army might be waiting the winter out, but they had patrols and spies everywhere. This island was part of Ulster, not Scotland, yet that didn't mean they were entirely beyond the enemy's reach.

And it wouldn't stop Aymer de Valence from sending out a raiding party if he discovered the Bruce's location.

Deciding it was best not to answer Stewart, Breanna kept her gaze upon the boat. It crested another swell, and she caught sight of two figures—one of whom was hauling in a net.

Tension unfurled from her shoulders at the sight. "Aye ... ye are right. They're fishermen, not English scouts."

"I doubt we'll see any English on these seas at present," Stewart replied. "Not this time of year, anyway."

Breanna cut the mercenary a look. "Did the Bruce say anything to ye yestereve about how long he intends to stay upon Rathlin?"

She heard the sharpness in her voice and inwardly chastised herself for letting her irritation show. Robert Bruce might have welcomed her into his ranks as a fighter, yet that didn't mean he wished to have a woman's counsel.

Stewart had been invited to meet with him and his brothers the night before—but not Breanna.

The rejection still stung.

As if sensing her ire, Stewart cast her an infuriating half-smile. "I've already told ye he said nothing of great interest last night. Ye missed little."

Breanna huffed an irritated sigh. She didn't believe him.

"What of ye?" he asked then. "While I was drinking with the Bruce, did ye use yer time productively?"

Breanna's mouth thinned. "What do ye mean?"

"Well … have ye been down to the kitchens yet to meet the servants? There could be a spy or a murderer among them."

The teasing note to his voice made her spine stiffen. Stewart had made it clear a few times now that he didn't believe anyone would make an attempt on the Bruce's life at Rathlin Castle. Although he'd taken her news about Robert the Bruce's destiny in his stride, he seemed less convinced about her warning that the outlaw king's life was in danger.

"Ye know I've already spoken to some of the servants," she said, injecting a chill to her voice. Turning, the pair of them resumed their patrol along the cliff-top. All the while, the snow fluttered down silently. "And none have aroused my suspicions."

"All the same," he murmured. "Ye should remain vigilant."

"We should *both* remain vigilant," she reminded him, her voice clipped.

"Aye," he agreed, irritatingly calm. "But a man asking questions around the keep will draw attention to himself. A woman won't."

Breanna clenched her jaw. She hated it when he was right. She longed to attend the Bruce's councils with Stewart, yet her frustration was more out of pride than anything else. It annoyed her that, even though she'd proven her fighting skill, Robert Bruce didn't see her as her husband's equal. However, there was nothing strange in that—most men would have treated her so. Having grown up in a female environment, Breanna still chafed at the world beyond the Wailing Widow Falls at times.

"I spent yestereve with Lady Bissett and her sister," Breanna admitted after a pause. "I listened to their gossip ... and asked a few questions. There doesn't seem anything amiss ... at present."

"Aye ... the danger will come once we return to the mainland," Stewart replied.

Breanna glanced his way to see that his gaze had shifted east, to where Scotland lay shrouded in clouds. Observing his profile, she wondered at the origins of the man she'd hired. Apart from his time as captain of the Stirling Guard, she knew little about him.

It's better that way, the voice of reason chastised her. *Ye don't need to know about his past.*

And yet she was curious. Things had been strained between them since their arrival here, and she wished to ease the situation a bit.

"Where do ye hail from?" she asked then. The Stewarts were both a Highland and Lowland clan, and unusual in that they didn't have a chief as most other clans did.

The mercenary glanced her way, and she noted the way his grey eyes veiled. For a moment, she thought he wouldn't answer her, but after a pause, he did. "Dundonald Castle."

Breanna took this in before nodding. "I know Dundonald ... it's in South Ayrshire?"

"Aye." His tone was cool and didn't invite questioning, yet Breanna ignored the warning.

"Are ye a close relation to the laird of Dundonald?"

Stewart's mouth pursed. He looked decidedly irritated now. "Aye, he's my brother."

Surprise feathered through Breanna. "Really?"

He nodded.

Breanna raised an eyebrow, favoring the mercenary with an assessing look. "Surely, the laird's brother doesn't need to work as a sellsword?"

"He does, if he has cut ties with his kin."

Breanna took these words in, as well as the hard edge to Cameron Stewart's voice. There was definitely more to this tale. Curiosity spiked within her. "And why did ye do that?"

Stewart's gaze snared hers. His expression was inscrutable, however, his eyes were hard. "It doesn't matter," he replied curtly. "It's all in the past now anyway."

The snow was falling heavily by the time they returned to the castle. It swirled around Cameron and Breanna in a thick white cloud, making visibility low. Blinking to dislodge flakes from his eyelashes, Cameron led the way into the outer ward under the portcullis and raised a hand in greeting to the guards posted there.

"We were wondering when ye two would return," one of the men called out. "I'm surprised ye didn't fall off a cliff in this blizzard."

"Aye, we thought it best to turn back," Cameron replied. "No one's going to bother us in a snowstorm." He glanced then over his shoulder at where Breanna had just entered the outer-ward.

Fur framed her face. Her cheeks were flushed with cold, and snow encrusted her shoulders and hair.

She was beautiful, in a wild way that made Breanna quite unlike any other woman he'd ever known. She was proud, independent—and entirely too nosy. When she'd started questioning him about his kin, he'd made it clear he wouldn't be answering.

Breanna had imposed clear physical boundaries between them, and he would do the same when it came to revealing personal details.

There were some things Cameron Stewart never spoke about.

The journey back to the castle had passed in silence, and he'd been grateful for it. Like Breanna, he too was impatient to know when Robert Bruce planned to return to Scotland. The sooner they were on the move, the sooner this mission would be completed. Then Cameron could take his leave of Breanna and return to his former existence. And in future, he'd be more careful about the jobs he accepted. Ever since departing from Perth, he'd been constantly reminded of why he worked alone.

He liked making decisions without being questioned and answering to no one but himself. And he also preferred to keep his contact with women limited to serving wenches and whores.

Breanna was a distraction—and because they were pretending to be husband and wife, the pair of them spent far too much time together. He wasn't surprised she'd eventually interrogated him about his origins. After all, she'd revealed details about hers.

Nonetheless, it put him on edge.

"I need a cup of warmed wine," Breanna muttered, hurrying past him, her boots crunching on fresh snow. "I'm frozen to the marrow."

"The noon meal will have just started, Lady Stewart," the guard called out once more. "Mutton stew and dumplings!"

Breanna twisted around, the discomfort easing from her face as she flashed the guard a smile. "That will be welcome indeed."

Watching her, Cameron felt a tickle of irritation. She never favored *him* with smiles like that. He also still hadn't gotten used to the men calling her 'Lady Stewart'. It was just another unwelcome reminder of where he was from, and of his decision to never take a wife. Aye, all of this was just mummery, yet he didn't like pretending to be wed. Sometimes, it felt too real.

There were times, as they sat in the great hall, elbows brushing while they ate and drank, when a sense of ease and contentment would filter over him. And in those moments, he wondered at the choices he'd made in his life.

Such thoughts were unbidden and unwelcome and were banished as soon as they appeared. Yet it left him uneasy all the same.

Breanna glanced Cameron's way then, waiting till he stepped up alongside her before she linked her arm through his. "Come, husband," she said, falling into her usual role whenever they were being observed. "Let's go inside."

18

SPINNING A WEB

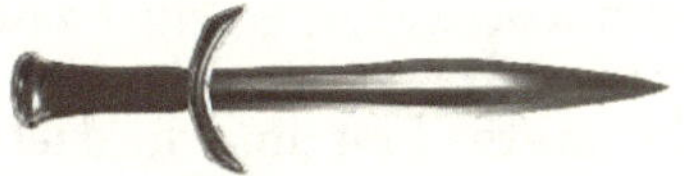

Six weeks later ...

"CAN I HAVE a word with ye, Stewart?"

Pushing his sweat-damp hair from his face, Cameron lowered his wooden sword and stepped back from his opponent, turning to where Robert Bruce stood a few yards away, watching them train. "Aye, Sire," he replied.

As always, a biting wind whipped through the inner-ward of Rathlin Castle. There was rarely a still day upon the island this time of year. For weeks, the North wind had brought flurries of snow, which had turned the isle into a frozen rock for the month following Yule. Thankfully, the worst of the weather was now behind them.

Turning, Cameron retrieved his gambeson from Breanna. She was standing a few feet from where he'd been fighting, awaiting her turn in the sparring ring. Their fingers brushed as he took the padded tunic from her, and Cameron's breathing caught, lust slamming into his gut as if she'd just punched him.

It was the first time they'd touched in weeks, accidentally or otherwise, and the light brush of her skin against his only served to remind him how much he missed it.

Aye, they sat with each other at mealtimes, and sometimes he would put an arm around her shoulders for show—but this was the first time in a while that their skin had actually touched. They still shared a bed, but ever since that fateful first evening, he kept his distance from her.

And Breanna had no idea what it was costing him.

Their gazes met now, briefly, and he imagined he saw her pupils dilate. Her lips parted then, and he heard her swift intake of breath.

Was this sham marriage, this celibate relationship, tormenting her as well?

If it was, this was the first time she'd let on.

Stepping back from Breanna, Cameron shrugged on his gambeson and turned away from her. He then approached Robert Bruce.

"Walk with me," the Bruce greeted him.

Cameron did as bid, and the two of them took the slippery stone steps up to the walls. Casting a glance over his shoulder, Cameron saw that Breanna was watching them, a groove between her dark brows. She'd clearly recovered from their accidental touch. Maybe he'd imagined the need he'd glimpsed in her eyes. Instead, she now appeared worried he'd done something to anger the Bruce. Or maybe she was just vexed because she couldn't overhear their conversation.

In the weeks since they'd arrived at Rathlin Castle, they'd settled into a routine. They both kept an eye on the Bruce's men and the Bissett household—yet there appeared little to worry about. Cameron had started to believe Breanna's concern that the Bruce's life was in danger was unfounded.

At Rathlin, Robert Bruce was safe from harm. However, the time was coming when he would have to decide upon his return to the mainland. He couldn't remain in exile forever.

Cameron grew increasingly certain that it was the English he had to worry about, not the plotting of enemies from within.

The wind whistled across the ramparts when they reached the top of the walls, and the Bruce pulled his thick fur cloak about him. Meanwhile, Cameron clenched his jaw. That wind felt as if it were knifing straight through his quilted gambeson. He hoped the Bruce would keep this chat brief.

"Ye have settled in here well, Stewart," Bruce said, turning to him. "The men respect ye."

The king fixed him with a solemn gaze, his expression stern. The seriousness of Robert Bruce's look didn't concern Cameron. In his time here, he'd noted that the king didn't smile often. Perhaps it was the loss of his brother—or the fact that his wife, daughter, and sister were still English captives—but worries clearly weighed upon the man. The Bruce spent a lot of time alone, often visiting a nearby cave to ponder matters.

His behavior had caused concern to ripple through the ranks of the men following him.

Was the king losing heart? Did he believe it hopeless to rally after the crushing disappointment of the previous year?

Cameron's gut tightened at the thought. Strangely, although he'd long told himself that he would never ally himself, heart and soul, to a cause, he didn't like to think of Robert Bruce despairing. If he did that, all was most certainly lost.

With a jolt, Cameron realized he didn't want to see his people crushed.

Scotland needed their outlaw king to rise from the ashes of defeat and strike back.

Cameron favored Bruce with a smile. "Aye, well ... they are a hardy lot ... and impatient to fight for ye once more."

The two men's gazes met then, and a rare smile curved the Bruce's lips. He wasn't old, around Cameron's own age in fact, yet lines of strain marred his face, and crow's feet crinkled around his eyes as he smiled.

"I'd like ye to captain them," the Bruce announced then.

Cameron's breathing stilled, a chill that had nothing to do with the freezing wind slithering down his spine.

"But that's Edward's role, is it not?" he asked, deliberately keeping his tone off-hand.

Robert Bruce pulled a face. "Aye, but I don't know whether ye've noticed ... my brother is a hot-head."

Cameron gave a thin smile. It hadn't escaped him. Twice now, he'd had to help break up a brawl between Edward and other warriors during training. The man's temper was permanently on a short leash, and he turned aggressive when questioned.

If he were honest, Cameron didn't like Edward Bruce much. Not that it mattered though.

"He won't take kindly to someone else leading yer men," Cameron pointed out. "Are ye sure ye wish to make an enemy of him?"

The Bruce barked a laugh, the sound carrying over the walls. Beyond, the sea was as dark as slate against a heavy blanket of racing clouds. Even so, Cameron could just make out the dark smudge on the eastern horizon: Scotland. "Edward will do as he is told," he replied, the iron edge to his voice making it clear that the younger Bruce brother would indeed. "I'll not have his reckless ways put my campaign at risk."

Cameron arched an eyebrow. "Have ye decided our next move then, Sire?"

"Aye." Robert Bruce's gaze fused with his. "This has been a bitter winter for me, Stewart, in more ways than one, and I'll admit to ye that I have struggled." His strong-featured face grew strained as he continued. "I have needed much time alone, to meditate on what must be done ... and so I've been visiting the caves near here."

He paused there and tore his gaze from Cameron's, looking out to sea. "As I sat there a few days ago, listening to the crash of waves and the drip of water in the caves, I spied a small spider attempting to weave a web. It tried and failed over and over again. Whenever I returned to the caves, it seemed no further ahead. But it never gave up. Each time the spider fell, it climbed back up to try again ... and finally, the spider's silk took hold." He paused then, a tight smile curving his lips. "This morning I saw that it had managed to spin its web."

He turned back to Cameron, his gaze glinting. "I too will never give up. We have tarried upon Rathlin long

enough. Tomorrow is the first day of February ... it's time
I returned to Scotland and took back what was taken
from me."

"Such a promotion is a compliment indeed," Breanna
said as the pair of them walked along the shingle beach
beneath the castle. After the noon meal, Cameron had
suggested they take a stroll together.

It wasn't the weather for it, for the wind now howled
like a banshee and brought with it stinging needles of ice,
yet she'd agreed. She was curious to know what the
Bruce had wished to talk to Cameron about in private.

Tugging her fur mantle close, she peered at her
companion's face. Cameron wore a pinched expression.
"However, ye don't appear pleased by it?"

"I'm not," he muttered.

"Whyever not, Cam?"

Cam. Not 'Stewart', or even 'Cameron'. He too had
started to call her 'Bree'. Over the past weeks, she'd
gotten used to having this man in her life, and they'd
even developed a friendship of sorts. Theirs was an odd
relationship. They shared a bed every night yet hadn't
repeated the intimacy of their first evening at Rathlin
Castle.

Breanna had initially been surprised that Stewart
hadn't tried to seduce her. And then she'd been irritated
by the disappointment that had crept over her as the
weeks slid by and the mercenary remained on his side of
the bed.

This was what she wanted, wasn't it? She'd been
ready to rebuff his advances, to coldly remind the man
that their coupling had been a gross error of judgment
on her part.

But her reminder hadn't been necessary, for he now
treated her like a sister.

Still, there were times when she imagined she saw desire darken his eyes, times when she thought she'd caught him watching her, yet then he'd glanced away, and she'd told herself it was just fanciful thinking.

Fanciful? Her fickleness vexed her. It was better this way. Neater. Easier.

But then, earlier, just after the Bruce had called for Cameron, their fingers had touched—and a wave of dizzying need had swept over her. And she'd heard his sharp intake of breath too, had seen hunger flare in his eyes.

It still smoldered after all—this fire between them. The knowledge made Breanna uncomfortable in his presence in the aftermath.

Cameron glanced her way, his gaze narrowing. "The last time I captained a group of men, it didn't go well."

Breanna tensed. Of course, she knew what he was referring to.

For a short spell, they walked in silence, side by side upon a shifting strand of tiny pebbles. Nearby, the waves rolled in, while seabirds screeched overhead.

"This isn't like Stirling," she said eventually. "Surely, ye realize that?"

Cameron's shoulder-length black hair whipped around his face as he shot her an irritated look. "Isn't it? I led a garrison of loyal men, Bree ... and then watched them die—one by one—before we all suffered a bitter defeat." He paused, hauling his fur cloak under his chin. "I can still recall the bleakness in their eyes as we were herded like sheep from Stirling Castle and into the English camp." His face twisted then, and Breanna saw the bitterness etched upon it.

Tightness constricted Breanna's chest, and she looked away from him, her gaze fixing on the caves at the end of the shore—where Robert Bruce sought refuge to think most days.

After weeks in the company of the outlaw king and his loyal men, she'd hoped that Cameron might have let go of his cynicism. However, she realized that the scars this man bore were deeper than she'd thought.

"Ye did yer best," she said softly.

"Maybe," he growled back. "But it wasn't enough. I don't want that kind of responsibility again."

"And so, why didn't ye refuse the Bruce?"

He cut her an irritated look. "Ye know why," he bit out. "Ye hired me to do a job, and I will see it done."

19

MAKING PLANS

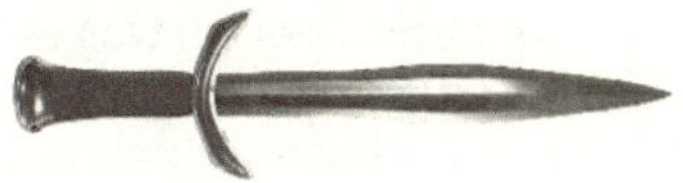

Ayr
Ayrshire, Scotland

HEAD BENT AGAINST the wind that raced in from the sea, Lamia hurried across the wide timber bridge spanning the tidal waters of the River Ayr.

Hades, these Scottish winters are bitter.

The wind seemed to cut right through the many layers of wool she wore. She could tell Fantôme was suffering; the grass snake had slithered up her arm, seeking the heat at her armpit. She had to be careful not to accidentally crush her familiar.

Pulling up the hood of her cloak, Lamia vowed to hunt down an inn after her visit to Ayr's busy market square. She would order a hot meal and some warmed wine and hopefully find a seat near a roaring fire.

Leaving the bridge behind, she navigated the tangle of narrow streets, overhung by buildings of timber and stone, and entered a wide space.

Despite the freezing wind, the hardy folk of Ayr were out in force. Ruddy-faced women with baskets under their arms wove in and out of stalls. Many of the vendors had put up awnings to shield them a little from the weather, and the hide billowed and snapped as another gelid gust barreled through the square.

Teeth clenched, Lamia joined them.

Cries from hawkers selling everything from fresh fish and smoked herrings, to live fowl and geese, carried across the square.

But Lamia wasn't here for food—but information.

She tightened her fingers around the small, clear quartz stone she carried and whispered a witching to strengthen the working upon her. It was one she'd used often of late, a glamor charm that changed her from a slender, pale-blonde, high-born French lady to a stocky Scottish lass with hair the color of straw.

"Greetings, lass ... what will it be?" A thin woman with a long red nose, who was selling hot pies and cakes, favored Lamia with a warm smile.

Lamia's belly rumbled in response. She hadn't yet eaten today, for she'd awoken with a queasy belly. It was strange, for the moment she'd left the English camp, the burning pains in her stomach had ceased—now that she'd taken action, frustration and anger no longer gnawed at her. But instead, she'd taken to feeling peaky first thing, only to develop a ravenous hunger later on. It wouldn't hurt to buy something while she asked her questions.

"One of yer mutton pies, please," she replied. Her Gaelic was halting, yet the glamor made the woman think otherwise. Lamia hadn't been idle in the years since Stirling. She already spoke both English and French yet had realized that, without a knowledge of Gaelic, she'd be limited in her ability to hunt down the Bruce. Philip had humored her request for a tutor shortly after their wedding.

"A fine choice." The woman took the coin she passed before handing her a pie. Lamia took a tentative bite, careful not to burn her mouth, and glanced around. Fortunately, there wasn't anyone else queuing up to buy pies at present.

It was the right time to start her interrogation.

"I hear the English are moving again," she said, brushing crumbs off her mouth. The pie really was delicious. "Do ye think they know where the Bruce is?"

The woman's thin face pinched. "Lord, I hope not, lass."

Lamia sighed. "Folk are saying he'll be back with the spring."

The pie-seller nodded, her eyes gleaming. "I've heard the rumors too."

"Have ye heard anything about where he might be hiding?"

The woman shook her head. "No." She leaned in then, her gaze darting from left to right. She was right to be prudent, for a number of English soldiers drifted through the crowd.

Lamia wondered if some of them would be looking for her.

Six weeks had passed since she'd slipped from her husband's pavilion and from the English camp. Would Philip have given up yet?

A strange sensation pulled at Lamia's chest then, a tightness just under her breast bone. Curse the man, but she actually missed him.

The realization caused her breathing to still. However, she quickly reined in her wayward emotions.

She was finally nearing her goals—would finally taste the glory she sought. She wouldn't let the memory of Philip de Eynsford's melting oak-colored eyes, the rough timbre of his voice, or his protective, reassuring touch distract her.

"There are rumors he's fled to Ulster," the woman murmured.

Tension rippled through Lamia, although she was careful not to let frustration show on her face.

Ulster?

She had no wish to brave the wild sea and cross to Ireland. She'd hoped the Bruce would be in hiding somewhere in the Scottish Highlands. He'd be easier to reach there.

"Will he remain long in Ireland?" she asked, taking a step closer to the pie-seller.

"Och, no, lass." The woman shook her head. "Not the Bruce. He'll want to take back his earldom."

Lamia stilled. Aye, she too had thought as much. That was why she was here in Ayrshire. The wolf always returned to its lair.

"My husband and I used to live at Turnberry," the woman went on, garrulous now that she'd found a sympathetic ear. "Bruce is loved there and still has many supporters waiting for his return." Her gaze glinted then. "My husband intends to join them. He's sure that's where our king will strike first."

Rathlin Castle
Rathlin Island—Off the Coast of Ulster

"We shall make a two-pronged return to the mainland," Robert Bruce announced, his finger tracing the map spread out across the table before him. "Edward and I will land at Turnberry in the southwest, while Thomas and Alex will land farther south still, at Loch Ryan."

The Bruce's words echoed around the silent solar.

Excitement twisted under Breanna's ribs at this news. Finally, after a long and tense winter, Robert Bruce was going to strike back against their oppressors.

A smile tugged at her mouth. He was moving, once more, toward his destiny.

Breanna was the only woman present in the solar this afternoon. And she was only there because of Cameron. As captain of the Bruce's fighting force, he now stood with the Bruce, Bissett, and the three other Bruce brothers: Edward, Thomas, and Alexander.

Finally, after weeks of being kept out of these meetings, the Bruce had allowed her to attend one.

"Is splitting our strength a good idea?" Edward muttered. "Those men ye send to Carlisle should be put to use taking back Turnberry."

Across the table, the Bruce shook his head. "We have plenty enough for that ... but it's vital we cut off the English to the south as well and let the folk there know that I have returned." His expression hardened. "We must strike hard this time. I will not let Aymer de Valence take advantage of my 'honor' again."

Breanna's mouth thinned. Indeed, she'd heard about the humiliating and tragic defeat at Methven. Bruce had drawn his army up outside the walls of Perth and called on de Valence to come out and do battle. De Valence, who had the reputation of 'a man of honor' had made the excuse that it was too late in the day to fight. Instead, he'd assured them he would accept the challenge the following day. Only he hadn't—instead, unbeknown to the Bruce, Longshanks had instructed de Valence that no mercy was to be given.

As such, the English had attacked while the Scots camped overnight in woodland outside Perth.

Viewing the hard light in Robert Bruce's eyes, Breanna could see he didn't intend to let Aymer de Valence best him ever again.

"We will see it done, Rob." Thomas Bruce spoke up, his voice sharp with purpose, while next to him, Alexander nodded. Both warriors, although young, wore determined expressions.

"At least send Stewart with those two wet-behind-the-ears pups," Edward replied. He folded his arms across his chest and cast his younger brothers a withering look. "They shouldn't be left in charge of so many men."

Alex muttered a curse, while Thomas's lips parted as he readied himself to argue the point.

Meanwhile, Breanna tensed. Wherever Cameron went, she would also have to go. She didn't want to be at Loch Ryan while the Bruce was in Turnberry. How could she protect him if she was fighting elsewhere?

However, the Bruce cut in before anyone else could speak. "Thomas has just passed his twenty-third winter ... and Alex his twenty-second," he replied, his gaze narrowing. "At the same age, both ye and I were leading men into battle. Don't patronize them ... or me." He shifted his attention to Cameron then, as did Breanna. The mercenary hadn't spoken since entering the solar. Instead, like Bissett, he'd been observing the exchange between the Bruce brothers. He now met the king's eye. "Ye will travel with me, Stewart ... and will lead my men. Do ye—"

"What?" Edward exploded, his face flushing. "He doesn't—"

"Don't interrupt me, Ed." The Bruce's tone turned flinty then, even as he continued to hold Cameron's eye. "Do ye have any suggestions on how we should approach this campaign?"

Cameron stared back at him, tension rippling around the now silent solar. Breanna held her breath. There was no mistaking the challenge in Robert Bruce's tone. He'd given Cameron his trust, and now he wished him to prove himself.

To his credit, Cameron didn't look cowed by the king's challenge.

Moments passed before he stepped close to the table, looking down at the detailed map unfurled in front of him.

"We must avoid meeting the English in open battle for the moment," he said softly, his gaze scanning the map. "Their numbers are greater than ours ... and they are better armed." He reached out, his fingertip running from the southwestern coast inland. "Instead, we should play to our strengths ... and use our knowledge of the mountains, forests, and glens to our advantage." Cameron leaned in, his face tensing as he peered closer at the map. "Once we take Turnberry, I suggest we move inland to rougher terrain before we draw de Valence into our net. The Galloway hills should provide the cover we require."

Silence followed these words.

Cameron spoke with the calm authority of someone who understood war. He also knew the English, having fought them on a number of occasions. He was a man with presence—a man others listened to.

Even Edward, who was still flushed, his eyes glittering with resentment, didn't speak up to contradict the advice.

Watching Stewart, Breanna's breathing slowed, and the skin on the back of her arms prickled. She knew then that she'd just caught a glimpse of the man Cameron Stewart had once been.

At that moment, she could forget that he was a mercenary and not a freedom fighter—and that he was only here because he was being paid handsomely. She could forget the reluctance he'd shared with her to captain the Bruce's men. She'd been disappointed by the things he'd said on the beach. But she wasn't now.

What mattered were actions, not words—and right from the beginning, Cameron Stewart had shown his quality. His quick thinking had saved their lives when they'd been forced to swim to shore during that storm. He'd protected her that day and championed her ever since.

And in the past weeks, she'd grown to like him, to respect him.

Breanna's chest started to ache.

The Three strike her down, she'd fought this from the very beginning. She'd thought herself immune to the man, yet she wasn't. Instead, he dominated her thoughts far more than he should.

Oblivious to Breanna's churning thoughts, the other occupants of the solar all watched Cameron with keen gazes. Moments passed, and a hard smile slashed across Robert the Bruce's face. "Excellent advice, Stewart ... and I shall heed it."

20

INCONVENIENT

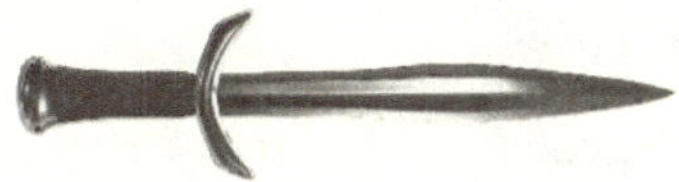

KNEELING DOWN UPON the icy flagstones at the foot of the bed, Breanna opened the pouch she held and emptied its contents onto her palm. The clink of rattling bones filled the small chamber.

Cameron shifted position on the bed and peered at the yellowed chunks of bone. He'd seen her use her 'telling bones' a few times now since leaving Perth. It was an unusual and slightly unnerving ritual—one that reminded him that Breanna wasn't just a warrior but a druidess.

A woman quite unlike any other.

"Are ye going to ask yer Goddesses what lies ahead?" he asked. He couldn't help inject a teasing note into his voice. Breanna's expression was so grave this eve.

"Aye," she replied, her gaze shuttered. Strangely, she didn't bite as she usually did when he teased her. "Since we are leaving on the morrow ... it is wise."

Her reminder made unease feather through Cameron.

He was only doing what she was paying him to do, and yet he'd felt excitement and determination coil within him as he'd stood in the solar with Bruce and the others. When he'd spoken about facing the English again, a fire had caught alight in his veins—one he'd thought was long since dead.

For a short while, he'd forgotten that he was a paid mercenary and that he'd sworn never again to ally himself to a cause. Instead, he'd stared into the outlaw king's eyes and made a silent vow that he'd die, if necessary, to help this man gain back Scotland.

Rein it in, Stewart, he silently warned himself as he shifted into a crossed-legged position and watched as Breanna closed her eyes, murmuring words in the ancient tongue she used for her workings. *Ye know where this road leads.*

Aye, he did—to bitter disappointment—but he'd been unable to stop himself.

His attention settled upon Breanna's face. She'd been oddly quiet throughout supper, and he wondered if she was sore with him after their exchange on the beach. He'd been unnecessarily curt with her.

Breanna cast the bones, and he heard them rattle and clack across the flagstone floor. She then leaned forward, her brows winging over her dark eyes.

Noting her strained expression, Cameron craned his neck to see where the telling bones had fallen. He didn't know why he was bothering, for they didn't make any sense to him. "What do they tell ye?"

Breanna's mouth thinned. "I'm not sure," she murmured. "In truth, I've never received such confusing messages. The bones rarely fall like this ... they utterly contradict themselves."

Cameron raised an eyebrow, even if worry tightened in his gut. He was superstitious enough to be bothered by her words. "For example?"

"Well, if the full moon and the lion are to be believed, the Goddesses favor us," she murmured. "We have just entered the Storm Moon ... a good time to strike back against our oppressors." Relief fluttered up under Cameron's ribs at this news. However, Breanna wasn't yet finished. "But the crone and the crow have also fallen together."

"And that means?"

Breanna glanced up, her peat-dark eyes almost black in the guttering light of the cresset behind her. "That a great slaughter is coming."

Cameron's skin prickled, and he resisted the urge to rub the goose-flesh that had risen on his arms. "A 'great slaughter' ... of the English?"

A nerve flickered in her cheek. "Perhaps."

"Ye are doubtful?"

Breanna shook her head, her attention shifting back to the scattered bones. "The way the bones have fallen, it's impossible to tell who will be the victor." She made an impatient sound in the back of her throat. "I should have drawn a pentagram first," she muttered. "Maybe I should cast the bones again."

Cameron had seen her etch out those strange five-pointed stars surrounded by a circle with a nub of charcoal when she did her witching.

"Isn't it a bit late for that?" he asked.

Breanna frowned. "What do ye mean?"

"Well, if ye've already asked the bones for guidance ... ye can't just ask again because ye didn't like what they told ye."

Her jaw clenched. "Since when did ye become an expert on such things?"

He flashed her a smile, enjoying seeing fire ignite in her eyes. It was better than concern. "I've watched ye cast the bones a number of times now, Bree," he replied. "And as ye might have noted, I'm an observant man."

Muttering an oath under her breath, she scooped up the bones and put them away in the drawstring pouch, which she looped about the belt at her waist. She then rose to her feet and dusted herself off. "Well, next time I cast the bones, I'll do it on my own," she muttered. "Ye put me off."

Cameron reclined on the bed then, crossing his feet at the ankle and placing his hands under his head. "So, I'm to blame, am I?"

"Aye." She was scowling at him now. "Ye usually are."

Their gazes met then and held.

And curse him, if lust didn't flare to life like a pitch torch in his belly.

"So, my advice to the Bruce earlier didn't please ye?" The question was a challenge.

Her brow smoothed, although she still held her body rigid. "Of course it did," she said, her voice lowering. "Hume was right to suggest ye for this mission, Cam. Ye have the skills we need."

Cameron tensed. He knew she was complimenting him, yet Breanna's words rankled. Foolishly, he'd hoped she'd be less practical about the matter. It dawned on him then that it mattered to him that she was impressed.

Pushing the realization aside, he watched as she turned from him and began to disrobe for bed.

Cameron knew he shouldn't, but he continued to observe her.

He usually looked away while she undressed. But not this eve.

Tonight his gaze devoured the long, strong length of her back, visible under the thin material of the lèine she wore beneath her kirtle, and the firm swell of her backside.

His mouth went dry as, still facing away from him, she undid her hair and teased out the braid, combing it with her fingers so that it rippled in dark, heavy waves down her back.

Cameron's groin hardened, and he glanced down to see an erection tenting his braies. Any moment, Breanna would turn around and spy it.

His hunger for her roared to be sated.

It had grown unbearable of late. His body had been behaving as it had when he'd been a youth. He'd be doing something completely unrelated—such as sharpening his weapons, patrolling the shores of the isle, training with the men, or taking watch on the walls— when his thoughts would turn to Breanna.

An instant later, his rod would rise like a Schiltron pike ready for battle. There had been a number of occasions when he'd been forced to abandon his post and hurry back to this chamber—the only place in the castle that afforded him any privacy. There, he'd taken himself in hand and dealt with his inconvenient arousal.

However, his hand was no substitute for Breanna's slick heat, and the hunger didn't abate.

At the thought of the honey-pot between Breanna's thighs, his rod started to throb.

Cameron clenched his jaw and rolled off the bed. He pressed the knuckles of one hand to his aching shaft as he started to unbuckle his belt with the other hand. To quell his arousal, he tried to think on unpleasant things: the rotting carcass of the hugest rat he'd ever seen just two days earlier in the castle's outer-ward and the ripe smell of the privy in the guardhouse.

It worked, for the pulsing ache ebbed just a little. But his rod was still rock-hard.

Teeth gritted, he undressed. He usually went to bed dressed in nothing but woolen leggings these days, yet tonight, he left his lèine on, for it covered his groin.

Then, not glancing Breanna's way, lest his body betray him once more, he yanked back the covers and climbed into bed.

Breanna was already there, tucked in within arm's reach of him.

Thankfully, she was not looking his way. Instead, she was staring up at the rafters, her expression strained, her gaze veiled.

They lay there in silence for a few moments while Cameron gained control of his body. Did this woman have any inkling how many times during the night he'd awaken and fight the urge to reach for her? How he stared at her mouth every time she spoke or ate, warring with the need to kiss it?

He'd never shown as much restraint as this. In the past, if he wanted a woman, he let his appetite rule, but with Breanna, it was different. They had to share a bed, a life. If things soured between them—as they eventually would if he gave in to his urges—life would get difficult for them both. It might put this mission, and his silver, in jeopardy.

Not only that, she'd made her feelings toward him clear, and he intended to respect her wishes.

Cameron had thought about attempting to sleep on the floor instead of the bed—but the icy flagstones held little appeal and such behavior would just likely draw attention to his discomfort around Breanna.

He drew in a deep, steadying breath. As she'd just reminded him, this was a business arrangement. He needed to keep his rod in his braies and his focus on the mission.

Breanna couldn't relax. Lying there, just a foot from Cameron, she longed to slide her hand across the mattress and touch him.

Her realization—as she'd stood in the solar, watching him continue his discussion with the Bruces—had left her shaken and on-edge.

Curse her, but she cared for the mercenary. Deeply.

She didn't want to dwell on the ache that had risen under her breast bone in the moments following that dawning, or the way her belly had twisted in yearning. Those sensations were too uncomfortable.

She'd done her best this evening not to let her feelings show. Yet all the while, her body and heart had betrayed her.

The former had hummed with awareness at his nearness as she'd cast the bones and tried to concentrate. And the latter had pounded wildly when she'd met his eye afterward.

And to her chagrin, Cameron Stewart had spoken with his usual careless air. That was—until he'd asked her about her reaction to his advice to the Bruce. Then, he'd seemed almost boyishly earnest.

She'd wanted to tell him that he was brilliant and bold—that she could see why the Bruce's men already respected him far more than they did Edward Bruce. She'd longed to reveal that he plagued her waking thoughts and that she burned for his touch.

And she ached to reveal that loneliness swept over her when she thought about the day their arrangement would end and he'd walk out of her life.

But she said none of that.

Rolling over onto her side, she faced the wall and prayed to The Three to rid her of this affliction.

21

HONORING THE DEAD

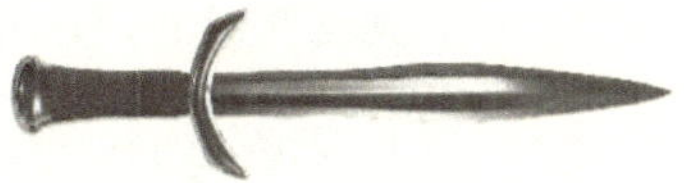

TURNBERRY CASTLE DREW closer, its high walls basking in the afternoon light.

Pushing back a strand of hair that had escaped her braid, Breanna shifted her attention from the mighty fortress—and seat of the Bruce clan—and glanced to where Cameron sat at her shoulder upon the rowboat. The thirty-three galleys they'd all sailed here on had dropped anchor just offshore, and now a swarm of rowboats rushed toward shore.

Perched there, his black hair whipping around his face, his lean frame encased in leather and chainmail, the man appeared in his element. He looked *alive.*

This is who he truly is, she thought, her pulse quickening. *Not a mercenary, but a leader of men.*

Cameron's gaze remained upon the castle, his iron-grey eyes narrowed. "Bastards," he murmured. "They're flying the Plantagenet flag."

Breanna looked back to see that, indeed, the red and gold flag of the English king fluttered from one of the towers. "Aye," she muttered. "But not for much longer."

"They've lowered the sea gate, Stewart," Edward Bruce called from behind them. Breanna twisted around to look at the king's brother. Edward's brown hair whipped around his face. He then cast a scowl in Cameron's direction. "I told ye we should have come ashore farther down the coast ... so we could surprise them."

Cameron glanced his way before favoring Edward with a harsh smile. "They were always going to lower that gate before our arrival ... whether it was by sea or land," he pointed out. "Ye were never going to get in that way."

Breanna frowned at the Bruce's younger brother. Ever since they'd set sail from Rathlin Island, Edward had questioned the captain's every decision. To Cameron's credit though, he merely shrugged the man's barbed comments off.

Ahead, the castle loomed nearer still.

Perched upon a rocky headland, and surrounded by the sea on three sides, Turnberry was quite a sight. The castle had been built over the water. The sea gate—a great archway, with the portcullis currently lowered—yawned like an open mouth, letting the tide wash in. Within the shadowy recesses of the archway, Breanna spied stone steps leading up into the belly of the castle.

Aye, it would have helped them greatly if that gate had been open—but Cameron was right. It would be the first thing the English closed upon spying them.

And as their rowboat swept in toward shore on an incoming tide, the clanging of bells mingled with the shriek of gulls.

Breanna's jaw firmed. Aye, the English knew they were here.

Jamming on a metal domed helmet and latching it under the chin, she checked to make sure her weapons—a sword at her right hip and a dirk at her left—were secure. She was the only one on board this boat bearing a longsword, and as such, she also carried a shield. The other warriors wielded Schiltrons—heavy pikes—or claidheamh-mòrs—great Scottish broadswords. These blades were designed to be wielded two-handed, and so the warriors had no shields. Breanna had been taught how to wield a claidheamh-mòr, yet she preferred the lighter longsword. It suited her nimble fighting style.

Twisting once more, she saw that the other rowboats clustered close by. The Bruce perched at the bow of the boat directly aft of theirs, his bearded face fierce as his gaze remained riveted upon his castle.

A roar went up then, and turning back to shore, Breanna spied a column of soldiers, their helmets and plate armor glinting in the weak February sun, snaking its way down the hill to meet them.

"Are ye ready, wife?"

Cameron's voice drew her attention then, and she caught his eye. He wore a hard smile, yet something shadowed his eyes.

Was it concern for her welfare?

Drawing her sword, Breanna shot him a fierce answering smile. Better he looked after his own hide than worry about hers. "Aye, husband."

Night fell over Turnberry, bringing with it an eerie silence.

Breanna knew this hush well—for she'd fought in a number of skirmishes over the years. It was the time when the battle song finally died and blood-lust drained from men's veins. The frenzy of the fight had ended, and carnage remained.

Walking across the battlefield, Breanna's gaze swept over the tangled limbs and gaping faces of the dead.

Was I part of this?

A shiver rippled down her spine. It wasn't easy walking amongst the dead after battle, but it was something she always forced herself to do.

It was a reminder that foe or not, the English were men of flesh, blood, and bone, just like her compatriots. Aye, she hated them, but she refused to let herself see them as faceless.

An icy breeze feathered against her cheeks then, bringing with it the stench of gore and the metallic odor of blood. In the morning, crows would start to circle, but tonight the dead lay unmolested.

Breanna halted before one of the corpses: a big English knight in a knee-length hauberk, his once splendid white and red surcoat a ruin. His gaze stared skyward, a look of angry disbelief upon his face.

Staring down at him, Breanna wondered if Nessa's knight looked anything like this one. She'd been shocked and angry when her sister had admitted that she'd lost her heart to one of the enemy. Truthfully, she hadn't understood Nessa's choice at all—until just a couple of days ago.

Now, she realized that the heart was a fickle thing. Nessa hadn't wanted to fall for Hugh de Burgh and had indeed fought it.

Just as Breanna was now doing with Cameron Stewart.

Breanna's mouth thinned, and she shifted her attention to where a Saint George cross banner listed, illuminated by the last rays of the setting sun.

At least Cameron isn't English.

Aye, she'd seen him in combat today. He'd fought shoulder-to-shoulder with the Bruce and his men, savage and proud.

A familiar ache rose under her breastbone, and she frowned.

Reaching up to rub at the ache with her knuckles, Breanna looked northwest to where the walls of Turnberry castle rose. The lower levels lay in shadow, although fires now burned on the ramparts, casting a golden hue over the stone and outlining the silhouettes of sentries upon the walls.

Breanna tensed at the sight.

They'd defeated the English outside the walls but hadn't managed to take the castle itself. A large army had camped before the gates, and once they'd pushed back the soldiers on the shore, the Scots had flooded into the camp, leaving a path of devastation behind them.

The English had held their ground for as long as they could before their commander had ordered a retreat.

They'd learned from one of the men they'd taken prisoner that an English baron named Henry de Percy led the English forces. He'd gathered what survivors remained and fled south.

The Scots had been the victors today, although—as Cameron had warned them—the castle would be harder to take.

"There ye are."

A male voice made Breanna turn, her gaze alighting upon a tall figure, his shoulder-length black hair rippling in the breeze.

Cameron approached her, his face cast in shadow. "What are ye doing out here, Bree?"

She cleared her throat, suddenly on edge at his presence. "It's something I do after battle," she replied. She gestured then to the dead knight at her feet. "To remind me of the consequences of dealing out death."

Cameron drew close, the fires on the walls casting a warm glow over his features now. "Ye fought well," he said, his mouth quirking. However, his gaze was solemn. The soldiers were all used to killing—it was a way of life for many of them—but it didn't prevent a shadow lying over them for a short spell in the aftermath. "Are ye sorry for it?"

Breanna huffed a humorless laugh. "No." She stretched then, in an attempt to loosen the aching muscles in her back, shoulders, and arms. Her right bicep throbbed from a blow she'd taken during the melee; she'd need to take a look at it later. "But I took lives ... and The Three remind me that I must honor those I cut down."

Cameron glanced down at the knight. "Did ye kill this brute?"

Breanna's mouth twisted, her attention returning to the dead man between them. "Aye."

The knight had nearly bested her too—she'd sought him out for that reason.

"So, what now?" she asked, her voice subdued. "Will the Bruce lay siege to the castle?"

"Edward is keen to do so," Cameron replied. "But I've advised the king not to."

Breanna glanced up, her gaze meeting his. "Why not?"

Cameron flashed her another hard smile before gesturing to the high curtain wall behind him. "Ye forget ... I have experience with long sieges. We don't have Warwolf at our disposal. Breaching this castle could take months ... and when Edward hears of what's happened here, he'll send reinforcements." Cameron paused then, his handsome face strained. "As I said back on Rathlin ... the best way to defeat the English is to take to the hills and use our knowledge of this landscape to our advantage."

Breanna inclined her head. "And what does the Bruce say?"

"He agrees. We won't linger here. With the dawn, we shall bury our dead and move inland."

It was growing late when Cameron retired to their pavilion.

They'd hastily erected tents at dusk, on the edge of the battleground and the ruin of the English camp. After supper, Cameron had met with Robert and Edward and two other lairds, James Douglas and Robert Boyd, who'd joined their ranks. They'd discussed their next move at length—something made more tiresome than it needed to be due to Edward's heckling—before eventually deciding that they would indeed make for the Galloway hills, a rugged inland region and Scotland's 'cradle of independence'.

The English would have difficulty besting them there.

Limping slightly, Cameron closed the last yards to their tent. He'd turned his ankle during the fight, and it now ached dully. He reached the pavilion, drew aside the flap, and went inside.

He'd expected to see Breanna huddled under the blankets of the narrow cot they were to share tonight, but instead, she sat on the edge of it. Dressed in a sleeveless tunic and leggings, her hair brushed out,

Breanna was a comely sight. She'd been inspecting an unsightly bruise upon her upper arm when he entered, yet she halted, her gaze swiveling to him.

"I thought ye'd be asleep," he said gruffly.

Cameron didn't mean to be curt with her—yet Edward's constant aggression had soured his mood.

As did the thought of the struggle that lay before them.

Cameron would definitely earn every piece of silver Breanna had already given him, and that which she had promised him too. Aye, he'd agreed to this—but he hadn't dwelled on what giving his sword to Robert the Bruce might cost him personally.

For he found himself *caring* about the outcome.

"I couldn't," she replied with a grimace. "I find it hard to sleep the night after battle."

"It's the opposite for me," he admitted after a pause. "After a skirmish, I slumber like one of the fallen."

"I wish I did." Her gaze shadowed. "But the noise, the violence ... and the stench of death ... all take a while to fade."

"Aye ... they do," he murmured. Nearing the cot, Cameron frowned, his attention resting upon her arm. "That's quite a bruise."

Breanna pulled another face. "Aye, and it'll be twice as pretty by the morn."

"Have yet put salve on it?"

"No." She gestured to the small clay pot sitting upon the coverlet. "I was about to."

"Here." Cameron lowered himself onto the cot, and she shifted over to make space for him. "Let me do it."

It was a task Breanna could easily do herself, and he'd have been wise to let her, but Cameron hadn't been able to stop himself. He felt the need to touch her tonight, even though he knew he shouldn't. After the day's violence, he craved closeness with this woman. He was only tending to an injury for pity's sake, and he was bone-weary. Surely, his body would behave itself?

Even so, he felt the stirrings of excitement in his belly at her nearness. Breanna had bathed while he'd been

meeting with the Bruce and the others. The scent of
lavender and lye wrapped itself around him.

Trying not to inhale the scent deep into his lungs, he
reached for the pot of salve and unstoppered it. The
woodsy aroma of herbs greeted him. He dipped in his
finger, scooped up some salve, and spread it gently upon
the purpling bruise on Breanna's upper arm.

She shivered under his touch.

Cameron halted, his brow furrowing. "Are ye cold?" A
brazier burned in the tent, yet it wasn't overly warm in
here.

She shook her head. Cameron slid his fingertips
across the bruise once more, rubbing in the salve, and he
heard her slight intake of breath. He stilled. "Am I
hurting ye?" he asked softly.

She shook her head once more.

22

FOOLISH HEARTS

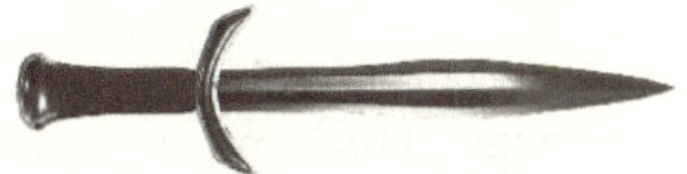

PERHAPS HE SHOULDN'T have touched her.

Hunger shivered through the air between them, unspoken. It turned the cool air inside the pavilion heated.

Her tremor, her swiftly indrawn breath, made the need that smoldered like an ember in Cameron's belly burst into flames. He'd been worried for her today. He knew the woman could handle herself as well as he could with a blade. But even so, he'd found himself looking for her during the battle.

It was dangerous. Such distraction could easily get a man killed.

And this evening, as he'd stood discussing the way forward with the Bruce and his men, all Cameron could think about was the woman waiting for him in their tent. The woman everyone thought was his wife.

And as Cameron's fingers trailed across the naked skin of her upper arm once more, he wished it were true.

He'd sworn off marriage—and love—a long time ago. But right now, he found it difficult to remember why.

Instead, Breanna filled his senses. Want drowned out any voice of reason. After so much death, he needed something life-affirming. He needed this woman.

And she was as affected by his nearness as he was by hers.

Slowly, he trailed his fingertips down her arm.

"Cam," she whispered, the tremble in her voice giving her away. "I don't think we should be doing this."

"No, we shouldn't," he murmured before reaching out and cupping her face. He then tilted it toward him. "Do ye wish to stop?"

Their gazes met before she whispered, "No."

His mouth slanted over hers.

Breanna's groan of surrender was all he needed to hear.

One moment she was seated beside him, the next he'd hauled her into his arms. His hands were everywhere—touching the warmth, firmness, and softness of her delicious body and the curves he'd been forbidden for weeks now.

Her lips opened under his, welcoming his questing tongue. She was exploring him too, her hands roaming over his leather vest, fumbling in their eagerness to touch his skin.

Cameron plundered her mouth, kissing her wildly.

This woman tasted of heaven, even better than he remembered. He couldn't stay away from her, and now that he'd started kissing her, caressing her, he couldn't stop.

And she didn't seem to want him to.

Breanna shifted off the bed, and to his surprise, moved to sit astride him.

The act was bold, lusty—and it made Cameron's shaft strain against his leather trews. Perched astride him, clad in only a thin tunic and leggings that hugged her shapely legs, Breanna was driving him insane.

She grabbed his shoulders, her fingertips digging into his skin even through the leather, wool, and linen of his clothing. Her kisses were wild, her tongue dueling with his. She lowered herself against him, grinding their groins together in a sensual roll that made a growl rumble through Cameron's throat.

Christ's bones—was this woman trying to kill him?

Weeks earlier, she'd told him that he would not be swiving her, ever again. And yet she now writhed against him with sensual abandon and kissed him with a hunger that made him forget all else.

He'd sensed that she'd wanted him, of course, but had been determined to deny her attraction.

But he hadn't realized the true extent of the hunger she was keeping leashed.

It matched his own.

Yanking up her tunic, he pulled it up over her head. Breanna's breasts—heavy, with milky skin and dark nipples—thrust into his face, and he lost himself in them, feasting on the swollen peaks and burying his face in the musky scent of her cleavage.

Lord, a bolt of lightning could strike him right now, and he'd go a happy man.

Breathing hard, Breanna leaned back from him and, with fumbling fingers, started to unlace his vest.

Cameron helped her, for he was as eager as she was to strip his clothes off—and hers.

Once they were both naked to the waist, Cameron rose to his feet, taking Breanna with him. He then stripped off her leggings and pushed her down onto all fours upon the sheepskin that covered the floor of their tent.

The ragged rasp of Breanna's breathing, and the sight of her there naked before him—her round, pale bottom facing him—made animal lust rear up within Cameron. He heeled off his boots, ripped off his trews, and fell to his knees behind her, parting her thighs with his knee.

And then, he drove into her.

Breanna's hoarse cry filled the pavilion.

Holding himself up over his lover, he watched her fingers clench around the sheepskin as her hips arched up to meet him. The walls of her core tightened along the length of his rod.

Buried deep inside her tight, wet heat, Cameron nearly unraveled there and then.

Groaning her name, he withdrew slowly and attempted to rein his impulses in. But, heedless of how close he teetered to the edge, Breanna gave a soft whimper and rotated her hips wantonly against him.

Cameron snapped.

Gripping her hips, he took her in deep, savage thrusts.

And Breanna matched him, her hips rising to take each plunge as her cries echoed through the tent. Leaning over her, Cameron reached down between her legs with one hand, stroking the slickness between her thighs, while with the other he held himself up.

And all the while he plowed her.

He didn't restrain himself at all. For the first time in years, he gave himself up to the need to possess a woman, body and soul, and to be possessed in return. And as he took her, this woman who both beguiled and infuriated him, his need for her coiling and growing with each thrust, Cameron Stewart also surrendered.

Breanna shattered against him then, tremors wracking her body—and if he hadn't been holding her up, his hand splaying across her belly now—she'd have collapsed. Pulling her hard against him, Cameron drove into her again and again before he too climaxed.

It barreled into him, making his belly muscles clench. Heat flowered across his lower back and pleasure ripped through him. And when he hoarsely cried out her name once more, his voice didn't sound like his own.

Panting from the force of the pleasure that had torn through her, leaving her limbs weak and molten, Breanna hung in Cameron's arms.

Maiden's blood. She'd thought their first coupling weeks earlier had been earth-shattering—but it paled compared to this.

Even now, her core ached with want.

She could never have enough of this man, she realized then.

And when he slowly withdrew from her, loss feathered through her. She wasn't ready for him to go just yet.

She wanted to cling to this moment for a while longer.

"Come, Bree," Cameron murmured, his voice oddly rough. "Let us get into bed ... the night is cold, and it grows late."

His words—not the promise of undying love her foolish heart craved—made the sensual veil that had wrapped itself around them draw back.

Goose-flesh prickled her skin. Aye, it was cold in here, although ever since Cameron had taken a seat at her side and rubbed salve on her bruised arm, she'd forgotten.

Wordlessly, she allowed him to help her to her feet.

She turned to him then, her gaze meeting his for the first time since he'd pushed her to the ground. The impact of looking at him full in the face now made her breathing still, her pulse quicken.

A flush highlighted Cameron's cheekbones, and desire still smoldered in his grey eyes, along with concern.

"I was rough," he said, his voice still husky. "Did I hurt ye?"

She shook her head. The opposite was true—she'd reveled in his lustiness, his dominance. She was a woman who liked to be in control, yet just now, she'd welcomed relinquishing it. She wanted to do so again—all night, in fact. Who cared about losing sleep?

Heat pooled in the cradle of her hips, and the tender flesh between her thighs began to ache once more. Did this man have any idea what he did to her?

A blush traveled up her chest and crept up her neck. Perhaps he did now. "I liked it," she whispered. "Although ye'll be thinking I'm fickle ... after telling ye that we would never again lie together."

His mouth quirked, although his grey eyes turned solemn. Reaching out, he cupped her cheek, his thumb sliding down to trace the curve of her bottom lip. "Not at all. Ye are quite a woman, Bree," he murmured. "One I find impossible to resist."

Was she imagining it, or was there a trace of regret in his voice.

The melting heat ebbed. Surely, not?

Taking Breanna by the hand, Cameron led her to the rickety cot, one they'd salvaged from the English tents. Pulling back the blankets, he climbed in and made space for her. "This cot is a little more cramped than our bed back at Rathlin," he said with a roguish wink that made her belly flip-flop, "but worry not ... I shall keep ye warm."

Breanna favored him with a smile in return, even if worry had started to gnaw at her, stealing the joy their coupling had brought.

Maybe Cameron didn't have remorse about what they'd just done, but he had emotionally withdrawn from her—behind that devil-may-care mask that he'd worn in their first days together.

He was retreating, and there was nothing Breanna could do about it.

Climbing into the cot with him, she sank against the warmth of his body, a sigh escaping her when his arms encircled her. She snuggled into him, reveling in his warmth and strength. How she'd longed for this over the past weeks. Ever since that night when he'd shown her what her own body was capable of feeling.

But traitorously, her reaction to this man went far deeper than that.

And she'd wanted to tell him so. She'd nearly blurted it out as she'd climbed to her peak earlier, yet in the aftermath was relieved she hadn't. She'd been impetuous in love once before, and it had nearly destroyed her. She was surprised she had it in her to trust again—and, in fact, had believed that part of her dead.

But Cameron Stewart had crept up on her.

And watching him fight today, she'd let herself believe he'd given himself to the cause. But had he?

Breanna swallowed hard then, in an attempt to loosen her suddenly tight throat. Squeezing her eyes shut, she willed the stinging tears to subside. The last thing she wanted to do now was start weeping.

The last thing she wanted was to love a man whose loyalty she'd bought—but she did.

23

SOME THINGS CANNOT BE FEIGNED

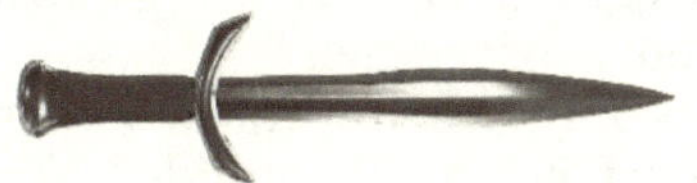

"THERE'S AN ARMY of the bastards … at least a thousand of them … bivouacked around fifty furlongs south from us." The scout's voice carried through the crowd.

Breanna watched Robert the Bruce's face split into a weary smile. However, his gaze remained somber. "Excellent … they've taken the bait."

He didn't seem remotely concerned that they were grossly outnumbered—for they all knew that the rough terrain here would make it difficult for the English to unleash their full strength against them.

Pushing a wet lock of hair off her face, Breanna also allowed herself a smile. It had been her first all day, for the march into the Galloway hills had been exhausting and cold.

Two days had passed since their victory at Turnberry, and they'd left the fortress upon a grey, drizzly dawn. The rain hadn't let up since. It fell now in a cloak, the clouds wrapping the world like a dense blanket of wool. The light had been poor all day and was fading now. Like the English, they too had recently made camp.

"The timing is perfect," Cameron spoke up then. He stood a few feet away from the Bruce, his dark hair slicked back from his face. The mercenary's eyes gleamed, his mouth curved in that arrogant smile that Breanna had come to know so well.

Her chest constricted. Had come to *love*.

Thrice-cursed goose-wit. Did ye want yer heart broken again?

"We know their location ... and they know ours," Cameron went on. "All we have to do is wait for them to come to us."

"It's a difficult position to approach," James Douglas pointed out, his grizzled face creasing into a smile. "The loch takes up much of the glen."

"And there's only a narrow track, bordered by a steep slope, to approach it," the Bruce added. "They won't have much ground to maneuver before the hill rises sharply."

"The 'Steps of Trool' will outwit them," Douglas replied, his smile widening into a grin.

Turning, Breanna's gaze alighted upon the precipitous hill rearing above them. "We shall lead them up there?" she asked. She couldn't help the incredulous note to her voice, for from this angle, the slope looked dangerously steep. She couldn't imagine engaging the enemy upon such terrain.

"Aye," Cameron answered her. "I climbed the path earlier ... there are boulders of granite we should be able to loosen and send down to give the English a rousing welcome."

Laughter greeted these words, although Robert Bruce wasn't smiling any longer. Instead, his walnut-brown eyes glinted. "Aye," he murmured when the mirth died down. "We shall make our stand here."

The rain eased with the coming of night, the clouds drawing back and the white sliver of the moon reflecting off the glistening waters of Loch Trool.

Peering across the water, Cameron shifted his weight from one hip to the other. Nearby, he heard a sentry muffle a cough. Cameron frowned. Sound traveled across the water. However, he reminded himself that the English knew where they were and that things were all going to plan.

They were unlikely to organize a raid at night, either—for even in daylight, this terrain was perilous.

Standing there, Cameron let the night's stillness wash over him. After days of gusting wind, it felt strangely quiet, and for the first time in a while, he sat with his own thoughts. Since Turnberry, he'd spent no time alone, although he'd welcomed the distraction.

It stopped him from dwelling on Breanna and their pretend marriage that was fast becoming something else entirely.

He didn't regret taking her the night they took Turnberry, yet a boulder now settled in his gut as he dwelled on the fact that there would likely be consequences. He'd noted the softness in Breanna's usually fierce eyes when she looked upon him, the tenderness of her touch, and the way she curled against him at night, sighing when he wrapped his arms about her.

Back at Rathlin Castle, she'd deliberately physically distanced herself from him—something that had frustrated him no end. But now that she'd succumbed once more to the attraction that pulsed between them, he could see the signs of a woman in love.

Unease danced down Cameron's spine. Christ's teeth, he'd gotten himself into a complicated situation. And if he didn't do something—and soon—he'd be lost. With each passing day, he found himself caring less and less about the silver he'd earn for this mission. Instead, his heartbeat quickened when he saw the fire in Robert the Bruce's eyes, patriotism igniting in his veins when he listened to the other men speak about taking back Scotland from the English. And whenever he looked Breanna's way, something squeezed deep inside his chest.

"All's well?" A gruff voice roused him from his brooding, and Cameron glanced up to see the Bruce standing at his shoulder, the strong planes of his face frosted by starlight.

"Aye," Cameron murmured. "They'll not bother us tonight."

Bruce nodded, his gaze glinting as he stared out across the gleaming surface of the loch. "I wonder how Thomas and Alex are faring," he said after a pause. "They should be making their way north to meet us." His brow furrowed then. "I was hoping our paths would have crossed by now."

"Give them time, Sire," Cameron replied. "They'll join ye."

Silence fell between the two men then. It was companionable, and Cameron felt no need to shatter it with trivial conversation. The Bruce wasn't a garrulous man, and Cameron had the sense that he'd grown even less so of late.

The trials of the last year would have broken a weaker soul.

"Ye are a fortunate man indeed, Stewart," Robert Bruce said eventually. His voice was unusually subdued, as if he'd been ruminating during the silence. "To have yer wife at yer side ... especially one so fierce. I swear I've never seen a woman handle herself like Breanna."

Cameron smiled, even if his belly knotted. The Bruce had no idea that it was all a ruse. To an outsider, Cameron and Breanna seemed perfectly matched—and he supposed they were.

"Aye," he murmured. "I am blessed ... however, Bree wouldn't suffer being left at home."

"Eight months have passed since I last saw my wife," the Bruce said then, his voice roughening. "Or my daughter and sister." Brittleness crept in as he continued. "I sometimes feel that I have failed them."

"Ye haven't," Cameron answered.

"But what if Longshanks has them executed ... like Neil?" His big frame shuddered, for no doubt, he was imagining Elizabeth being hanged, drawn, and quartered. However, Cameron believed it unlikely that Edward of England would treat the Bruce's wife thus.

Longshanks had a brutal reputation, yet Breanna had told him that he also had a chivalrous streak. Her sisters, Nessa and Fyfa, had noted such during the brief contact they'd had with the English king.

Nonetheless, he understood why the Bruce might fear he'd never see his womenfolk again.

"Last I heard, yer wife, daughter, and sister are all still live," Cameron assured him. Indeed, during his stay in Perth, Cameron had caught whispers that Elizabeth was being held somewhere in Yorkshire.

The Bruce grunted, signaling that he too had heard the rumors. All the same, he feared for their safety. "I won't rest until I have them back," he said, his voice hardening with the iron that Cameron had come to know well. "Even if I have to destroy everything in my path."

A shiver rippled through Cameron at these words, for he believed them.

Gasping for breath, her skin slick from sweat despite the cold, damp air inside the tent, Breanna collapsed upon Cameron's chest.

She'd just ridden him, his hands on her hips guiding her as she'd impaled herself on him. And when she'd shattered, throwing her head back as pleasure throbbed out from deep in her womb, the world had spun.

But now, as she lay, limp and boneless against her lover's thundering heart, her surroundings came back into focus.

Wordlessly, Cameron pulled the blankets over them both before he stroked her back. The touch of his fingertips sent delightful shivers through Breanna. Even now, just after coupling, her body still responded to him. He was the musician, and she was his lyre.

He has too much sway over ye, a voice whispered in the back of her mind. *He shall break yer heart, just as Grant did.*

Breanna shut her eyes, willing the voice away. She didn't want the harsh realities of life to intrude, not now. Couldn't her fears give her peace, just for one night?

They continued to lie there in silence, and as the moments stretched out, uneasiness settled over Breanna.

She worried when Cameron didn't speak to her. And indeed, after they'd coupled at Turnberry, and when he'd taken her since, he seemed to have very little to say in the aftermath.

Knowing that she should probably leave things be, but unable to prevent herself, Breanna opened her eyes and propped herself up on an elbow, her gaze settling on Cameron's face.

He hadn't been dozing as she'd thought. But instead was staring up at the roof of the pavilion, his gaze shadowed.

The seriousness of his expression made misgiving tighten her belly.

"Are ye worried about tomorrow?" she asked, breaking the heavy hush.

Cameron's gaze shifted to her, and then his mouth lifted at the corners. "Not particularly."

"I hear the English outnumber us significantly."

"Aye ... but we have the higher ground."

Breanna held his eye. "Then why the stern look?"

He raised an eyebrow. "Was I looking stern?"

"Aye."

He huffed a laugh, although she felt him tense against her. "I never thought I'd let myself get embroiled in the Scottish cause," he said after a pause. "Not after Stirling."

Breanna studied his face. As often, the mercenary's expression was veiled.

"And yet ye did," she reminded him.

"Aye ... for a price."

Tension rippled through Breanna. Why did he have to say that—why remind them both why he was here?

"So, if ye did it only for coin, why the troubled gaze?" she asked, her tone sharper than she'd intended.

He favored her with an arch look. "I think ye mistake tiredness for something else, Bree."

No, she hadn't.

"Why do ye pretend ye don't care, when it's evident ye do?" she asked, trying to ignore the ache in her belly.

I warned ye this is folly. The nasty wee voice was back. *Ye'd be best to let this matter drop, lass … before ye say too much.*

But she couldn't. "Some things cannot be feigned, Cam," Breanna pressed on, cursing the way her voice caught. "Ye have come alive of late. And ye are a natural leader too. I see the way the men respect ye … how the Bruce heeds ye. There's no crime in admitting the outcome of this campaign matters to ye."

24

WE FIGHT NOT FOR GLORY

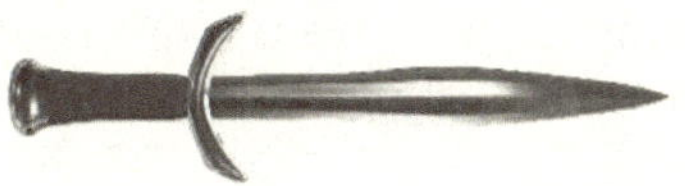

THERE'S NO CRIME in admitting the outcome of this campaign matters to ye.

Breanna's heartfelt comment tormented Cameron the next morning as he readied himself for battle.

He'd snorted at her words, brushed them aside like cobwebs—and had seen the hurt that flowered in her expressive peat-brown eyes as a result.

He was a callous bastard and had been unable to stop himself.

Breanna had questioned him at a weak moment. After lying with her, he often felt dangerously exposed. Not physically—for the feel of their naked limbs entwined gave him a sensation of completeness he'd never before experienced—but emotionally. When she met his gaze afterward, it was as if she were looking into his soul. As if she could see all his deepest, darkest secrets and knew all his fears.

The sensation unbalanced him. It also reminded him of the mistake he'd made in allowing his attraction to Breanna to override his good sense.

Sooner or later, things were going to get too intense, too complicated. Sooner or later, he was going to have to step back from the edge of the abyss he was teetering upon.

Sheathing the blade he'd just sharpened, into the scabbard across his back, Cameron strode out of the camp, following the line of warriors making their way up the 'Steps of Trool', to where their king awaited them.

Breanna was already there, shield slung over one shoulder and a longbow and quiver of arrows over the other, her longsword sheathed at her hip. She looked on as men loosened boulders of granite with pikes and iron bars, yet glanced up as Cameron approached, her expression shuttered.

She'd withdrawn a little from him since their conversation the night before.

"The English are on their way!" James Douglas puffed his way up the hill, his cheeks ruddy in the icy morning air. "They approach along the lakeshore."

Cameron turned and let his gaze travel down the steep hillside to where the waters of Loch Trool sparkled in the morning sun. Around them, a frost glittered and the sky above was clear, promising a fine, if cold, day.

And as Douglas had warned, he spotted the column of men approaching. The soldiers traveled on foot, and there were no drums or pennants fluttering in the breeze.

Cameron's mouth stretched into a thin smile. "It's a raiding party," he called out. "I'd wager that de Valence has sent them on ahead to deal with us before he follows."

Muttered oaths followed this comment, while hatred coiled in Cameron's belly. He remembered the Earl of Pembroke from Stirling. He'd never forget the evening Edward's commander had delivered the news that his king wouldn't accept their surrender—not until he'd used his new weapon on them. The knight had appeared a fiend from hell that evening, faceless in his helm and seated on a huge destrier while thunder rolled overhead and lightning flashed across the sky.

Sir Aymer had mocked them, and Cameron had longed to jab his dirk in the bastard's belly. The knight had escorted them all out of Stirling the following day, after Warwolf had brought down the eastern curtain wall in one shot.

The man's goading words still echoed in Cameron's ears.

Cameron had hoped to face him today, yet it made sense that the knight wouldn't move his full force against them—not when that raiding party looked to be over four hundred strong. *Twice the size of our own force.*

"Are the boulders ready, Edward?" The Bruce asked.

Cameron turned back, his gaze traveling to where the king's brother stood a few yards away. Edward flashed him a wolfish grin. "Aye, brother."

Cameron's gut tensed, as it always did before a fight. This would be an interesting one indeed, for although they held the high ground, the rough slope was dangerously steep.

He glanced over at Breanna once more, to find her attention riveted upon the king. He'd seen her fight and knew she could hold her own. Yet he wished she would keep to the back today, out of harm's way.

Of course, she wouldn't. That wasn't Breanna's way.

He'd come across her that morning, when he'd returned to their tent after breaking his fast, murmuring a charm as she held her hand over the flickering flames of the brazier. "Ensuring a rousing victory for us, are ye, Bree?" he'd teased.

She'd glanced up, her mouth pursing and her dark eyes narrowing. "If I were that powerful, the English would already be cowering south of the border," she'd replied, her voice clipped. "It's a sain … a protection against harm in battle … for us both."

Cameron had flashed her a cocky smile, even as his chest constricted at the gesture. He'd then patted the dirk at his hip. "Yer charm is appreciated, Bree … but it's no substitute for this."

Now, as he stood upon the rocky slope, awaiting the Bruce's final words before they turned their attention to the enemy, Cameron wished he hadn't been so glib.

He'd seen the hurt in Breanna's eyes before her jaw set in that way he'd come to know well over the past two months.

He really could be an arse at times.

"The enemy is at our door once again." Robert Bruce drew his heavy claidheamh-mòr, his chainmail clinking.

"But this time, they will not best us." His gaze swept the faces of the warriors surrounding him. "Remember, we fight not for glory, nor for wealth, nor honor," he continued, his voice ringing out over the hillside, "but only and alone for freedom ... which no good man surrenders but with his life."

Cameron's skin prickled at these words, and around him, he felt the air change. His gaze swept the faces of the Bruce's men and saw his own tension, his own pride, reflected back at him.

The night before, he'd scoffed at Breanna's words, yet he couldn't deny them now—not when the Bruce had just reminded him what really mattered.

We fight not for glory, nor for wealth, nor honor.

Heart kicking against his ribs, Cameron tried to remember that he was indeed doing this for coin, yet the assurance seemed feeble and false.

He couldn't lie to the wild beat of his heart or to the pressure in his chest that made him feel as if he would burst with pride.

Curse it ... I was a fool to agree to this mission.

Shoving the thought aside, Cameron swiveled then, watching as the English drew nearer. As they approached the 'Steps of Trool', they were forced to travel in single file up the defile.

Moving down to where warriors were struggling to loosen the first of the boulders, Cameron loaned them his shoulder.

Moments later, a huge rock was hurtling down the slope.

Straightening up, Cameron turned to see Robert the Bruce had stridden to where his men were heaving against the other boulders. "Loose the lot of them!" the king shouted. "Bring down hell."

Instants later, the rumble of stone filled the air— followed by panicked shouts from below.

Tearing her gaze from Cameron Stewart, Breanna notched an arrow and drew back her bowstring, sighting one of the hauberk-clad men who'd escaped being crushed by a granite boulder.

She needed to focus on the task at hand and not on the man who now dominated her thoughts far more than he should.

The twang of the bow releasing cut through the bellows of both her countrymen and the English. An instant later, the quarrel lodged in the soldier's throat.

Arms cartwheeling, he fell backward and toppled off the path.

Another soldier replaced him. But he too was cut down, by the bowman at Breanna's right. There were a line of them positioned at the top of the hill. They'd waited until the last of the boulders crashed down the defile, taking with them a number of the enemy, before loosing their arrows.

More English soldiers fell, lurching off the path, but many others continued on, kite shields aloft. Arrows clattered off wood and iron, and frustration surged through Breanna. The longbows had managed to do some damage, but the English were tenacious.

They weren't giving up. Not yet.

When the last of her arrows were spent, she cast her bow and empty quiver aside before picking up her shield and drawing her sword.

A number of her countrymen, Robert and Edward Bruce and Cameron among them, had already surged down the hillside, claidheamh-mòrs swinging, to engage the enemy.

Breanna followed them.

The knot of fighting farther down prevented her from getting any closer. Her jaw clenched—as the need to spill English blood rose within her. She'd been too slow in racing down the hill to meet the enemy and couldn't push into the fray without risking a fall from the path.

Yet, as she looked on, Breanna saw that the Scots were quickly gaining the advantage. Indeed, they'd chosen this spot well. The narrowness of the path prevented support from either the front or the rear.

Without room to maneuver, the attack took a downward spiral for the English. One by one, they fell—until, as their numbers dwindled, those surviving withdrew.

Breanna watched them from above, her blade still unbloodied, as men fled along the lake edge. One or two Scots harried them, their shouts echoing through the glen, yet the rest let them go.

25

CELEBRATING VICTORY

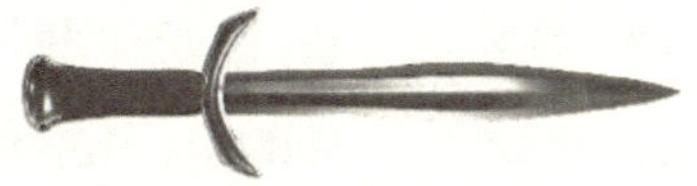

"HERE'S TO THE first of many victories to come!"

Cheering followed James Douglas's toast, the roar echoing high amongst the rafters of the hall of Cree Castle. Located half a day's march from Glen Trool, the small fortress—which sat on the banks of the River Cree, with thick woodland behind it—was home to Ian Douglas, one of Lord Douglas's clansmen.

One of the few fortresses in the area not occupied by the English, Douglas had insisted his cousin would welcome them. Indeed, the laird had taken them in without hesitation.

Seated next to Cameron at one of the long trestle tables in the crowded hall, Breanna also raised her cup of ale aloft. Her gaze traveled the length and breadth of the hall, observing those seated. She didn't believe the Bruce was in danger here, yet she'd gotten into the habit of scanning the faces of folk surrounding the king. After all, the last attempt on his life had occurred during a banquet.

Nonetheless, despite her honed senses, lightness filled Breanna's heart this eve, hope that Robert the Bruce had weathered his darkest hour and had now started on the road toward liberating Scotland of the English.

She took a gulp of ale, a smile curving her lips. Hope had returned to the hearts of the Scots. She knew the Guardians of Alba had allies at Cree too; first thing tomorrow, she would seek them out and ask one to carry word to Assynt.

Colina and the others would be wondering how the campaign fared. The High Bandruì would have sent her crow, Eclipse, to gain word, if she'd known Breanna's whereabouts. However, Breanna had moved about so much over the past two months, there was little chance of Colina's familiar finding her.

"Looking pleased with yerself this eve," Cameron noted from beside her. "And rightly so."

Breanna glanced the mercenary's way. Although he was teasing her, his gaze shone with a pride that couldn't be feigned. She'd seen the elation on his face after battle. Cameron had hauled her into his arms afterward and kissed her passionately, not heeding the catcalls and heckling from the other men.

His reaction had pleased her, as did the look in his eyes now.

Perhaps, despite his evasion the night before, Cameron Stewart had finally admitted to himself that this mission wasn't just another job.

"I am ... although I can hardly say I contributed much," she huffed before taking another gulp of ale. The brew was cold and bitter, quenching her thirst after a long day. "I couldn't get near the fighting."

"Aye ... but I saw ye with that longbow," Cameron replied with a wink. "Ye weren't boasting when ye said yer aim was deadly."

Breanna laughed, a little of the tension she'd been carrying inside her unraveling. "Women don't make empty boasts like men," she told him with mock seriousness. "Surely, ye realize that by now?"

His gaze met hers and held. "Aye," he replied.

Hidden in the shadows in the yard behind the kitchens, Lamia awaited her chance. It was getting late. Night had settled over the Galloway hills and the dark forests around Cree, and the sound of drunken laughter and revelry drifted from the squat stone keep.

Lamia ground her teeth. Curse it, she was foot-sore and hungry and longed to be indoors out of the damp and cold.

The past few days had been exhausting.

She'd arrived at Turnberry just a day before the Bruce and had looked on from a distance as the Scots trounced the English garrison. She'd been hoping for a chance to get close to Robert Bruce then, yet he hadn't lingered. Turnberry Castle hadn't yet been taken, and instead, the outlaw king and the force of around two hundred men who followed him had journeyed inland.

Desperate not to lose her quarry, Lamia had followed them.

Shifting from a crouch to a standing position to ease the numbness in her legs, she scowled. Her belly growled, and she placed a hand over it, willing it to settle.

She frowned then, as her thoughts turned to her predicament. After leaving Ayr, her morning queasiness had persisted. And finally, with dread in her heart, she'd visited a healer just outside Turnberry.

The woman had confirmed her suspicions. She was with child.

She'd taken precautions ever since she'd first lain with her husband, yet somehow Philip de Eynsford's seed had taken root in her belly.

Lamia's hand remained upon her flat stomach. She'd heard that carrying a child turned a woman a bit witless, and she was no exception: she often felt oddly tearful, and tiredness dragged down upon her. She didn't want children, and yet ever since she'd learned she would bear Philip's child, she'd found herself wondering if it would be a girl or boy. She envisaged Philip's reaction—once he got over his rage at her running off into the wild.

He'd make a good father.

Lamia's jaw clenched. Hades. Where had that come from? She removed her hand from her belly and squinted at the darkened doorway to the castle kitchens.

Enough simpering womanly thoughts. She had to remain focused. Her goal was finally within reach. For the first time in two and half years, Robert the Bruce was within her grasp. This was her chance to end him, and this time, she wouldn't fail.

Her skin prickled then as she imagined Sir Aymer's shocked face when she returned to the English, victorious. Philip would forget to be angry with her when he learned what she'd achieved.

And perhaps history *would* record her bold deed. The mysterious lady who brought down the outlaw king.

However, she was getting ahead of herself. In order for her to kill the Bruce, she needed to get close to him.

"Surely, the wench will venture outdoors again?" she murmured to her familiar. "I tire of waiting."

Fantôme shifted against her arm, warning her to be patient. They'd been hiding here ever since dusk, and Lamia had taken note of a small mousy-haired scullery maid who'd ventured outdoors to empty some slops.

Surely, she would do so again before the eve was up?

As if heeding Lamia's thoughts, a small figure emerged from the doorway.

Whistling to herself, the lass descended the steps, hauling a bucket with her. Lamia's gaze tracked her. The young woman was the ideal disguise. Lamia would use her identity, cloak herself in a powerful glamor that would fool most folk. Unfortunately though, there couldn't be two of them moving around the castle.

It was regrettable, yet this hapless lass would have to be dealt with.

Oblivious to Lamia's presence or intent, the young woman continued to whistle a merry tune as she emptied the pail of vegetable scraps onto a compost heap. Above, within the keep, the wail of a Highland pipe followed by singing drifted out into the night.

Lamia's mouth thinned. The Scots wouldn't be celebrating for much longer.

She straightened up to her full height, the fingers of her right hand clenching around the small knife she'd brought with her. Violence was a crude method indeed. But right now, witching wasn't what was needed.

The River Cree rushed past, just a few yards from where they stood. Once she threw the girl's body in, she would be swept away.

And then Lamia would be able to assume her identity.

Cameron shifted in his seat, disquiet coiling in the pit of his gut and making the meal of roast boar stew he'd just consumed churn uneasily. Around him, the hall boomed with laughter, singing, and the screech of the Highland pipe. Mead and ale flowed, and two of the Bruce's men— one of them Edward Bruce—were dancing on the tables.

Next to him, Breanna clapped along in time with the music and singing.

She, like everyone else in the hall, was unaware of the battle that raged within him.

The war he'd been fighting for days now.

It seemed that with every step forward, every victory—no matter how small—the panic within him grew, rolling in like ominous storm clouds.

Soon the storm would break.

Cameron clenched his jaw and raised the half-full cup of mead before him to his lips, taking a sip. The cloying, sweet taste—usually one he liked—just made his bile rise this evening.

His state of mind was poor indeed if he couldn't make merry and enjoy the revelry like everyone else.

But he couldn't.

All he could think about was that, in the aftermath of the battle upon the 'Steps of Trool', hope had flared within him like a beacon. Hope for the Bruce. For Scotland. For himself.

He'd dared believe that he could be part of this, that he could make a difference. And then when Breanna had approached him, her cheeks flushed with pride, he'd dared imagine a life with this fierce, loyal, and lovely woman at his side.

And then, like the great fool he was, he'd gone and kissed her, not caring when the other warriors heckled him.

But in the hours that followed, a chill had stolen over him.

What was he doing?

At thirty-five winters, Cameron Stewart had learned the hard way what a cruel mistress fate could be. She gave, and then she took away. He'd once loved without reservation, and once given himself whole-heartedly to defending Scotland. But in both instances, he'd been left with nothing but ashes in his mouth.

He couldn't go through that again.

If he had nothing, he could lose nothing—that was the motto he'd lived by over the past years, and it had served him well.

And now, because of Robert the Bruce, and because of the woman seated at his side, he was at risk of throwing himself off the precipice.

Cameron broke out in a cold sweat, his fingers clenching around the cup he still held.

It was no good, he couldn't go on this way.

Breanna had certainly drunk too much ale this evening, far more than she was used to. Her head was starting to swim, and the urge to find somewhere flat to stretch out and rest her weary bones stole over her.

Around her, the revelry and celebrations were still in full swing.

On the dais, seated between James Douglas and the laird of this castle, Ian Douglas, Robert the Bruce looked the most relaxed Breanna had seen him. The severe lines that had worn grooves on either side of his mouth and nose had softened, making him look younger. A half-smile curved his lips now as he watched his brother make a complete arse of himself.

Edward had slipped on a patch of spilled drink and toppled forward. He would have had a nasty fall too if three warriors hadn't caught him.

Laughter rolled over the hall, and Breanna's mouth twitched.

Life was good. Finally, after so much waiting, the tide appeared to be taking a turn in their favor.

She glanced Cameron's way, expecting to see the same contentedness that she felt on his face as well. Earlier, he'd appeared in high spirits, but a shadow fell over Breanna when she saw her lover's expression was now hooded.

He was watching the revelry with a look of detachment that made misgiving seep over her in a cold tide.

Crone's tears, this man was so mercurial. The last time she'd glanced his way, he'd seemed as caught up in the celebrations as the rest of them.

"Is all well, Cam?" she asked, reaching out and placing a hand over his forearm.

Cameron shifted his attention to her. A moment later, he favored her with a warm smile, one that made her wonder if she'd just been imagining things. "Aye, lass."

Breanna's lips parted as she readied herself to ask him something more. However, a commotion upon the dais drew her attention.

Her gaze swept to where a serving lass had just fallen onto Robert the Bruce's lap.

Small, with mousy brown hair, the girl was red in the face. Wine had spilled over the table, running like blood across the surface and dripping on the floor.

"Fenella!" Ian Douglas's voice boomed across the hall. "Clumsy wench!"

The wail of the Highland pipe cut off as the mortified servant scrambled off the Bruce. "I'm so sorry, Sire," she gasped, her pale grey eyes bright with tears. She was halfway to her feet when she slipped once more and grabbed hold of the Bruce's shoulder to steady herself. "I tripped."

The king wore a bemused expression as he brushed her apology away with a wave of the hand. "Fret not, lass," he rumbled. "There's no harm done."

"Ye shouldn't even be out here, Fenella," the laird of Cree Castle grumbled, glaring at the young woman. "Get yerself back into the kitchens. There are pots to be scrubbed!"

26

ENTANGLED

IT WAS LATE when they retired to their bed-chamber. The laird's wife had given them a room high in one of the two towers rising from the keep. It was a tiny, drafty chamber, but fortunately, it had a small fire burning in the hearth, which took the edge off the chill.

Muttering an oath under her breath, Breanna hurried to the fireplace and held her hands out over it. After the warmth of the hall—where the heat of two massive hearths and many bodies had kept the cold at bay—the rest of the keep felt as cold as a tomb.

Nevertheless, Breanna was ready to retire for the night. Her eyes were gritty with fatigue, and she was starting to feel a little queasy after all the ale and mead she'd consumed.

Fortunately, none of them had an early start the following morning.

It was just as well, for she wagered most of the Bruce's party—herself included—would awaken with a sore head.

Glancing over her shoulder, she saw that the bed looked a lot more comfortable than the rickety cot they'd slept upon of late. She was looking forward to crawling into it.

"I feel like I could sleep for a week," she murmured, stifling a yawn. She turned then, shifting her gaze to where Cameron had just closed the door behind him. "Do ye think we ..."

Her voice died off when her attention came to rest upon his face.

The mercenary wore a grim expression.

"Cam?" she asked, misgiving fluttering in her belly. "What is it?"

Cameron halted, his gaze spearing hers. He then muttered a curse under his breath before raking a hand through his hair.

Breanna's misgiving slid into worry. She'd never seen him so agitated.

He tore his gaze from hers then, focusing his attention upon the glowing lump of peat in the hearth.

Breanna's belly twisted. He was avoiding her eye now—something was most definitely amiss with the man. Her instinct earlier in the eve had been right after all.

"I can't do this," he ground out, his voice unusually rough. "Not anymore."

A chill prickled Breanna's skin. It surprised her that when she replied, her voice was steady, "Can't do *what*, exactly?"

His attention swept back to her, and the desolation she saw there made her draw in a sharp breath. She hadn't thought Cameron Stewart capable of such a look. She was used to his confident front, his arrogance. The look he wore now made her realize that she didn't know him at all.

Cold seeped into her bones. She wished she hadn't asked him that question for, suddenly, she didn't want to know the answer.

"Any of it." His voice was as bleak as his expression. "I can't continue this campaign with the Bruce ... and I can't pretend to be yer husband any longer." He drew in a harsh breath. "I'm leaving."

A heavy silence fell in the bed-chamber, and with it, the already cold air grew frosty.

Breanna stared back at Cameron, her pulse hammering in her ears. "Ye can't leave," she said finally, once again marveling at the steadiness of her voice.

Inside, she was in turmoil, yet she managed to keep it leashed. "The mission isn't complete."

"It is for me."

Breanna inhaled deeply and slowly as she felt anger kindle. The heat of it washed over her, making her forget the coldness inside this chamber and the chill in her heart. She welcomed the heat; it galvanized her.

"How can it be?" she asked, her voice catching then as desperation boiled to the surface and threatened to break through. "Today was only the beginning, Cam. We still have so much work to do ... the Bruce needs ye by his side."

I need ye.

The words screamed in her head, yet she didn't voice them. Not yet. Breanna was proud—too proud at times. Nessa and Fyfa had teased her about her hubris growing up. How she refused to admit any weakness, even to her own detriment.

But neither of her sisters had seen the spectacle she'd made of herself over Grant. They hadn't seen how she'd fallen to her knees before him, tears streaming down his face as he'd insulted her.

Afterward, when she'd fled from him, she'd vowed that she would never again leave herself so vulnerable with a man.

But even if she managed to keep her composure, here she was—reliving the past. She'd let Cameron Stewart in. And like her former lover, he was now betraying her trust.

And as she stared into the mercenary's eyes, she cursed herself for making another poor choice.

Cameron's mouth twisted. "The Bruce survived without my assistance ... and he will do so again."

Breanna folded her arms across her chest. The defensive gesture helped her keep her brave face on— even as she crumbled within. "Ye agreed to stay the course, Stewart," she said, her voice flint-edged now. "Ye gave me yer word."

He stared back at her. "I did, and now I must break it, Bree."

Her throat tightened. "Ye won't get the rest of yer silver." The words ripped from her.

His gaze never left hers. "I don't expect to." He went to where his leather pack sat against the wall, reached in, and fished out a drawstring pouch. He then crossed to her and held it out. "Here are the sixty silver pennies ye gave me in Perth. Ye can have them back."

When Breanna made no move to take the pouch, he reached out, gently pried one of her hands free of their clasp across her chest, and placed the pouch in her palm. It clinked as he wrapped her fingers around it. "Take it," he said softly. "I haven't earned this coin."

The tightness in Breanna's throat increased. It now felt as if she had a plum lodged there. Queasiness rolled over her, even as panic beat like a trapped raven in her chest.

"I can't believe ye are doing this."

"I'm sorry … I thought I could go through with this mission, but I can't."

Breanna's throat worked. "Was pretending to be my husband such a chore?"

His mouth quirked, although there was no humor in his eyes. "No," he said, his voice lowering. "And there lies part of the problem."

Breanna frowned, even as her pulse started to race. "I don't understand. What do ye mean?"

Cameron's face shuttered, and he stepped back from her. "I told myself a long time ago that I would avoid entanglements, Bree … but with ye, things are becoming …"

His voice died off then, although Breanna silently completed the sentence for him.

Complicated.

"It's become clear to me that this arrangement of ours … this pretense that we are wed … isn't feigned on yer part," he continued, "not any longer."

Breanna flinched as if he'd just struck her. "What?"

He took another step back from her, his gaze narrowing. "Ye have developed an attachment to me, Bree … and it will only end messily if I let it continue."

He paused there, a nerve flickering under one eye. "I don't want that to happen … and that's why I'm leaving."

Breanna swallowed before closing her eyes. Nausea pitched in her belly, and dizziness assailed her.

"It's too late," she rasped. She opened her eyes then, stepped close to the fire, and put out her hand on the wall to steady herself. "Ye great dolt … I'm already in love with ye … although I dearly wish I wasn't." The words tore out of her.

She turned her baleful stare upon Cameron, seeing the horror in his eyes at her words. Humiliation washed through her in a hot wave.

Heedless she plowed on. "Ye are a fazart. Ye can stand there and tell me that ye don't want to be *entangled* … with the Bruce's cause or with me … but the truth is ye are scared. And ye'd rather walk away than face yer fears like a man."

Her words were harsh, cruel even, but she'd had enough. She didn't want his excuses or his masks. Who exactly was Cameron Stewart? She didn't know at all. She'd lost her heart to an empty shell of a man.

It wasn't just him she was angry with, but herself.

Turning from him, she clamped her eyes shut once more. They burned, yet she kept the tears at bay. She wouldn't weep. Not yet, not in front of him.

"Go on then," she said, her voice barely above a whisper. "Now ye are done with yer speech, ye can leave."

Silence followed, and when Cameron spoke, his voice was brittle. "Bree, please. I don't want—"

"No," she cut him off. "Ye've made yer choice … and I've made mine. Get. Out."

Another hush fell.

Breanna's breathing became shallow. The Three give her strength; if the man tried to reach for, or touch, her, she'd break his nose. She'd had enough of listening to him. She just wanted him gone. He'd made his position clear. There was nothing more to say.

The moments drew out, the quiet within the bed-chamber broken only by the crackle of the embers in the hearth.

The skin between Breanna's shoulder blades burned as she felt his gaze boring into her, willing her to turn around. But she didn't.

Eventually, the scape of his boots filled the chamber, and she heard the whisper of his footsteps as he moved and the rustle that followed when he retrieved his pack.

"Goodbye, Bree," he said softly.

And with that, the door to the chamber opened and then thudded shut as he let himself out into the stairwell.

An instant later, she heard his retreating footsteps.

Breanna stood there by the hearth for a long while afterward. Her ragged breathing and thundering pulse deafened her. Eventually, she came out of her trance and pushed herself off the wall. Then, glancing down at her other hand, she saw that she still clutched the leather pouch of silver the mercenary had returned to her.

Fury spiraled within her, even as tears blurred her vision and spilled down her cheeks. Snarling a curse, she whirled and hurled the coin purse across the room.

27

SOMETHING AMISS

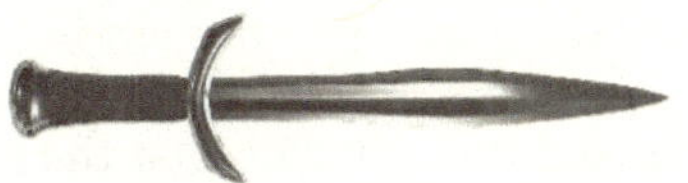

"THE BRUCE HAS fallen ill."

James Douglas's greeting when Breanna entered the hall for the noon meal made her draw to a halt. The Lord of Douglas stood next to one of the great hearths inside the hall, a wolfhound at his feet. At the graveness of his expression, Breanna's breathing quickened.

For an instant, she completely forgot the crushing weight that pressed down upon her breastbone like a lump of lead. She'd wept for most of the night and had only ventured from her bed-chamber once her red, puffy eyes had gone down.

Breanna frowned, alarm flickering to life within her. "What ails him?"

"No one's rightly sure," Douglas rumbled. "He was hale when he retired yestereve ... but Edward can't even get him to rise from his bed today." He paused then. "The healer's with him now."

Breanna nodded, taking this in, even as her skin started to prickle. "Perhaps he ate something that disagreed with him?"

Douglas shook his head. "He ate from the same platter as Ian and me... and we are both well." The man's gaze settled on her face then, a groove appearing between his greying brows. "Are ye poorly as well, Lady Stewart ... ye are deathly pale?"

Breanna swallowed.

Lady Stewart.

It was a bitter reminder of the ruse she and Cameron had woven. Breanna forced a tight smile, even if the pressure on her breastbone increased. "I fear I overdid it on the ale last night ... and am still recovering."

"Yer husband must be too," Douglas replied, "for I haven't spied him yet today."

Breanna forced her smile to remain in place. "Aye ... Cameron's love for mead has left him with a sore head indeed." She paused then, noting that the hall was starting to fill up, the greasy odor of mutton drifting across the space as servants carried in tureens of stew.

Bile stung the back of her throat. She had no appetite today, and the news about the Bruce's illness closed her belly entirely. She'd sworn to protect him, but some foes were easier to defeat than others. Perhaps it was nothing, but it was better to be sure. "I should visit our king," she murmured.

Turning from James Douglas, she hurried from the hall. She probably should have told him that Cameron Stewart had left Cree Castle and wouldn't be returning— but it could wait for now.

Soon though, she'd have to inform them. None of the men would understand, least of all Robert Bruce. Cameron had likely left without bidding any of them farewell. What would she tell them? Would she make up some excuse as to why her husband had slipped from Cree Castle in the night? Or would she simply tell them the bald truth: that she'd hired the mercenary to pretend to be her husband so that the Bruce would accept her sword. And that Cameron Stewart had decided he'd had enough of fighting for Scotland's freedom?

She'd called Cameron a coward, yet she wasn't sure she had the courage to look the Bruce in the eye and tell him the truth. The king genuinely liked Cameron and respected him. Better that she came up with an excuse, some reason why he'd been compelled to leave so suddenly.

Jaw clenched as she pushed aside thoughts of the mercenary and focused instead on Robert Bruce's sudden sickness, Breanna alighted the steps that took her up to the first floor of the keep. Upon the landing, she met a servant. It was a surprise to see the lass who'd fallen on the Bruce's lap the night before and spilled wine all over the table, for Breanna had thought she was a scullery maid, and as such would spend most of her days downstairs in the kitchen. But nonetheless, Breanna asked her where she'd find the Bruce's chamber.

"It's at the end of the hall, my lady," the girl mumbled, her eyes downcast. "The last door on the left."

"Thank ye." Breanna's gaze roamed over the maid's stooped shoulders and cowed face. The lass seemed a nervous creature. She hoped the laird of the castle hadn't been too harsh with her over the incident of the night before.

The maid glanced up then, and Breanna was struck by what strange eyes she had—pale grey, almost silver in the flickering light of the nearby cressets. Breanna had never seen eyes of the like before.

Something tickled at the back of her mind then, a memory she couldn't quite place. There was an odd scent in this hallway too, a musky scent mixed with the odor of hot iron. It was strange, for the forge wouldn't be located nearby.

Frowning, Breanna bid the maid 'good day' and followed the hallway down to the door the lass had indicated. As she approached, an elderly woman emerged from the bed-chamber. She carried a basket of herbs under one arm, her wrinkled face creased in severe lines.

"How is he?" Breanna asked the healer.

The elderly woman paused, peering shortsightedly at Breanna. The gesture reminded her of Colina. The High Bandruì's sight had worsened over the years. Breanna's throat constricted. It had been a few months since she'd been home to the Wailing Widow Falls and seen her mother and sisters. She missed them—and her aching heart longed to find solace amongst her order once more. The Guardians of Alba were her refuge, her haven from a harsh world.

"It's the strangest thing," the woman murmured, her voice whispery with age. "He has pains all over his body, yet I cannot determine what the problem is."

"Does he have a fever?"

The healer shook her head. "He is weak, full of aches, and unable to bear sunlight … I have given him a draft to calm him and help him rest … but I'm afraid I can do little else at present."

Breanna nodded, even if her earlier misgiving tightened into a hard knot of fear under her ribcage. She'd never heard an illness come on so swiftly— especially without a fever. It made no sense. How she wished Nessa were present at Cree Castle. Her sister was gifted at using witching for curing most ailments. Over the years, she'd taught Breanna a few tricks, yet she felt woefully inept compared to Nessa.

Pushing open the door, Breanna took a tentative step inside the chamber. It was shadowy, illuminated only by the light of a single cresset upon the far wall. The shutters were closed, blocking out the noon sun. Outdoors, it was a windy, bright day, yet one wouldn't have thought so in this chamber.

Edward Bruce sat by his brother's bed, and the furrow upon his forehead grew deeper still when his gaze alighted upon Breanna.

Breanna tensed. Even nearly two months on, Edward hadn't forgiven her for beating him in their duel at Rathlin Castle. Losing to a woman had embittered him.

Ignoring Edward's scowl, Breanna approached the foot of the bed, her gaze shifting to the Bruce. He lay propped up in a nest of pillows, his strong-featured face flushed and taut.

A moment later, Robert Bruce grimaced, a groan escaping between clenched teeth.

"Sire." Breanna moved to his side before reaching out and grasping one of his hands. As the healer had said, his palms weren't clammy or hot. Yet she felt a tremor pass through his body, and his grip tightened as another bout of pains assailed him.

"Christ's teeth," he grunted. "What's wrong with me?"

"That useless cunning woman has no idea," Edward muttered. "We need a proper physician."

Breanna's mouth thinned. As often, the Bruce's younger brother's aggression grated upon her. Was it really necessary to lock horns with everyone who crossed his path?

Deliberately ignoring his comment, she focused instead upon Robert Bruce's strained face. "When did this come on, Sire?" she asked gently.

"In the middle of the night," he replied roughly. "I was asleep, and then stabbing pains assailed me … woke me from my sleep."

"Are they centered on one part of yer body in particular?"

"No … they're everywhere."

Breanna's mouth thinned. She noted then the strange scent she'd smelled upon the landing: the whiff of musk and hot iron.

Bending over the Bruce, she inhaled deeply, her brow furrowing when she realized the smell was also upon his skin.

Uneasiness prickled the backs of her arms then.

"What are ye doing?" Edward demanded.

Breanna's chin kicked up; she'd almost forgotten that the Bruce's brother was present.

"My mother taught me a little of healing," she replied. It wasn't a lie, although Colina had been exasperated by Breanna's lack of aptitude for the healing arts. Her talent lay in divination, like the High Bandruì. "She told me that a patient's smell can tell ye much."

"And?" There was no mistaking the challenge in Edward's voice.

Breanna straightened up and stepped away from the bed. "I think I shall seek that healer out and speak to her once more."

Edward's mouth pursed, making it clear that he thought the pair of them useless. However, Breanna paid him no mind.

She was already heading toward the door.

Leaving the Bruce's sick room, she didn't go in search of the healer. Instead, she hurried back to her tower chamber, her pulse thundering in her ears.

The moment she stepped inside the small space, memories of the night before crashed over her. The last words she and Cameron had spoken. The tearing pain in her chest as she'd listening to his receding footsteps.

Clenching her teeth, Breanna banished the thoughts. Now wasn't the time for letting sorrow overwhelm her.

The Bruce's life was in danger. She had to focus.

Fingers fumbling in haste, she dug into one of the pouches at her waist and withdrew her telling bones and a nub of charcoal. Then, kneeling upon the flagstone floor, she drew a pentagram. Each point of the star represented one of the five elements—spirit, air, earth, water, and fire—and the circle symbolized the universe, which contained and connected them all.

Finishing the design, Breanna then leaned back on her heels and clenched her fingers over the bones. Closing her eyes, she began to murmur the ancient words Colina had taught her many years earlier.

The words and the deep breathing that accompanied them calmed her, cleared her thoughts, and sharpened her senses. She needed to reach a state of openness and fluidity; otherwise, the Goddesses would not speak to her.

Time drew out as Breanna's words died away and her breathing deepened. And then she opened her eyes, leaned forward, and cast the bones. She watched the yellowed lumps, each one inscribed with a different symbol, roll and bounce across the flagstones before coming to rest.

Leaning forward, Breanna studied them. The most accurate divinations required the drawing of a pentagram, for it gave them more clarity.

And with Robert Bruce abed with this mystery illness, Breanna needed answers.

That strange scent had bothered her. And once again, she had the nagging feeling something was amiss—that she was overlooking something important.

Her gaze roved over the scattered bones, taking in their position—both in relation to each other and to where they'd fallen upon the pentagram. The symbols upon the bones represented many things: the phases of the moon; the seasons; the Mother, The Maiden, and The Crone; as well as love, protection, honor, loyalty, and danger, among others.

They'd just reached the first quarter of a Storm Moon—a time for decision-making.

And as Breanna studied the bones, misgiving knotted her belly.

She did regular divinations and had managed to keep up the practice even on campaign with Cameron and the Bruce. The mercenary had often teased her over it, yet like most men, he didn't understand the ritual.

She'd been frustrated of late though, for the bones hadn't yielded much. Their messages had been vague, conflicting.

Not so today.

The three bones that had fallen together upon the point of the star that symbolized fire presented a clear message.

The Yew Tree.

The Torch.

The Sword.

Breanna's breath gusted out of her, her heart now beating wildly. An instant later, she muttered an oath. Death, change, betrayal—all wrapped in witching.

Someone has cursed Robert the Bruce.

28

ILL-TIDINGS FROM THE SOUTH

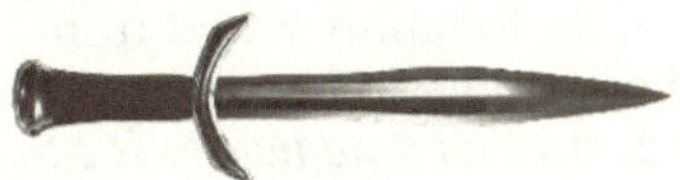

THE SUN WARMED Cameron's face as he walked south. For the first time in months, the air held the promise of warmer weather. They were still in winter, yet there was no sting in the wind.

But Cameron hardly noticed the mild morning.

He hadn't stopped walking since leaving Cree Castle the night before. The waxing moon had lit his way, and his thick fur cloak had kept the cold at bay. Dawn brought a heavy frost with it, and Cameron's breathing had steamed as streaks of red and pink blazed across the sky—an ominous sunrise indeed.

But he'd kept walking.

The road south took him over hills and valleys, alongside the path of the wide River Cree. Eventually, the road would take him to a village, where he intended to find himself an alehouse.

There, he planned to drink until he forgot everything.

Forgot the pain on Breanna's face. Forgot the rawness of her words. Forgot how each furlong he walked that took him from her made him feel as if a knife were being twisted in his gut.

The only thing he didn't wish to forget was how much he loathed himself. He deserved such punishment.

Fazart.

Aye, he was a coward. Breanna was right to have turned her back on him.

He'd wanted to go to her, wanted to pull her into his arms and tell her he was sorry for hurting her—that she deserved so much better.

But she'd likely have shoved his teeth down his throat.

And so he'd picked up his pack and his cloak and slipped out of the bed-chamber, and from her life.

It's for the best, he'd told himself as he left Cree Castle. *Better to end this now before it's too late.*

And he actually believed it, for the first furlongs south.

But now, as he spied a hawk gliding overhead, regret cramped Cameron Stewart's belly.

Panic had assailed him back at Cree, and now that he'd had time to think upon his decision and its consequences, he realized he'd made a terrible mistake.

A cold sweat rose to his skin, and queasiness swept over him.

What have I done?

His step faltered then, but he pushed himself on. It was too late for remorse. He should have thought about the consequences the night before—before he'd said things that couldn't be taken back.

Aye, panic no longer consumed him. He no longer fought for Scotland or shared a bed with the most remarkable woman he'd ever met. But now that his fears had subsided, a yawning gulf had opened up within him.

One that grew deeper with each step.

Cursing, Cameron lengthened his stride. Satan's cods, he needed to find himself an alehouse fast and drink himself to oblivion.

He didn't want to dwell upon what he'd done and the ruin that was now his life.

Ahead, two figures appeared upon the road, traveling north.

Spying them, Cameron's hand instinctively went to the hilt of his dirk. It was habit, for although he hadn't passed many travelers this morning, there were a number of outlaws in these hills—besides the Bruce and his men—and ones that weren't fighting for Scottish freedom.

It was wise to be wary.

But as the two travelers drew nearer still, Cameron's brow furrowed. They were limping, and their clothing was muddied and stained with blood. Both men had hollowed cheeks and haunted gazes.

And when they were but a few yards distant, one of the men called to him. "Captain Stewart!"

Cameron halted, his pulse quickening. His gaze narrowed. Did he know these men?

"Aye," he replied cautiously. He was tempted to tell them that he was no longer captain of anything, yet the wild look on the men's faces, as they limped toward him, checked the impulse.

"We sailed south and landed with Thomas and Alexander Bruce at Loch Ryan," the second of the men spoke up then, his voice hoarse.

Cameron tensed, his gaze sweeping over their ravaged faces. "Where are the others?"

"We were ambushed," the first warrior rasped, the desolate look in his eyes revealing more than words ever could. "When we landed, the MacDougals attacked." His throat bobbed. "They are allied with the Comyns ... and have been waiting for their chance to strike back at the Bruce."

Cameron breathed a curse. This was ill news indeed. The Bruce had been wondering why his brothers hadn't yet joined him. But, instead of being waylaid by the English, they'd been attacked by their own countrymen.

Bitterness filled his mouth. How would they ever defend Scotland from outside threats when they fought so viciously with each other?

What does it matter to ye, Cameron? A voice jeered in his head. *Ye threw it all aside, remember?*

He had, but it didn't mean that he'd stopped caring.

A chill filtered over him then—as he recalled Breanna's warnings that the Bruce's life was in danger. She was right. And it wasn't just the English they had to watch out for.

It was just as well Robert had landed farther north.

"And Thomas and Alex Bruce?" Cameron asked, dreading the answer. He knew without being told that these two were the only survivors. Yet he needed to hear the rest.

Both men's faces twisted, their eyes glinting with grief and rage. "Those bastard MacDougals handed them over to the English," the first warrior said, choking out the words. "Where they met the same fate as Neil Bruce."

Nausea rolled over Cameron before heat ignited under his ribcage, his anger quickening like dry tinder to a flame. He swore again, this time viciously.

Hanged, drawn, and quartered.

He remembered Thomas and Alexander Bruce's eager faces, their gazes gleaming with pride as they'd farewelled Robert and Edward and boarded the galley that would take them south.

Two warriors in their prime—both gone.

Cameron's temper flared hotter until it threatened to consume him. His desire to find an alehouse, to leave his mistakes behind him, suddenly paled to insignificance.

His voice, when he spoke, was flint-hard. "Ye are both half a day's walk from the Bruce," he told them. "Come ... I will take ye to him."

Swiveling on his heel, Cameron turned north and began retracing his steps.

Think, Bree ... think.

Breanna entered the hall and headed toward one of the long tables. She deliberately sat with men she didn't know, hoping that they wouldn't question her about Cameron's conspicuous absence this eve.

Ye must discover who's behind this.

Lowering herself onto the end of the bench seat, her gaze settled upon the plate of bread, cheese, and braised onions before her. Her belly growled, reminding her that although her insides felt tied up in knots, she was indeed hungry.

Even so, she began her meal without enthusiasm, her gaze sweeping around the rapidly filling hall. Unlike the day before, the rumble of conversation was low, subdued. Did everyone within the keep know that the Bruce was seriously unwell? The worried looks on many of the surrounding faces told her that they likely did.

Her brow furrowed. She'd spent the entire afternoon searching for answers, trying to figure out how Robert the Bruce had come to be cursed and who was behind it.

She'd even resorted to dowsing, a skill she was a little rusty at, using a feather. She'd hoped it would draw her to the source of the curse, but the dowsing hadn't given her the answers she craved either.

Her gaze settled now upon the dais, where James and Ian Douglas sat, side by side, talking together in low voices. Their expressions were strained, and without listening to their conversation, Breanna knew they would be discussing the Bruce's illness.

The healer had told her that his condition was worsening. He'd even had a fit earlier and would have fallen from the bed if Edward and the Douglases hadn't held him down.

If it was a curse, and Breanna was sure it was, then whoever had cast it must have used an item of the Bruce's clothing, a lock of his hair, or a sliver of one of his fingernails.

How had they managed to get close enough to Robert the Bruce to do so?

Breanna's gaze remained upon the dais, where two serving lasses passed behind the men, topping up their cups with wine.

She stilled then, recalling the incident of the night before.

The small, mousy lass who'd sprawled on the Bruce's lap.

Ian Douglas had told her off for being in the hall. She was a scullery maid and shouldn't have been out here.

Breanna froze as she recalled the young woman's odd silver-grey eyes when she'd briefly glanced up that morning on the landing.

And then she remembered.

Both Nessa and Fyfa had told her that Lamia Delamare possessed eyes of that color. They'd also told her that Lamia's witching didn't smell like theirs. A Scottish druidess carried with her the scent of pine and freshly-turned earth, a smell particularly evident when she cast a working. Breanna recalled then that Fyfa had mentioned how odd Lamia had smelled, how it had reminded her of a blacksmith's forge.

Hot iron.

Breanna's heart started bucking against her ribs.

Of course, Lamia Delamare was a skilled witch—Fyfa had described how artfully she'd used misdirection at that banquet where she'd tried to poison the Bruce and Fyfa at Stirling.

The misdirection spell meant that Lamia could move in plain sight without being noticed, but that wasn't what the witch had used this time. Instead, she'd worked a powerful glamor—a disguise so complete that even when she'd been standing before her earlier, Breanna hadn't seen through it.

Thrice-cursed fool. She'd let heartbreak distract her, cloud her usually sharp senses.

Pushing aside the dish of food, Breanna ignored the surprised glances of the men surrounding her and rose to her feet.

She couldn't remain here, forcing down food while the Bruce's condition slowly worsened. If Lamia had indeed worked a hex upon the man, things looked bleak for him indeed.

The Bruce wouldn't likely last the night.

Breanna made for the door, paying no heed to James Douglas as he called out to her.

She had no time to explain herself or make some feeble excuse as to Cameron's whereabouts. Instead, she had a witch to track down.

29

FIGHTING THE WIND

BREANNA STEPPED OUT into the castle's bailey, her gaze sweeping left and right. Her pulse was racing. Although the days were starting to lengthen, dusk still came far too early. She'd just been to the kitchens to see if the maid Fenella was there, but the cooks had said she was outside scrubbing pots near the well.

Moving silently in her hunting boots, Breanna peered across the shadowy bailey. The nights were still bitterly cold this time of year, but there had been no time to retrieve her cloak before going outdoors. Besides, she had more freedom of movement in the leggings and gambeson she wore, without a cloak hindering her. She carried a dirk at her hip, and her fingers curled around it now.

Once she spied the witch, she would need to move fast.

A small stone well, encrusted with lichen, sat under the shadow of the wall.

Breanna spied a pile of dirty pots and an abandoned pail and hog-bristle brush. But her quarry was nowhere to be seen.

Pulse quickening, Breanna glanced around her.

Curse her, where had Lamia gone?

Men's voices made her turn then, and she spied three cloaked figures talking with the guards at the gate.

Her heart leaped into her throat when she recognized one of them.

What is that dung rat doing back here?

As if feeling the force of her stare, Cameron Stewart shifted his attention from the guard and looked across the bailey, his gaze fusing with hers.

Breanna's breathing hitched.

The Three be damned, she couldn't believe it. Even after what he'd done, her soul ached for him.

Breanna's hands curled into fists at her sides. She wouldn't give in to this weakness, not again.

With a quick word to the other men, Cameron headed toward her.

Breanna's spine stiffened, and she drew herself up, readying herself to face him.

"Did ye forget something?" she greeted him, her voice harsh. "Yer honor perhaps?"

She didn't want to be here, bandying words with this man. Not with Lamia at large. She needed to get rid of him.

"Thomas and Alex Bruce are dead," he replied, his gaze never leaving hers. His face was strained, his gaze shadowed. "They were ambushed by the MacDougals in retribution for John Comyn's murder."

The angry words that had been building within Breanna choked off, and she gaped at Cameron. She wanted to have misheard, yet there was no mistaking the bluntness of this news. Nor the grim expression on his face.

Bitterness filled her mouth, *The MacDougals*. Her former lover's clan had turned on the Bruces.

Cameron then gestured to the two ragged figures who now limped across the bailey toward the keep. "These two men are the only survivors. They're going to the Bruce now."

Breanna swallowed in an attempt to ease the sudden tightness in her throat. "He's unwell ... it's probably not the best time to give him such news."

Cameron's dark brows knitted together. "Unwell?"

Breanna cleared her throat. She needed to get away from Cameron, to find Lamia, and yet her feet felt welded to the spot. And when she spoke once more, the truth poured out of her. "He's been cursed."

Cameron's eyes flew wide. "What?"

"That witch I told ye of is here ... posing as a servant. I'm looking for her now." Breanna's pulse was hammering in her ears as she gestured to the dirty pots next to the well. "She's supposed to be out here."

Cameron stared back at her before his gaze narrowed. "Have ye checked the yard behind the keep ... next to the river?" he asked.

"Not yet."

He took her by the arm, steering her toward the postern gate that led out of the bailey and the back of the keep. "Come ... we must be swift."

Breanna fell into step with him, although she jerked her arm from his grip as if scalded. She was aware they needed to move quickly. And if he hadn't reappeared like a portent of doom, she would already be checking the rear of the keep.

Even so, she didn't argue with him.

She'd rail at Cameron Stewart later. Right now, his presence was reassuring. She wasn't sure why she'd confided in him, only that he alone would understand. After all, he knew about Lamia and the danger she presented.

The gloaming was deepening now, the last of the light fading from the western sky. Breanna and Cameron slipped into the yard. The odor of livestock, fowl and goats, drifted across the space, as did the ripe stench of compost.

Breanna halted, her gaze sweeping from one side of the yard to the other.

Her belly clenched. *No sign of Lamia here either.* A gate, currently ajar, led to the narrow path down to the river. Was that where she had gone?

However, a moment later, Breanna's attention settled upon a row of low-slung out-buildings: grain and food stores.

Her witch-will stirred, the fine hair rising on the back of her neck.

Lamia Delamare was within.

Without a word to Cameron, she strode across the dirt yard, drawing her dirk as she went. She then murmured a charm under her breath, one that she often used before a fight. It sharpened the senses and quickened the reflexes.

Once they surprised the witch, they'd have little time.

Behind her, she caught Cameron's whispered curse. He wanted her to wait, to let him go first. But she wouldn't. This was her fight. She didn't know why the feckless bastard was even back here.

With her free hand, Breanna withdrew her cairn stone of persuasion and protection, her fingers clenching tight around the smoky quartz. She'd never fought another witch before and didn't want to do so without added security.

Sensing her intention, the cairn stone warmed.

Breanna ripped open the door to the grain store and burst inside.

A figure knelt on the floor, whispering muffled words over an object before her. A small white snake lay curled up on the floor next to where a lantern had been set down, a forked tongue darting from its flat mouth.

The snake reared up in warning at Breanna's sudden entrance, and the woman leaped to her feet, whirling to face her.

In an instant, the glamor dissolved.

The small, plain scullery maid disappeared, replaced by a willowy woman with hair the color of sea-foam, dressed in a dove-grey, travel-stained cotehardie.

The eyes were the same. As silver as two bright pennies.

Lamia Delamare cursed in French and made a grab for something at her belt. The musty air around Breanna shifted then, growing heavy as the odor of hot iron and cloying musk settled over them.

Breanna was dimly aware of Cameron growling something behind her, yet all of a sudden, it was as if she were moving through porridge.

Whispering to the cairn stone, Breanna felt it grow hot against her palm. An instant later, her pine-scented witch-wind gusted through the storeroom, making the lantern Lamia had brought with her gutter.

The white snake slithered away, diving into a gap between two sacks of grain at the back of the store.

The heaviness lifted, and Breanna moved, covering the space between her and Lamia in two long strides. The witch reeled back, but Breanna was quicker. Her dirk-blade flashed, slicing into Lamia's left flank. Sometimes, there was no substitute for hard Scottish steel.

The woman's hiss of pain filled the store, even as her silver eyes flashed with ire.

She growled out a string of words in French, while she clutched at her side, crimson seeping through her fingers.

A hot wind gusted through the store, the reek of iron so strong that it burned the throat. It knocked Breanna backward, slamming her up against the wall. Her breath gusted out of her, and twisting, she saw that the wind had thrown Cameron off his feet. His head had collided with one of the supports holding up the roof, and he now sagged to his knees, his eyes fluttering closed.

Breanna's chest constricted. The urge to go to him reared up, yet she shoved it aside.

She had to focus on Lamia. Her attention snapped then to the object that Lamia had been crouched over when they'd entered the grain store. It was a small clay pot filled with liquid. Something floated on the surface.

Breanna lunged toward it, shoved Lamia aside, and kicked the pot over.

Lamia cursed once more and another gust of wind howled through the store.

Breanna grabbed hold of Lamia's arm, to prevent the wind from flinging her across the space once more. She'd had to drop her cairn stone to do so, yet she wouldn't let this devious witch best her. If Lamia wanted to get to the spilled contents of that pot, she'd have to kill her first.

Snarling, Lamia struggled against her, her nails raking down Breanna's face.

Breanna reeled back, fire stinging down one cheek. She took a swipe at Lamia with her dirk as she did so, and the sound of ripping material followed as the blade tore through the bell-sleeve of the witch's cotehardie.

Dropping to a crouch, Breanna swiped up her fallen cairn stone—and its heat pulsed against her skin, making her witch-will sing in her veins once more.

Lamia backed away. She glared at Breanna, fury contorting her face.

Lamia Delamare was faced with a difficult decision. Remain here and attempt to recover the items she needed to kill Robert the Bruce or flee into the gathering dusk.

And as their gazes fused, Breanna knew which one the witch would choose.

Lamia would receive a blade to the gut if she took one step closer. A hot wind continued to shriek through the store, pummeling Breanna like angry fists, yet the cairn stone held her fast within its protection now.

Lamia would not defeat her.

Face ashen, Lamia turned, still clutching her injured side, and dodged Cameron's clumsy grasp. Struggling against the wind, his hair whipping across his cheeks, Cameron's expression was set in strained lines. Blood trickled down his temple from where he'd collided with the support.

Lamia gasped another witching, and the wind slammed him back against the wall, pinning him there.

And then the witch fled.

Breanna tried to follow her, but the wind shoved her back and sent her sprawling over the floor. Her own witch-wind couldn't compete.

Lamia disappeared through the door.

And a heartbeat later, the wind subsided.

Cursing, Cameron unpeeled himself from the wall and staggered to his feet. He then went to follow her.

"Stay here!" Breanna choked out the command. "Don't touch anything ... but if that snake reappears, kill it." She couldn't risk the witch's familiar interfering with whatever Lamia was using to curse the Bruce. But neither could she risk the witch escaping.

Not waiting to see his response, Breanna raced after Lamia.

Outside, the light of pitch torches burning on the walls illuminated the yard. Lamia was nowhere to be seen, yet the postern gate leading down to the river was now wide open.

Breanna knew exactly where her quarry had gone.

Diving through the gate, Breanna raced down the narrow path toward the River Cree. On the way, she met two servants carrying heavy buckets of water, making their way back up to the castle.

As she approached, Breanna hid her drawn dirk behind her so as not to alarm them. "Did ye see a woman?" she asked. "Slender and pale?"

Both lasses shook their heads, their gazes bemused.

Frustrated, Breanna continued down to the riverbank. Of course, Lamia might have used misdirection or a glamor to fool those two—even if her injury would have weakened her.

Stopping before the swiftly flowing water, Breanna's gaze scanned her surroundings.

This section of the River Cree flowed fast. As the river neared the coast, it became wider and tidal, yet there were rapids up here in the hills.

Breanna's gaze narrowed. Had Lamia thrown herself in?

Jaw clenched, she knelt upon the bank, murmuring a charm as she reached out with her witch-will and let it see things she could not.

It guided her back up the riverbank, toward the postern gate, and drew her gaze to a dark patch on the earth upon the bank. Breanna moved to it and touched the spot, her fingers coming away wet and sticky.

Blood.

Lamia had indeed been here, and she'd used the river to escape.

"Scheming bitch," Breanna muttered straightening up. Her gaze swept the dark surface of the river. The

currents would be perilous, even for a strong swimmer.
And Lamia Delamare was injured and without the aid of
her familiar. "It's a better death than ye deserve."

30

IN THE STAIRWELL

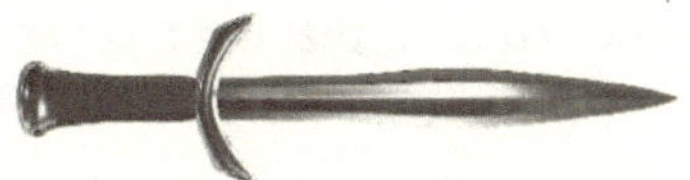

OUT OF BREATH, Breanna re-entered the grain store. She found Cameron standing over the fallen clay pot. One look at his set expression and smoldering gaze, and she knew he was vexed. However, she paid that no mind.

"I lost her," she announced, sheathing her dirk. She then crossed to the items Lamia had left behind. "She jumped into the river and was swept away ... with any luck, she will drown." Her gaze shifted to the sacks of grain piled up behind Cameron. "Any sign of that snake?"

He shook his head, a muscle bunching in his jaw. Aye, the man was truly infuriated. So much so that he couldn't bring himself to speak.

Good. Let him know what that tastes like. Cameron Stewart was entirely too smug.

Picking up the lantern, Breanna crouched down next to the clay pot and peered at the contents it had spilled over the dirt floor.

Her brow furrowed.

A wet lock of brown hair lay there.

Breanna picked up the pot and sniffed it, her nose wrinkling. "Vinegar."

"What?" Cameron asked gruffly, his curiosity getting the better of his anger.

She glanced up, meeting his gaze. "Aye, she placed a lock of the Bruce's hair in vinegar and then worked a hex upon it. Once the vinegar dissolves the hair, Robert Bruce will die." She paused, her mouth pursing. Colina had warned her daughters numerous times to be wary of using hexes. There was always a price to be paid—something Lamia was surely aware of.

Cameron's brows crashed together. "But surely, ye have broken the curse?"

"Not yet." Breanna tore her gaze from his and scooped up the lock of hair, placing it carefully in the palm of her hand. "Only fire will do that ... and we must hurry."

"What about that snake of hers?"

Breanna rose to her feet, her gaze shifting once more to the sacks of grain. "It is powerless without its witch," she murmured. "I was afraid it would try to interfere with this." She jerked her chin toward the lock of hair she grasped. "But now I have it, the serpent can't cause any more trouble."

With that, she spun on her heel and hurried from the grain store.

She was aware of Cameron following her, although he did so without another word. Breanna ignored him then—her entire focus was upon reaching the hall of Cree Castle and one of the great hearths that burned within.

Folk were amassing for supper when she entered, the murmur of conversation enveloping the newcomers. Breanna spied serious faces and shadowed gazes this eve, and a brief glance to the dais told her that Ian and James Douglas, and Edward Bruce, were absent.

Her throat constricted. They would all be with the Bruce—watching as the mystery illness claimed his life.

Shifting her attention from the hall's inhabitants, Breanna moved to the hearth nearest, where two of Ian Douglas's wolfhounds lounged.

And then, without hesitating, she tossed the hair into the flames.

A moment later, Cameron was at her side. She glanced his way, to see that his features were set as he watched the flames roar. He then caught Breanna's eye. "Is it done?"

"I believe so," she replied, her tone clipped. "But I must go upstairs now to reassure myself."

"We thought he was done for." James Douglas's gravelly voice filtered through the bed-chamber.

"Aye," Edward Bruce added with a shake of his head. "When he started frothing at the mouth, I believed he was possessed by the devil." Edward crossed himself before glancing to where his elder brother was sitting, propped up in a nest of pillows.

All those gathered around the outlaw king's bed wore stunned expressions. When Breanna and Cameron had entered the chamber, they'd interrupted gasps of amazement and muttered oaths.

The Bruce's face was pale and gaunt. He appeared exhausted, but fortunately, he was no longer fitting or in the spasms of pain the men had described.

A priest had been called for, word spreading through the keep that the Bruce's end was near. And then, all of a sudden, the seizures and agony that had wracked his body had simply ceased.

"What manner of illness was that?" Robert Bruce rasped, his hollowed gaze focusing upon the healer. However, the elderly woman could only shake her head, her face a study in bemusement. "I have no idea, Sire," she murmured. She then cast Edward Bruce a wary look. "My grandmother once told me that folk who'd been cursed or possessed by Satan fall prey to such illness."

Listening to the healer's words, Breanna suppressed a shiver. The men in the bed-chamber—save Cameron Stewart of course—would likely scoff at such folk tales, yet the woman was closer to the truth than any of them realized.

But Breanna would not tell them that.

Indeed, it was best if the Bruce and his men knew nothing of what had transpired here this evening or of Lamia Delamare.

The Guardians of Alba preferred to remain hidden. And besides, some things were difficult to explain.

The healer cleared her throat then, perhaps noticing the dark looks she was receiving from Ian Douglas. "However, those are just tales ... what matters now is that ye are recovering. Whatever ailed ye has passed. A good night's sleep and a hearty meal in the morning ... and ye will soon be back to yer former strength."

"I'm glad to see ye are on the mend, Sire," Breanna said, favoring the king with a smile.

Likewise, she could see the relief on the surrounding men's faces. Now that their shock had subsided, and it was clear the Bruce wasn't going to die, they looked like they wished to down a few ales in celebration. Breanna realized then that she didn't see the two newcomers who'd arrived with Cameron among the occupants of the chamber.

Her belly clenched. The Bruce didn't yet know about his brothers. Glancing back at the king, Breanna noted his fragile state. No, now wasn't the time to tell him about the MacDougals' betrayal.

"Thank ye, Lady Stewart," Robert Bruce answered, his voice still husky. "It was as if I were lost in a terrible dream ... as if my body were no longer my own."

Breanna nodded, even as she swallowed to ease the tightness in her throat. Lamia Delamare had come very close to killing him—closer than she should have.

Tension rippled through her. If she hadn't been so focused on the situation with Cameron, she might have noticed something was amiss sooner.

Across the chamber, Edward Bruce was looking at her, his gaze narrowed. "What happened to ye, woman?" he asked. "It looks as if a cat flew at yer face."

Breanna raised a hand to her cheek. It still stung, yet she'd been so focused on saving the Bruce, she'd forgotten the injury Lamia had inflicted upon her.

Unfortunately, Edward hadn't finished his observations. His attention swiveled to Cameron, and his frown deepened to a scowl. "And ye, Stewart. Yer forehead is bloodied."

Swallowing, Breanna turned to where Cameron stood to her right. Indeed, the cut above his left eyebrow was deeper than she'd thought, although the bleeding had now staunched.

To her surprise, Cameron's mouth quirked as he held Edward's eye. The mercenary's gaze then glinted. "Aye … well, that's what comes of having a feisty wife," he replied. "Bree and I were sparring earlier … and things got a little … heated." He then cast her a long, sensual look. "She likes it rough."

Embarrassment flushed through Breanna in a hot tide. She clenched her teeth. *Bastard … ye shall pay for that.*

And now the other men were grinning. Even Robert Bruce managed a weak smile.

Breanna wasn't amused though; she was sure her face was now flaming like a beacon. Her hands clenched into fists at her sides, and she wondered how they'd all react if she punched Cameron Stewart in the face. He wouldn't be grinning like a fool with a broken nose.

But this wasn't the time or place for a confrontation. That would come later, once they didn't have an audience.

With a jerky nod to the Bruce, she swiveled on her heel and made for the door.

"Lady Stewart … wait," the healer called after her. "I should really dress those cuts for ye."

But Breanna couldn't wait. She had to get out of that bed-chamber.

Outside, she stormed down the hallway, making for her tower room. She needed to get away from the rest of this keep—and from the man who in the space of a day had managed to break her heart *and* humiliate her.

However, she was halfway up the narrow stairs when she realized that Cameron Stewart was coming after her.

Drawing her dirk, she whipped around to face him.

Seeing the blade glinting in the light of the cresset above, the mercenary halted. His expression was serious although his grey eyes still glinted. The shit-weasel had enjoyed embarrassing her.

"What are ye going to do?" he asked gently. "Gut me?"

"I should," she bit out between clenched teeth. "After what ye just did."

"I did it to save ye having to make excuses," he replied. "Edward Bruce was suspicious ... and I had to throw him off the scent."

"By humiliating me?"

His eyes shadowed. "That wasn't my intention, Bree."

"Don't use that name," she growled back, even as her throat thickened. Crone's tears, she wouldn't weep. Not now. "Ye no longer have the right."

His gaze held hers. "I'm sorry," he murmured. There was no trace of humor upon his face or in his gaze now. "I was wrong to leave ye."

"So why are ye back?" she snarled back. "Did ye discover ye have a conscience after all?"

Silence fell then, and to her consternation, Cameron moved up the stairwell toward her, heedless of the blade she still raised between them. He halted upon the step below her, his chest just an inch from the dirk tip.

"I discovered that I can't give ye up," he said, his voice husky now, his face pained. "Without ye, the world is a grey, empty place. Without ye, I am a lesser man. I love ye, Bree ... I'm just sorry it took me so long to admit it to myself."

Breanna stared into his face. There was no trace of teasing in his eyes, no mask. Even so, fury coiled in her belly, looking for a chance to strike out, to wound. "Ye sound as if ye've just accepted ye have some awful affliction," she ground out. "Is that what love is to ye?"

"Aye," he replied, his tone roughening. "It is."

Breanna sucked in a breath. She couldn't believe he'd admit as such. The man had taken a declaration of love and turned it into an insult.

"Well, my heart bleeds for ye, Stewart." She pressed the tip of her dirk to the collar of his leather vest. A warning. "But as touched as I am, I need ye to leave now."

His throat bobbed. "No, I can't do that."

Her heart started to thunder in her ears, and she applied more pressure to the dirk, feeling it press into the leather. However, Cameron didn't flinch. He merely stared up at her, his grey eyes dark in the shadowy stairwell.

"I won't go until I have told ye my story," he continued, his voice catching. "If ye spurn me ... ye should have *all* the facts when ye do so."

Her mouth twisted. "I don't need to know anything else."

His gaze held hers. "Aye, ye do."

31

STAY

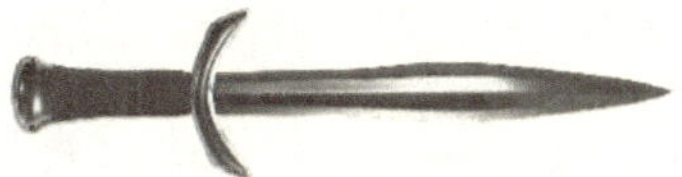

"BACK ON RATHLIN, I told ye I'm from Dundonald Castle," Cameron began. "And that I am estranged from my kin."

Breanna didn't reply, instead waiting for him to continue. She recalled the conversation on that day they'd been out on patrol, and how he'd made it clear he wouldn't be divulging anything else about his past. She'd known then that he was even more guarded than she was.

"I am the younger of two brothers," he continued. His mouth curved, although there was no humor in his gaze. "My brother was destined to become laird, not me ... but I was the one blessed with the looks ... the charm. My elder brother, Murray, is dour and disapproving. Despite that he was the first-born, he resented me."

Breanna clenched her jaw. She hadn't met Murray Stewart, yet she couldn't blame him for disliking his cocky younger brother.

"I cared not ... for I had no wish to take over from our father as laird," Cameron pressed on. "My life was carefree ... until we lost our parents when I was eighteen. They both succumbed to a deadly fever that carried them off one winter ... and Murray became laird of Dundonald." Cameron paused there, his gaze flattening. "I grieved for my mother and father ... but was distracted in the spring when I met a beauty by the name of Evina MacDonald." His voice faltered as he spoke the name, as if it was one he hadn't spoken in a long while, and one that he hesitated to repeat even now. Cameron dragged in a deep breath before raking a hand through his wild raven-hued hair. "Before Evina, lasses were just a bit of fun ... but she tamed my heart." His mouth twisted into a humorless smile. "By mid-summer, I was hopelessly in love in that way that lads get. Foolish. Blind. I was so besotted that I'd have walked across hot coals for her."

Silence fell then, and Breanna waited for him to continue. Anger still simmered within her, yet she held it in check. She'd let Cameron Stewart finish this tale. The raw edge to his voice as he spoke of his family, his love, hinted at the hidden depths to the man before her.

Eventually, Cameron broke the heavy silence. "My brother was betrothed ... to the daughter of the Boyd clan-chief ... Evina and I used to laugh at how, since the pair of them were humorless, they risked boring each other to death." His throat bobbed. "We entertained ourselves at their expense, but we didn't care. We were smug in the love the pair of us shared." He cleared his throat. "Ye can imagine my surprise then ... when at Samhuinn, my brother announced that he was breaking his betrothal and wedding someone else ... none other than Evina MacDonald." He halted then, letting his words fade, and when Cameron resumed speaking, his voice held a brittle edge.

"I went to Evina and begged her to tell me it was a mistake ... that my brother was deranged and she had no part in his madness. But it was no misunderstanding. Evina wished to be Lady of Dundonald, not the wife of the laird's feckless younger brother." Cameron's throat worked. "I made a laughing-stock of myself. I went down on my knees before her, clutched at her skirts, and pleaded and wept like a bairn. But it made no difference ... and in fact, it's possible my desperation made her realize she'd chosen the right brother after all. I'll never forget the scorn in her eyes."

Cameron's voice had lowered, and watching his face, an ache rose under Breanna's breastbone. The fury settled, leaving a hollow sensation in its wake. Aye, she too knew what it was like to humiliate oneself like that.

"So what happened between ye and yer brother?" she asked after a pause. "Did ye challenge him to a duel?"

"Aye," Cameron replied, his mouth twisting. "And he thrashed me. I might have had the looks and the charm … but he was the better warrior … and Evina knew it." His gaze never left Breanna's as he continued. "I left Dundonald Castle that day and never went back."

Breanna inclined her head. "Ye really have cut all ties with yer kin?"

He nodded. "The day I rode from Dundonald, I told myself I'd never let myself be humiliated again. I'd never love a woman again … and I'd train to be a warrior that others feared."

He let out a deep sigh as if telling this story had unburdened him. Even so, his face bore lines of strain, and his grey eyes were still shadowed.

"The defeat at Stirling was another blow," he admitted then. "Months of keeping the enemy at bay … before Warwolf took down our curtain wall in one shot. We were then paraded before Longshanks while he ground his victory into our faces." Cameron drew in a deep breath before continuing, "I swore that would be the last time I'd let myself care about *anything* … until I joined the Bruce's cause … until I met ye." He favored Breanna with a searing look. "I don't offer any of this as an excuse, Bree. Just as an explanation. But I meant what I said earlier … I love ye. Not with the desperate, hollow love of a callow youth … but with the love of a man who knows what a cruel bitch life is. I know all that, and I willingly offer ye my heart … ye can do with it what ye will."

Breanna sucked in a slow breath. The ache under her breastbone twisted, making it hard to breathe. She and Cameron had more in common than she'd realized: the pair of them had been humiliated by lovers and had both built walls around their hearts in the aftermath.

She drew back her dirk and resheathed it, cursing the way her hands now trembled. "Curse ye, Cameron Stewart," she murmured. "No man should be as good with words as ye are."

"I meant every one of them."

Swallowing a lump in her throat, she blinked. Her eyes were burning, and despite her best efforts to prevent it, a tear slid free, causing her scratched cheek to sting as it traveled down to her jaw.

"It wasn't my intention to make ye weep," he said huskily.

Cameron stepped up then, so the two of them stood upon the same level; they were so close their bodies were almost touching. Raising a hand, he brushed his knuckles along her jawline, scooping up the tears as they fell.

Breanna didn't answer; she couldn't. Her throat had constricted.

"I can leave now, if ye wish?" The way his voice caught as he said the words betrayed him.

Breanna lifted her chin, meeting his eye. His face was a blur through her tears, yet the tenderness in his voice caused something to give way within her.

Shaking her head, she reached up, her fingers closing around his. "Stay," she breathed.

Cameron's breath gusted out of him. "Ye are my heart, Bree," he admitted shakily. "If ye permit it, I will remain at yer side ... make ye my wife in truth rather than this mummery we have been playing. And, together, we will continue to fight for Scottish freedom."

Breanna nodded. She should really say something, and wasn't usually a woman lost for words, yet this man's admissions had rendered her mute. The Cameron Stewart who'd stood before her in their bed-chamber the night before had shunned all the things he was now promising.

"I don't understand," she finally managed to choke out. "Ye were so insistent on leaving all of this behind ... what made ye change yer mind?"

His mouth curved, a sensual quirk that as always made her lower belly melt. "Walking has a way of untangling the mind ... making ye see clearly. By the time morning came, I knew I was making the biggest mistake of my life, yet I still clung to my pride. But when I met the Bruce's men and learned of his brothers' fate, I realized that my pride didn't matter." He cupped her face with his hands. "*Ye* matter. *This cause* matters. And I will fight to preserve both with my dying breath."

Breanna stared back at him. "It terrifies me to love ye, Cam," she murmured. "I never told ye, but I too know what it means to be humiliated by a lover." She cleared her throat then. "His name was Grant MacDougal ... and he followed William Wallace ... as did I for a spell. We both fought with him at the Battle of Stirling Bridge."

"A great victory for Scotland," Cameron replied softly.

Swallowing hard, Breanna nodded. She stepped back then, and so he lowered his hands. She needed a little space between them while she told him this. "Grant and I became lovers just before that battle." It was difficult not to wince as she forced herself to relive those days. "I was determined that I could both serve the Guardians and remain with him ... after all, our goals were the same. I was with the Wallace and his men, and we were fighting for Scottish freedom. It was the perfect union."

And *had* felt perfect at first. Her fighting skills had been welcomed amongst Wallace's band, and her status as Grant MacDougal's lover earned her respect and protection.

"But after Stirling, my lover changed," she continued, her voice roughening. "And so did his attitude toward me ... and in the months that followed, he became increasingly distant. When I tried to talk to him about it, he grew belligerent and rude. And then he started frequenting brothels." Her cheeks started to burn. This wasn't an easy tale to tell, yet Cameron had been open with her, and she would do the same. "And when I discovered him with another woman in our bed, I knew that it was over."

Silence fell between them, and Breanna dragged in a shaky breath. She averted her gaze from Cameron's as she rallied herself to continue the story.

"I cringe now to admit how I lost control ... I railed at him, my screams echoing through the Wallace's camp. And then when he told me I was a poor lover and that was why he'd sought the arms of another, I humiliated myself further by pleading with him before fleeing the camp in tears. I wept myself ill afterward." Breanna broke off there. Aye, she was a woman who loved and grieved with the same passion, and her lover's betrayal had altered her forever.

"In the weeks following, I discovered my womb had quickened with Grant's bairn," she admitted huskily. "The news filled me with both grief and joy, yet I lost the child shortly after." She forced herself to raise her chin and look at Cameron once more. His expression was soft, as was his gaze. The understanding she saw there made her throat ache. "I've told no one about the bairn ... not even Colina, Nessa, and Fyfa," she whispered. "Even now, years later, it is too raw."

Her voice died away before she reached up and dragged a hand over her face. Unburdening herself of all that had wearied her; she suddenly felt as old as the Crone.

Silence fell once more between them, broken only by the whisper of their breathing.

"So ye can see why I don't trust easily these days," Breanna said eventually. "I never wanted to feel that way again."

Cameron reached out, cupping her face with his hands once more. His gaze ensnared hers, intense now. "I will prove myself worthy of yer trust, mo ghràdh," he murmured. "I swear it."

With that, he lowered his head, sweeping his lips across hers. It was a tender kiss, one that asked permission for him to continue.

Sighing, Breanna swayed toward him, demanding more.

Cameron gathered her in his arms, as gently as if she might break, and captured her mouth again.

This kiss was different to any other he'd given her. Cameron Stewart knew how to use his lips and tongue to excite a woman. Aye, his kisses in the past had driven her witless with desire. Yet this one held his heart. It was gentle, exploratory—as if he were tasting her for the first time.

Breanna melted into his arms.

They clung together, lost in the kiss, and tears flowed down Breanna's cheeks once more. She didn't know why she was weeping, only that his embrace stripped away every last defense she had, leaving her heart open.

Drawing back, they moved toward their tower chamber. Hand in hand, they climbed the last of the steps to the room. And once inside, Cameron swept her into his arms once more, his mouth taking hers in a kiss that was as possessive as it was passionate. Breanna drowned in it, her senses swimming as her hands slid across his chest, seeking the warm skin underneath.

Their clothing came off, pooling upon the floor, and they sprawled together on the bed.

Whispering words of love, Cameron traced his lips down her jaw and neck before he began an exquisitely gentle exploration of her body.

Breanna quivered under his touch, gasping his name and reaching for him. However, he merely favored her with a slow smile and continued his sensual study—not ceasing until she was a panting, whimpering wreck. Breanna's thighs now trembled uncontrollably. Sweat slicked her body as she stared down at him pleasuring her.

Her eyes fluttered closed then, and she arched up from the bed. Maiden's blood, how she needed this. She loved him with a fierceness that scared her.

And unlike Grant MacDougal, Cameron Stewart loved her in return.

He rose over her once more, their gazes locking. He slid into Breanna then, and started to move, taking her in long, languorous thrusts.

The intensity of his gaze, and the feel of his shaft filling her, relentless yet tender, was too much.

With a cry, Breanna shattered. Aching pleasure rippled through her, like a stone dropped into a pool— the waves traveling up from the cradle of her hips, through her belly and chest, and catching in her throat.

Trembling, she bucked against him, yet he didn't cease his thrusts. Instead, Cameron murmured tender words and leaned down for a long, sensual kiss, while he drove into her, deeper and harder.

His tongue mimicked the action of his shaft, and wet heat exploded deep within Breanna's core. And when she climaxed again, her lover joined her.

Cameron tore his lips from hers, throwing his head back—pleasure twisting his face. She watched it dance across his features, watched the man she loved unravel.

32

UNWAVERING

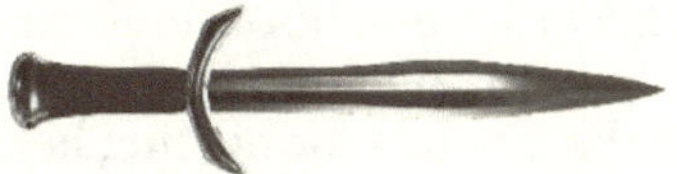

CAMERON AWOKE IN the early hours of the morning. Lying there, Breanna curled against him—her head nestled into the hollow of his neck—he basked in a feeling of well-being stronger than he'd ever experienced.

Who knew love could feel like this?

All the anger, hurt, and insecurity he'd carried inside him over the years was gone. He felt powerful, invincible, as if this woman's love could give him the strength to take on the world.

Cameron swallowed as his throat constricted. His only regret was that it had taken him too long to admit his love—to both himself and Breanna.

She deserved so much better.

Cameron closed his eyes, listening to the whisper of her breathing. It felt so right to sleep with her in his arms. He had meant it, too, earlier, when he'd told her he wished to wed her. This pretend marriage had taught him that he needed this woman in his life. He wanted to wake up every morning with her, to reach out in the night and know that she would be lying beside him.

The back of Cameron's eyelids burned then, and he blinked.

What was happening to him? He'd been numb for so long—but now it was as if a storm of emotion raged within him, so fierce that it made his chest ache.

He'd nearly wept the eve before when he'd seen the pain on Breanna's face and known that he'd been the cause.

She was the last person in the world he wished to hurt, but he had. His fears had turned him blind, had nearly ruined both their chances of happiness.

Tightening his grip upon his sleeping lover, Cameron buried his face in her rosemary-scented hair.

He would make amends for hurting her. He'd show her that his word was good.

Sunlight bathed Breanna's face when she awoke. Stretching under the covers, she opened her eyes and reached out a hand. However, the mattress beside her was cool. She turned to where Cameron had lain to find him gone.

Rubbing the sleep from her eyes, Breanna pushed herself up onto her elbows. The shutters were open, letting in the morning sun, and someone had placed a fresh log on the fire, ensuring that the chamber was warm.

But Cameron Stewart was nowhere to be seen.

Breanna's breathing quickened, tightness spreading across her chest.

Had the night before been a dream? Had she imagined his declarations and the way he'd loved her afterward?

Sitting up, Breanna pulled the blankets up around her chin, a shiver stealing through her.

Has he left again?

The door opened then, bringing with it a tall, lean leather-clad man. Cameron carried a platter and wore a boyish smile.

Breanna's heart bucked against her ribs. *Goose.* Did she trust him so little?

"I brought ye fresh bannocks, butter, and honey, mo ghràdh," he announced. "And a cup of milk to wash it all down."

Breanna's belly growled, reminding her that neither of them had eaten the eve before. Her mouth watered as he placed the tray down on the bed. He'd brought enough food to feed four—yet she was sure they could both do the bannocks justice.

"Did ye sleep well?" he asked, leaning down to kiss her.

"Like a bairn."

"Good." Cameron lowered himself onto the bed and reached for a wedge of bannock. The nutty aroma of the griddle cake wafted over Breanna, making her belly growl once more. "I take it ye would like both butter and honey?" he asked.

Breanna favored him with a smile, chiding herself for her earlier misgivings. "Aye, thank ye."

She watched him prepare the wedge of bannock for her, her gaze tracking his lean hands and nimble fingers. Hunger smoldered in her belly then, one that had nothing to do with the food he'd brought. She wanted to feel the touch of those hands on her naked skin again—and soon.

Biting into the bannock he passed her, Breanna let out a sigh of contentment. It was still warm from the griddle, and the floral taste of heather honey sang on her tongue.

The pair of them ate hungrily, not pausing to converse until only crumbs remained upon the tray. Fingers wrapped around her cup of milk, Breanna settled back against the pillows. She watched Cameron under lowered lids, aware that he kept stealing glances at her naked breasts.

"Keep looking at me like that, and we'll never leave this chamber today," he murmured, his grey eyes darkening.

Breanna's mouth curved. "Is that such a bad thing?"

He smiled back, although his gaze turned somber then. "The cook told me that the Bruce now knows about his brothers' fate ... we should go to him this morning."

Cameron's news made a chill feather over Breanna's naked skin. She'd been so taken up with him that she'd nearly forgotten the situation beyond their reconciliation.

Lamia foiled.

Thomas and Alexander Bruce dead.

She nodded, pushing back the blankets and swinging her legs off the bed. "Aye ... ye are right. I will get dressed."

A knock sounded on the door then. "Yer hot water," a female voice called out.

Cameron crossed to the door, opening it just enough to take the bowl and drying cloths from the woman outside. Thanking her, he closed the door with his foot and carried the items across to the low table beside the bed, where he set them down.

Breanna noted the small clay pot sitting upon the folded drying cloths. "What's that?"

"Salve for our injuries," he replied, his hand going to where the blood had long since dried on his face. "We'd better wash and tend to them ... as the healer advised." He met Breanna's eye then. "The kitchen servants were in a huddle this morning," he said quietly. "Apparently, one of the scullery maids ... a lass called Fenella ... has gone missing."

Breanna suppressed a shiver. "Lamia must have killed her when she assumed her identity."

Cameron's brow furrowed. "How did she manage to fool everyone into thinking she was the scullery maid?"

"Witching ... she used a powerful glamor ... something few druidesses have ever managed."

He raised an eyebrow. "Ye couldn't?"

Breanna shook her head. "Our abilities are more subtle, earthier, than that ... we can divine the future, cast charms that protect or even sway someone's will. But to change yer appearance isn't something a bandruì dabbles in."

"Should we worry that Lamia Delamare will try again?"

Breanna pondered this question before shaking her head. "No ... my blade struck deep. If she doesn't bleed out, she'll need to find a healer quickly. She won't be bothering us any time soon." She paused then before favoring Cameron with a determined look. "And we'll be at the Bruce's side anyway, just in case she does."

He held her eye, his gaze unwavering. "Aye, we will."

It was warm inside the solar, yet Robert the Bruce sat close to the fire, a fur wrapped around his broad shoulders. His walnut-brown eyes were haunted, his face set into harsh lines that made him look far older than he really was.

Grief had carved deep grooves on either side of his mouth and nose.

Seated opposite the king, Cameron and Breanna had offered their condolences, yet although their words had been sincere, they didn't seem enough.

Not after the loss Robert the Bruce had suffered.

A few feet away, Edward Bruce sat upon the window-ledge. The man had said little since they'd entered the laird's solar, but like Robert, his gaze was dark with sorrow.

Cameron's chest tightened.

There were only two of them left now. The Bruce had lost three of his brothers to his cause—and his sister, daughter, and wife were still prisoners of the English.

Right now, the surviving brothers must be pondering their own fates and whether they'd ever manage to win back Scotland.

Worry wreathed through Cameron, turning his breathing shallow.

That would be an irony—to have Robert the Bruce lose hope just when *he* had started to believe that victory was possible.

"Executed," the Bruce rasped, his gaze fixing upon the dancing flames in the hearth. "All three of them."

A chill slid down Cameron's spine. "Don't dwell upon it, Robert," he said quietly. "It will do ye no good ... and it won't bring Thomas and Alex back."

Robert the Bruce's chin kicked up, and his gaze swung around to meet Cameron's. His expression had turned fierce, although Cameron welcomed the anger. It was preferable to the despair he'd just witnessed in the king's eyes.

Anger could be channeled and used as fuel, but despair would only drag the Bruce down, as surely as if he'd just chained himself to a boulder and thrown himself into a deep, dark loch.

"They'll pay for this," Bruce ground out. "As will those traitorous MacDougals."

"Aye, they will," Edward agreed, his voice equally hard.

Cameron nodded. Next to him, Breanna remained silent. A quick glance in her direction confirmed that her gaze also smoldered.

Vengeance. Few things drove a man harder.

Except perhaps love.

"Ye will have yer reckoning," Cameron affirmed. Leaning forward, his gaze fused with the Bruce's once more. "And when we take our next victory ... when ye cut down yer enemies ... it will be yer brothers' names that we will be shouting."

33

HUMBLED

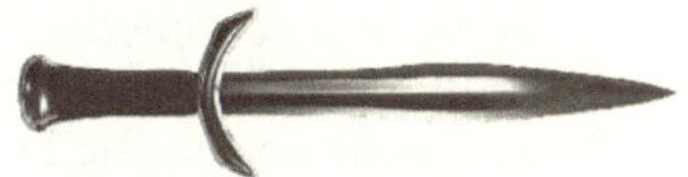

The English camp
Lauchentyre—Galloway, Scotland

Two weeks later ...

AN ICY WIND whipped across the camp, causing the sides of the pavilions to billow and the red and gold Plantagenet banners to snap.

Philip de Eynsford trudged across toward the largest of the tents, the one with the cross of Saint George flag flying from the top. His boots sank into the sticky mud, and he cast a narrow-eyed look up at the heavens.

The sun had shown its face briefly earlier, yet dark clouds had rolled in overhead. More rain was on its way.

Muttering a curse under his breath, Philip closed the final yards to his commander's pavilion.

Damn this campaign to the pits of hell. He was sick to the teeth of the endless, bone-numbing cold. Their defeat at Glen Trool recently, in which they'd lost far too many men, had been demoralizing. Even Sir Aymer had been in a dark mood ever since.

Robert the Bruce had emerged from hiding and was making his presence felt.

News of his victories at Turnberry and Glen Trool was racing through the Scottish countryside like the plague.

Philip's mouth thinned. The last thing they needed was the Bruce rallying the locals to his cause. Something had to be done.

Heaviness pressed down upon de Eynsford's shoulders then, one that had nothing to do with their recent defeat and the cold weather.

Something that was a constant distraction from this campaign.

Lamia had been gone for over two months now.

After she disappeared, he'd searched desperately for her. He'd even continued when Sir Aymer bid him stop, sending out men far and wide across the Lowlands looking for her.

But his wife had simply vanished.

And every morning since, he'd awoken with a pain lodged under his ribs.

He had no idea what had happened to Lamia. Had she deliberately fled, or had something befallen her?

Reaching the tent, Philip raised a hand, rubbing the familiar ache under his breastbone. He didn't understand it. He'd thought they'd been happy. However, in the past weeks, he'd started to wonder if he knew anything about his enigmatic French wife. He'd been drawn to Lamia from the first moment he'd set eyes upon her in Stirling. She'd been cool with him at first, but he'd eventually won her over.

Lamia had been a demanding wife, both in and out of bed, yet he'd enjoyed the challenge. He'd enjoyed doing things to please her, taking care of her.

But now she was gone and had left a yawning abyss where his heart had once been.

Entering the commander's pavilion, Philip found Sir Aymer standing in the center of the richly decorated space. The knight stared down at a missive he was reading. The commander of Edward's army was a big man—a man who dominated most spaces he entered. The light of the brazier he stood over made his hauberk glitter and illuminated the deep scowl upon his face.

Philip moved to the brazier and warmed his chilled fingers over the flames. "What's that?" he greeted Sir Aymer. "Word from the king?"

The commander shook his head, his mouth twisting. "No, it's from the Bruce."

Philip tensed, his gaze going to the scroll of parchment. "Who delivered it?"

"A blacksmith from Lauchentyre. Apparently, one of the Bruce's men dropped it off last night."

Philip frowned. "And what does it say?"

Sir Aymer straightened up, his gaze baleful. "I have brought you to the ring … now you must dance."

Philip's skin prickled. Robert the Bruce had just laid down the gauntlet, offering them a direct challenge. "Is that all?"

Sir Aymer muttered a curse. "It's enough." With that, his big hand closed over the parchment, crushing it into a ball. He then dropped it into the brazier, watching it burst into flames. "If the bastard wants a dance, he'll get one."

Philip's lips parted as he readied himself to respond. However, he was forestalled by the arrival of Nicholas Harrington, one of the other knights who'd traveled north on this Scottish campaign.

The knight's bald head gleamed in the glow of the brazier, although his gaze was keen when it fastened, not on Sir Aymer, but on his companion.

"Philip … there's someone here to see you."

Lamia moved through the inner circle of the English camp, limping heavily. Her feet were a ruin of blisters, and she knew that she was garnering a number of stares.

The Lady Lamia de Eynsford they remembered was always immaculate: dressed in fine cotehardies, her hair swept up onto her crown, and smelling of exotic perfume.

But not this Lamia. Her once fine dove-grey cotehardie was filthy and tattered, and her hair hung in a greasy, limp tangle down her back. She'd lost her cloak, and her boots were caked in mud. Not only that, but she reeked.

However, she was past the point of caring.

Her side hurt, her body ached, and her soul longed for a safe haven.

She'd failed. Robert the Bruce still lived, and once again, one of that mysterious coven of Scottish witches had foiled her plans.

Lamia hadn't realized that dark-haired warrior woman who'd traveled with the Bruce's men had been one of them. She was different to Nessa and Fyfa—and when they'd met briefly on that landing inside Cree Castle, Lamia hadn't smelled the scent of pine and peaty earth as she had with the other two witches. She couldn't understand why that was the case. Perhaps her focus on holding the glamor in place had dulled her usually sharp senses.

As such, Lamia had been caught completely off-guard when the woman and her male companion had burst into that grain store. If she'd realized another witch was in the vicinity, she'd have warded the door to keep her out.

But instead, she'd had to fight her—and witching hadn't been a match for a deftly wielded dirk-blade.

The wound, which was on the mend now thanks to the skill of a healer, twinged then. It was a reminder of how close she'd come to dying. Fleeing from the yard, she'd taken the path to the river. However, hearing voices approaching, she'd dived off the path and thrown herself into the current, letting the chill waters carry her south. Lamia hadn't fought the river; instead, she'd latched onto a floating oak-branch and let it carry her away. But when she'd eventually clambered onto the bank farther downriver, she'd been weak from blood loss. She'd only made it a few paces before collapsing.

She'd have died if a fisherman hadn't found her. He'd then carried her to the local healer.

Even now, it amazed Lamia that the woman—a complete stranger—had taken her in, tended to her wounds, fed her, and looked after her.

In the same position, Lamia wouldn't have done so.

For the first time in her life, she'd been truly humbled.

She'd lain upon the narrow cot, weakly taking sips of bone-broth, while the healer gently explained that she'd lost the bairn she'd carried.

Lamia hadn't welcomed her pregnancy, yet the news devastated her. Of course, the hex had demanded its price—something she hadn't even considered at the time. She knew that cursing someone had ramifications, but such was her determination to kill Robert the Bruce, she'd pushed all other thoughts from her mind.

And now she'd lost Philip's child—and it was all her doing.

It seemed there was a price too for taking the life of an innocent. Guilt knotted deep within her whenever she thought of how she'd slain Fenella. The scullery maid had done her no wrong, yet Lamia had merely seen her as a means to achieve her goal. Her life hadn't mattered.

A heavy mantle of loss had settled over Lamia, while remorse clawed at her breast. She'd wept bitterly at times while the kindly woman fussed over her.

She'd lost Fantôme too. Her familiar had been her companion for years now, and losing the grass snake felt as if she'd had a limb amputated. Her abilities were diminished without her familiar, but Fantôme was more than that to her—she was family.

Despair had swallowed Lamia for a few days, and for a while, she hadn't cared if she lived or died. She'd lain abed fighting a fever, and she'd been as weak as a newborn lamb when she finally rose from her bed.

The healer had insisted she stay on a few more days and regain her strength, and Lamia had acquiesced. But with the passing of the days, restlessness filled her.

Now that she'd earned a reprieve, just one instinct filled her.

It wasn't to track the Bruce down and finish what she'd started—for her desire for glory had died the day that witch had stuck a dirk-blade into her side. No, instead, she wished for nothing else but to see her husband.

She was bruised and battered, body and soul—and only Philip could ease her suffering. If he still wanted her that was.

But what if the hex has claimed his life too—or harmed him in some way?

A chill swept over Lamia at the thought as she stumbled in the mud.

What if he no longer wants me?

She'd been so focused on ending the Bruce's campaign that she'd arrogantly assumed that Philip would take her back once she succeeded in killing the outlaw king.

But now that she'd failed, she wasn't so sure of herself.

Nonetheless, she had to find her husband. And as soon as she was strong enough, she'd left the healer's cottage and traveled south. And when she'd spied the vast carpet of tents and fluttering pennants in the distance, Lamia had nearly wept with relief.

Ahead, a tall man with dark hair ducked out of the commander's tent and walked toward her.

Dressed in a hauberk and blood-red surcoat, Philip de Eynsford wore a severe expression as he approached.

Misgiving clenched in Lamia's belly.

He *was* furious with her—and had every right to be. She'd left without a word after all.

When they were a few yards apart, Philip halted, his gaze sweeping over her. Lamia held herself upright, although she inwardly cringed. What a fright she must look. Around her, she heard murmurs and muttered oaths. Others had noticed her return—and her bedraggled state.

However, Lamia paid none of them any mind. Instead, she stared at Philip. Too late, she'd realized what this man meant to her. Too late, she'd realized how much she wanted to bear his child.

If he cast her out of this camp, she'd deserve it. Yet the thought filled her with icy dread.

"Where have you been, Lamia?" he greeted her. His handsome face was all taut angles, his gaze hooded.

"North of here," she replied, her voice catching. "I took it upon myself to find the Bruce ... and kill him." She might as well tell him the truth. There was no other excuse she could make. "But I failed."

The murmurs around her increased, while Philip's gaze widened. "You did *what*?"

"He took refuge at Cree Castle after his victory at Glen Trool," she continued. "And I posed as a servant ... but my attempt on his life went awry." She grimaced as she cupped her side. "I was stabbed in the side and barely escaped with my life."

Long moments passed as a myriad of emotions flickered across Philip's face. He then folded his arms across his chest, his brow furrowing. "And now, you return to your faithful husband. The man you left without a backward glance." There was no mistaking the caustic edge to his tone.

The voices around them quietened. Lamia was aware that they'd attracted a crowd, including Sir Aymer and Sir Nicholas, who'd followed Philip out of the tent and were now watching the scene unfold with bemused looks.

Still, Lamia kept her gaze fixed upon her husband's face.

She didn't care they had an audience now. She was beyond worrying about her dignity. During the journey south, she'd wept, remorse dogging every step.

Moving closer to Philip, she wet her lips. "I don't deserve you, Philip," she murmured. "I know that."

His expression turned stony, a nerve flickering under one eye. Aye, he was angry, yet her husband was also upset, hurt.

"I didn't consider you when I left two months ago," she continued. "All I thought about was killing the Bruce and returning with news of victory."

He shook his head, confusion clouding his eyes. "Why the devil would you embark on such a quest, woman?"

Lamia choked out a bitter laugh. "It's not only men who have dreams of glory. Since girlhood, all I've ever wanted was to be part of history. When I came to live in

England, I decided that I would be part of Edward's victory over the Scots ... no matter what it took."

His jaw tensed. "And now?"

"I no longer care about any of it." She took another, hesitant, step toward him. "All I want is you, Philip. Please say you'll have me back. Please forgive your foolish wife." Lamia couldn't believe the words that were spilling from her. In the past, she would have rather had her tongue ripped out than admit weakness. But those days, and that woman, were gone.

Silence fell between them, and the surrounding crowd remained hushed.

Lamia became aware then of the coldness of the wind that buffeted her. She was chilled to the marrow, although she couldn't take her gaze off Philip de Eynsford's face.

It's too late. I've taken things too far.

Lamia swallowed and drew herself up, trying in vain to gather the shreds of her pride. But there was none left. She'd come before Philip humbled and broken. Indeed, he was right not to want her. The woman he'd fallen in love with was gone.

Taking a step back, she braced herself for his scorn.

To her surprise, Philip followed her. His arms dropped to his sides, and he moved close.

Lamia tensed. It was best he didn't come too near, for she stank like a barnyard. Nonetheless, Philip didn't seem to notice; his gaze never left her face. When they were less than a foot apart, he reached up, his hands folding gently over her shoulders.

"I've been going slowly mad over the past two months, Lamia," he admitted huskily. "At times, I believed you'd been taken ... and at others, I was sure you'd tired of me and run off."

Lamia's breathing hitched, her throat aching from the tenderness that welled up within her. She wanted to tell Philip about the child, but now wasn't the right time. Not with Sir Aymer and the other men looking on. Some things should stay between husband and wife.

"I can't make any excuse for my behavior," she whispered back. "Only that I was selfish and driven. I tried to kill the Bruce in Stirling ... and he's become an obsession ever since."

Her admission caused murmurs of surprise from Sir Aymer and Sir Nicholas, yet Lamia ignored them both. She didn't look away from Philip.

Shock rippled across her husband's face as he took her words in. Then his gaze fused with hers. "And now, you wish to simply be my wife?"

Lamia nodded. Tears stung her eyes, and her vision blurred. It was taking all her will not to crumple into a heap at his feet, not to plead for his forgiveness.

But Philip wouldn't wish her to make such a scene. She had to remain strong, even if she was falling to pieces inside.

"Can you find it in your heart to forgive me?" she asked, her voice catching.

Moments stretched out, and the silence around them grew deafening.

Lamia's heart started to pound, cold sweat beading upon her skin. He really was done with her.

But then Philip's handsome features softened. He reached up, cupping her cheek with a tenderness that made her tremble. How she'd missed his touch. And when he finally replied, there was no mistaking the pain, and the love, in his voice. "Aye, foolish woman. I can."

34

TO FREEDOM

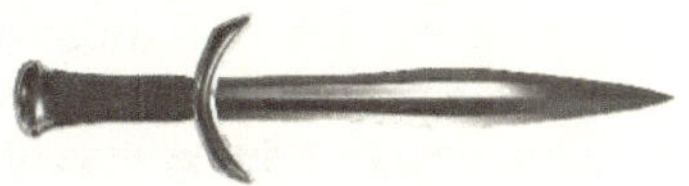

Loudoun Hill
Ayrshire, Scotland

Three months later ...

BREANNA WALKED ACROSS the battleground, amongst the dead.

It was quite a sight—a tangle of broken, bloodied bodies trampled into the mud.

Was this the battle that Colina foresaw?

Breanna had no way to truly know. However, this had been a rousing victory for the Scots.

A warm breeze feathered across her face. With everything that had happened of late, she'd barely noted the passing of time. It was now May, and they'd spent the last months moving through Ayrshire, gathering recruits as they went.

And then, upon this meadow, where the highway ran, bounded either side by treacherous bogs, they'd met the English army in battle.

Breanna walked to the edge of one of the deep ditches filled with iron spikes that crossed the highway. An English soldier had been impaled there, his gaping face splattered with mud.

Despite that she'd been among the Scots to deal out death here today, Breanna grimaced. The soldier hadn't received a clean death. Nonetheless, these ditches had been clever indeed.

As always, the enemy had outnumbered them, but the Bruce had used his knowledge of this land to his advantage. The bogs hemmed them in, and before the arrival of the English, he'd had his men dig three ditches, with the hope of weakening the enemy's strength as they pushed through.

Breanna's mouth curved into a tight smile. Glen Trool had shown all of them how utilizing the land to their advantage was the only way to defeat a larger and better-equipped army.

Sir Aymer had arrived at the head of a glittering column of mounted knights and men-at-arms. The sight of the English army's superior strength had turned Breanna's bowels to water. Of course, she'd fought this enemy before, but although they'd rallied a number of men to their cause, the Bruce's army appeared a dirty rabble compared to this force.

But in the end, they'd been the victors.

Her gaze shifted to the highway beyond the ditches. Dead horses and men, and listing banners, were all that remained. The survivors, Sir Aymer among them, had eventually fled with the remnants of his army when it became clear that the battle was lost.

Turning then, Breanna spied her husband picking his way through the dead toward her.

Warmth spread across Breanna's chest at the sight of him—dimming the sickly chill that always settled over her after battle.

Cameron Stewart had made her his wife two months earlier. They'd been camped near Kilbride, and the pair of them had sneaked away to the village to find a priest who would wed them. Of course, since the Bruce and his companions believed Breanna and Cameron were already wed, they'd had to find strangers at an alehouse in Kilbride to bear witness to their union. In truth, there had been something thrilling about being wed in secret.

Mud and blood still encrusted Cameron's face, even though he'd done his best to wipe it clean. Breanna scrutinized him as he approached, relief washing over her at the sight of her husband uninjured save a few superficial cuts.

Likewise, Breanna only bore minor injuries. Her right thigh throbbed from where the edge of a knight's shield had driven into it—she'd have a livid bruise there by morning—and a shallow cut to her right arm throbbed dully. She'd need to get the physician that traveled with them to take a look.

But first, she'd wanted to pay her respects to the dead—on both sides.

Nearing her, Cameron favored Breanna with a tired smile. "I thought I'd find ye here."

She smiled back. "Ye know me well."

Moving close, he slung an arm around her shoulders. Breanna leaned into him, reveling in the strength and warmth of his body. It was a solace after the violence.

This battle had been the most brutal one she'd ever taken part in.

"Are ye well, Bree?" he asked gently.

She nodded. "Just exhausted." Her mouth kicked up into another smile then. "We did it ... we sent those bastards running."

He grinned back, his eyes gleaming. "Aye, lass ... even the mighty de Valence himself looked a bit worse for wear once we were done with him."

Their gazes fused then, and for a moment, Breanna forgot they stood amongst the dead. "The tide has turned now, Cam," she whispered. "Robert Bruce is going to fulfill the destiny the head of my order prophesized."

Cameron nodded. "The English are a tenacious lot ... but ye are right ... support for the Bruce grows daily. They won't be able to hold onto the Lowlands forever." He tightened his grip about her shoulders, steering Breanna away from the battlefield and back toward where the Bruce's men were making camp under the lee of Loudoun Hill, a rocky outcrop that rose above the meadow and bogs below. "Come, love, let us join the others ... our king is preparing to give a speech."

They crossed the meadow, and Breanna's chest constricted when she spied the faces of men she recognized amongst the Scottish dead. Their fallen compatriots would be gathered up and given a cairn, but first, the Bruce would address the living.

Entering the circle of half-erected pavilions and awnings, they made their way to the center of the camp.

The Bruce stood amid his men, flanked on one side by his brother Edward and James Douglas on the other. The outlaw king was a formidable sight in his blood-splattered hauberk and greaves. His bearded face was still set in fierce lines, almost as if the blood-lust of battle had not yet left him. Next to Robert, Edward wore a savage grin.

Men were handing out cups of ale. Cameron and Breanna helped themselves to one each before taking their places amongst the crowd.

The rumble of voices quietened then, and silence fell, punctuated only by the whistling of the wind and the screech of a kestrel gliding above. Spying the bird, Breanna smiled once more.

The bird of prey was a good omen, especially at a time like this: they represented clear-sightedness and vision.

"Friends!" Robert the Bruce's voice rumbled over the crowd. "Today, we have taken the first step in winning freedom for our people ... in releasing ourselves from English serfdom. We still have a long road to travel, but on this battlefield, we showed Longshanks that we won't suffer his yoke." The king paused then, his narrowed gaze sweeping the faces of those amassed before him. "Every one of ye showed courage and honor today ... and I will never forget it. Ye have made me yer king, and I will continue to prove myself worthy. Historians from England will say I am a liar ... that I have no claim to the Scottish throne ... but history is written by those who have hanged heroes."

Breanna's skin prickled at these words, and her breathing caught. She glanced at Cameron, observing his profile as he stared at the Bruce. The fierce determination on her husband's face caused her pulse to quicken.

Cameron Stewart had given up after Stirling, but the cynical mercenary she'd once known was gone. It had only ever been a shield, she realized—an attempt to protect himself from further pain. But the defenses he'd built around his heart had nearly sabotaged both their chances of happiness.

Breanna swallowed to ease the sudden tightness in her throat. She too had built a high curtain wall around her heart. After Grant, she'd sworn never to be vulnerable with a man again—and certainly never let herself love one. But Cameron Stewart had been impossible to resist. Even when she'd wanted to rail at him, wanted to take her fists to him, he'd drawn her in.

The man's strength, his courage, was difficult to match.

"All of ye are heroes today," the Bruce continued, his voice ringing out across the hillside. "Now raise yer cups, and we shall honor our countrymen who have fallen. They gave their lives for our freedom, and we shall never forget them." The Bruce's gaze swept the crowd, searing and fierce. "To freedom!"

A roar went up, and the prickling across Breanna's skin intensified. Her eyes stung with pride as she raised her cup high. "To freedom!"

Taking a gulp of ale, she enjoyed the cool bite on her parched throat. Breanna then turned back to Cameron. He'd turned his attention from the Bruce now and was watching her. The intensity of his gaze held her fast, and for a moment, the pair of them merely stared at each other, their surroundings and the cheers of the other warriors fading.

"To freedom, mo ghràdh," Breanna murmured, stepping close to her husband.

His mouth quirked in that arrogant smile that had once so infuriated her. These days, such a smile made her want to drag him into their tent and rip off his clothes. Now was no exception.

"And to us, Bree," he replied. "May we live to fight at the Bruce's side until the final victory is his ... and may we then settle down, have bairns, and grow old and fat together.”

Breanna huffed a laugh, even as warmth suffused her. As much as she wished to remain with the Bruce until the last of the English were driven from this land, she also longed for hearth and home. There hadn’t been any time in the past three months to travel to the Highlands, to visit The Wailing Widow Falls, even though she’d managed to send word to the High Bandruì. The order had accepted Hume into their ranks, and they would accept Cameron as well.

“And one day, we shall do just that,” she promised.

Breanna stepped into Cameron then. Her hand wrapped around his neck, and she pulled him in for a searing kiss.

Around seven years later ...

EPILOGUE

OUR LEGACY

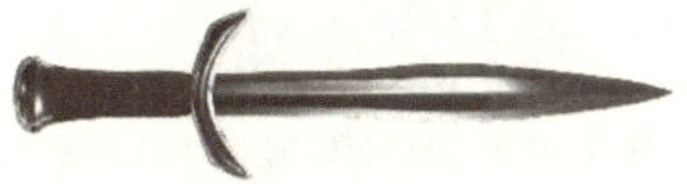

The Wailing Widow Falls
Assynt, Scotland

Late summer, 1314

"LACHLAN STEWART! STOP hitting yer sister!"

Breanna placed her hands on her hips and fixed the wee lad of six winters with a stern look. Lachlan, who had his father's wavy blue-black hair and her peat-brown eyes, had been clubbing his younger sister, Earie, with a branch he'd just fished out of the loch. Earie, who was almost four, had scrunched up her face and started to howl.

The sound drifted across the still, dark waters of Loch na Gainmhich and seemed to echo off the slopes of the mountain, Glas Bheinn, above them.

Her daughter wailed so loudly that Breanna was sure the druidesses residing within the cavern behind the nearby waterfalls would hear her.

Lachlan stilled his clubbing and glanced his mother's way, his gaze guileless. However, when Breanna saw the impish smile that curved his lips, she stepped forward and snatched the offending branch from his hands, throwing it into the loch. "Do that again, and I'll tan yer hide," she told him sternly.

"God's teeth, what's all this noise about?"

Breanna turned to see her husband emerge from behind their cottage. Naked to the waist, Cameron's torso gleamed with sweat. In one hand, he held an axe, for he'd been busy chopping wood.

Scooping up a still wailing Earie, Breanna stroked her daughter's back before rolling her eyes. "Just Lachlan bullying his sister."

Cameron's expression darkened at this, and the mischievous smile on Lachlan's face died. "It was just a game," he replied, his tone pleading.

Breanna cuffed him gently around the ear. "One yer sister wasn't enjoying."

"If the lad's idle, the twins could do with his help." Another male voice rumbled across the lakeshore. Breanna turned to see that Hume was standing over a pile of fishing nets, a few yards distant.

"Aye, Jean and Tara are picking brambles by Gainmhich creek," a woman's voice added.

Breanna realized that the commotion her bairns had been making had also drawn Fyfa from her cottage. The two dwellings sat just a few yards apart on the shore of the loch. For many years, the cottage where Hume, Fyfa, and their daughters lived had been a ruin. But Hume had patched it up and extended it.

When Breanna and Cameron had retired from campaigning with the Bruce, they'd decided to build their own cottage next door. They hadn't planned to return to Assynt so soon, but a year after the Battle of Loudoun Hill, Breanna's womb had quickened. Robert Bruce had insisted that the pair of them retire their blades and settle down together. "Ye have earned it," he'd told them, his gaze shining.

"A bonny idea," Cameron replied, his gaze still upon his son. "Maybe that will keep ye out of trouble, lad."

Lachlan wilted under his father's stern look. Digging a toe into the shingle shore, he was starting to look truly sorry for taking a branch to his wee sister. Breanna was pleased to see he was abashed. Her son was a sweet lad, but he had a mischievous edge to him—not surprising really since Cameron Stewart was his father.

"Off ye go then," she told her son. "And try not to eat too many berries."

Lachlan nodded before heading up the shore toward the creek that fed into the loch.

"Ma, I'm hungry," Earie announced after her brother departed, her tone plaintive.

Smiling, Breanna pushed her daughter's dark-brown hair off her damp cheeks. "Aye, noon isn't far away, my love ... auntie Fyfa is making us venison pie."

"Just as soon as I get the pastry done," Fyfa quipped.

Since they lived so close, Fyfa and Breanna took turns cooking for both families. They shared meals together most days, and although the bairns weren't actually related by blood, they saw each other as cousins. It was a surprisingly busy life. Breanna had thought she'd grow bored once she returned to the Highlands, especially since the Bruce still continued his campaign to take back Scotland, but pregnancy and childbirth changed her.

A contentment unlike any she'd ever known had settled over her upon the shores of Loch na Gainmhich. She hadn't expected to ever feel this happy, yet despite her quarreling bairns this morning, she did.

"Look, Ma!" Earie chirped once more, clutching at her arm. "Horses!"

Swiveling on her heel, Breanna reached for the dirk that she still carried at her hip. Fyfa often teased her about it, yet she'd replied that old habits died hard. And she was glad of her caution now. Likewise, Cameron had tightened his hold upon his axe as he moved to stand in front of his family. Wordlessly, Hume moved to his side.

Visitors were a rare occurrence here. The nearest village was half a day's walk, and apart from seeing the bandruìd who came up from the falls, they encountered few folk. Travelers didn't often pass near the Wailing Widow Falls.

Breanna's gaze narrowed. There were two of them, upon fine-looking bay coursers. And as the riders drew closer, Breanna's breathing quickened. It was a man and woman.

"It can't be," she breathed, her chest constricting.

But a moment later, she realized it indeed was.

Hugh and Nessa de Burgh were approaching.

Behind her, Breanna heard Fyfa murmur an oath. "Do my eyes deceive me?"

Breanna shook her head. "No."

Heart thundering against her ribs, she hurried forward, still clutching Earie, past Cameron and Hume—who both wore nonplussed expressions—to where Hugh and Nessa approached.

Breanna's attention seized upon Hugh de Burgh. The Marcher lord, who'd once been Edward of England's commander, wasn't what she expected. He had short light-brown hair, skin tanned golden by the summer, proud features, and a strong jaw. Piercing hazel eyes fastened upon her before his mouth lifted at the corners. And then, to her surprise, he spoke in fluent Gaelic. "Latha math, Breanna. Tha e math coinneachadh riut mu dheireadh."

Good day, Breanna. It's good to finally meet you.

Breanna's gaze flew wide. "How did ye know which one I was?" she asked.

His smile widened. "Nessa has spoken of ye and Fyfa many times over the years ... I feel as if I already know ye both."

"He's not lying." Nessa slid down from the saddle. "I prattle on about ye both regularly. He must tire of it."

"Never, my love," he replied, his smile sliding into a grin that made his eyes crinkle at the corners.

Setting down Earie, Breanna closed the gap between her and Nessa, throwing her arms around her. Nessa's eyes were glittering when they drew apart, and Breanna was blinking furiously in an effort to stem her own tears.

"Ye came!" Fyfa rushed in then, her cheeks flushed with joy, and embraced Nessa, nearly knocking Breanna over in her haste.

Nessa laughed as she drew back, tears running down her cheeks. "Of course ... ye invited me, didn't ye?"

"Aye, but it's been a while. I thought ye would never make the journey."

"We had to wait till things settled down on the border," Hugh said, interrupting their reunion. "We didn't want to attract any unwanted attention."

Breanna nodded, understanding. A month had passed since the English and Scots had clashed at Bannockburn—and the Bruce's victory had been a decisive one. Their sisters had brought word from the battlefield. Edward the Second, Longshanks's son, had fled with his bodyguards, while the rest of his troops flew into a panic. Edward had tried to seek refuge at Stirling Castle, but Sir Philip de Moubray, the English commander of the fortress, turned him away as Stirling would shortly be surrendered to the Scots. Edward had then made for Dunbar Castle, from which he'd taken a ship south.

"So, ye didn't have any trouble on the journey?" Cameron had approached and was watching Hugh with a hooded expression that Breanna knew well. He'd spent years fighting the English—and wasn't sure he wanted to welcome one of Longshanks's knights here. Hume had also come forward, and like Cameron, his expression was nakedly suspicious.

"None I couldn't handle," de Burgh replied with cool confidence.

"We wanted to bring our daughters with us but decided it was safer to leave them at Grosmont," Nessa added, her gaze flicking between her husband, Cameron, and Hume. Like Breanna, she'd noted the tension that crackled in the air.

"Aye, it was too dangerous a trip for Isabel and Margaret to make," her husband agreed. "We heard few of the English force reached the border. Save for a hardy group of Welsh archers."

Breanna nodded. She too had heard how Edward had abandoned his men to the wolves, saving his own hide instead.

"We also bring news that King Robert has secured the release of his wife, sister, and daughter," Hugh added. "They will be reunited with him within the month."

A weight that Breanna hadn't even realized she'd been carrying lifted from her shoulders. Robert Bruce had known so much tragedy—had lost much in his fight to take back Scotland. "This news is welcome indeed," she murmured. It hadn't been lost on her that Hugh had referred to the Bruce as 'King Robert'. And when she glanced back at her husband, she saw that both his and Hume's gazes had softened a little.

It hadn't been lost on them either.

Silence fell then, while the newcomers studied those they'd traveled to see. Breanna and the others did the same. Apart from a few fine lines around her eyes, Nessa didn't look that different at all. Breanna hoped that she too looked so youthful. Nessa still had those sharp green eyes and a knowing smile.

Wordlessly, Hugh de Burgh dismounted. The Marcher lord was a big man, Breanna noted, towering over his wife as he stepped up behind her.

Breanna met Nessa's eye once more, her breath catching. "I've missed ye so much."

"We both have," Fyfa added, her voice husky.

Nessa's throat bobbed. She reached out her hands then to Breanna and Fyfa, beckoning them closer.

They did as bid, each taking a hand.

"How long are ye planning to stay?" Hume asked, clearing his throat.

"A month at the least," de Burgh replied, meeting his eye. "If we are welcome?"

"Aye, of course ye are," Hume said gruffly. "We have a wing out the back for guests ... it will accommodate ye easily."

Hugh nodded in silent thanks.

Meanwhile, Nessa squeezed her sisters' hands. "I am happy at Grosmont, my sisters," she said, her voice a little raspy as she struggled to rein in her emotions. "But not a day has gone by that I haven't missed ye both."

"Of course," Breanna replied. She'd meant the reply to be airy, yet her own voice sounded raw to her ears. "Colina always said the three of us are connected ... even when we're apart."

"Aye, three foundlings," Fyfa added huskily, "who were left to die in the cold but lived and thrived against all the odds."

"And helped change history." Nessa favored them both with a soft smile. "Never forget that."

Breanna wouldn't. They'd all played their part in driving the English overlords from Scotland. History would not record their deeds, yet they needed no recognition from scribes. It was enough that they alone knew the truth. And along the way, all three of them had found love and now had families of their own.

Glancing over her shoulder, Breanna caught Cameron's eye. He'd scooped up Earie into his arms. Her husband wore a soft smile now and no longer held his axe in a death grip. To her relief, he winked at her, making it clear that he too welcomed their visitors.

Breanna turned back to her sisters before she reached out and took Fyfa's free hand, so the three of them formed a circle. "Aye," she said softly. "We are Guardians of Alba ... and we may work in the shadows, but our legacy will live on."

The End

FROM THE AUTHOR

Here we are at the end of the GUARDIANS OF ALBA. I hope you loved reading about three amazing women who helped shape Scottish history (well, in my version of history they did ... and who knows, they *could* have existed!). I'd been wanting to write a series like this for while—one where a group of women are integral to major historical events. The brains behind the brawn!

BREANNA'S SURRENDER was so much fun! Of course, I knew it would be—I mean, a fake relationship story with a roguish mercenary as the hero had to be. This was also a real 'on the road' tale (which, if you've read my previous books, you know I enjoy), and I loved being able to research the various (mostly real) locations that Breanna and Cameron visit during their adventures.

There's nothing more delicious (to me, at least) than heroes and heroines with painful pasts that have wounded them. I really felt for both Bree and Cam as I told their stories.

I also hope you enjoyed Lamia's side-story and conclusion. I do enjoy giving villainous characters a second chance (sometimes!) and hope of redemption.

Jayne x

HISTORICAL NOTES

If you've read the previous two books of the
GUARDIANS OF ALBA, you'll know I did a mountain of
research for this series!

Of course, this story-world blends a touch of fantasy with
real historical fact. However, I took care to base my
witches of the Guardians of Alba order on ancient Celtic
druidic and Wiccan practices, to give the order a feeling
of authenticity.

In BREANNA'S SURRENDER, we follow Robert the
Bruce on campaign and watch him rise from the ashes of
defeat (during his darkest period). I decided to begin the
story in the aftermath of the Battle of Methven.

The Battle of Methven took place on June 19, 1306, and
was a crushing defeat for the Scots. The Bruce had drawn
his army up outside the walls of Perth and called on
Aymer de Valence, the English commander, to come out
and fight. De Valence, who had the reputation of 'a man
of honor' had made the excuse that it was too late in the
day to do battle. Instead, he'd assured them he would
accept the challenge the following day. Only he hadn't—
instead, unbeknown to the Bruce, Edward of England
had instructed de Valence that no mercy was to be given.
As such, the English had attacked while the Scots
camped overnight in woodland outside Perth.

In the aftermath of Methven, Robert the Bruce lost his
brother Neil, and his wife, sister, and daughter were all
taken prisoner by the English. Neil had taken Robert's
womenfolk to safety at Kildrummy Castle, but,
unfortunately, they were betrayed from within by one of
their own—a blacksmith who was offered 'as much gold
as he could carry' if he set fire to the grain stores. The
man did as bid and with their food supply destroyed, the

men of Kildrummy were forced to surrender. Neil Bruce
was arrested before he was hanged, drawn, and
quartered. As a brutal post-script, the treacherous
blacksmith was caught—and then 'as much gold as he
could carry' was melted and poured down his throat.

When our story begins in December 1306, Robert the
Bruce was hiding out on Rathlin Island, off the coast of
Ulster. Previously he'd sought refuge at Dunaverty Castle
near the Mull of Kintyre (which is why Bree and Cam
head there first), but with his enemies closing in, he was
forced to move on.

His time at Rathlin was the Bruce's darkest hour—a
period in which he was reputed to nearly have lost hope.
In this story, I tell the tale about Robert the Bruce and
the spider. Some tales have him taking refuge in a cave
(which I also mention) rather than the castle, although
it's more probable that he was hosted by Hugh Bissett,
lord of this castle and island, and of the Glens of Antrim
in Ulster. In the cave, the Bruce was reputed to have
watched a spider try and fail numerous times before the
plucky insect finally built its web. Watching its struggle
and eventual success spurred him to return to the
mainland in February 1307 and take back his lands,
beginning with Turnberry.

Fun fact—did you know that some scholars have
attributed the phrase "If at first you don't succeed try, try
and try again," to Robert the Bruce. Apparently, he was
meant to have told his troops this shortly before beating
the English at Bannockburn in 1314.

And speaking of historical quotes attributed to the Bruce,
I have used three in this story:

*"We fight not for glory, nor for wealth, nor honor but
only and alone for freedom which no good man
surrenders but with his life."*

"I have brought you to the ring, now you must dance."

"Historians from England will say I am a liar, but history is written by those who have hanged heroes."

During the course of writing my novel, I tried to remain as true as possible to actual historical events. As stated above, the Bruce did defeat the English army camped outside Turnberry Castle (led by Henry de Percy, who was forced to flee after his defeat), although he didn't manage to take back the castle itself.

Tragedy continued to stalk Robert the Bruce though. One of his brothers, Edward (who was indeed reputed to be an aggressive hothead!) traveled with him when he returned to the mainland. However, he sent his two youngest brothers, Thomas and Alexander south with eighteen galleys to land at Loch Ryan farther south along the coast. Unfortunately, they were attacked by the MacDougals, allies of the Comyns, in retribution for the Bruce's murder of John Comyn a year earlier. Thomas and Alexander were then handed over to the English, where they were hanged, drawn, and quartered as their elder brother (and William Wallace) had been.

Heading into the Galloway hills the Bruce launched a successful campaign of guerilla warfare. Methven had taught him a few lessons. He knew that the English force was larger and better equipped—and as such he used his knowledge of the Scottish countryside to his advantage. This knowledge helped him gain the victory at Glen Trool (as shown in this story). Indeed, the Scots positioned themselves at the top of 'The Steps of Trool' and sent large boulders hurtling down the slope before they engaged the English with arrows and in hand-to-hand combat.

I have the Bruce learning of his brothers' deaths after his victory at Glen Trool, although it's likely he discovered it earlier.

The real turning point for the Bruce that year was his victory at Loudoun Hill on May 10, 1307. Once again, he used his knowledge of Scottish topography to his advantage, meeting the English force, led by Aymer de Valence, on a highway that led through a meadow bounded either side by treacherous bogs. He had three ditches dug across the highway, hindering the enemy and forcing them into a narrow space. Once the battle turned against them, de Valence fled with his surviving men.

Nonetheless, the Bruce wouldn't earn a definitive victory until June 1314 and the Battle of Bannockburn, when he defeated the English, led by Edward II. After this victory, his wife, sister, and daughter were finally returned to him.

All the settings in this novel are based on real locations:

Dunaverty Castle: this fortress is located at Southend at the southern end of the Kintyre peninsula in western Scotland. The site was once a fort belonging to the Clan Donald (MacDonald). Little remains of the castle. Its remains stand on a rocky headland, which formed a natural stronghold with the sea on three sides and is only approachable from the north. A narrow path would have led up to the castle, which would have been accessed by a drawbridge.

Rathlin Castle: the castle sits upon Rathlin Island, and today only a ruined shell remains. Rathlin is the only inhabited offshore island of Northern Ireland, and today has a population of approximately 150 people. In 1306, Robert the Bruce sought refuge upon Rathlin, which was then owned by the Irish Bissett family.

Turnberry Castle: like Dunaverty and Rathlin, Turnberry is little more than a ruin these days. However, it was once the seat of the Bruce family, and to Robert the Bruce himself. Turnberry Castle is surrounded on three sides by the sea, and although it took Robert Bruce many years to win back the castle from the English, he ordered the destruction of the castle in 1310, to prevent it from falling into the hands of the English ever again.

Glen Trool: this glen is located in the Southern Uplands, Galloway. It contains Loch Trool, which is fed by several burns and drained by the Water of Trool. It is also the site of the Battle of Glen Trool, a minor engagement in the First War of Scottish Independence, fought in April 1307 (you will note I set the battle around a month earlier in my story!).

The only fictional location in my story is Cree Castle, although River Cree itself does flow through Galloway.

I hope you enjoyed this window into the research, settings, and background to the novel. All these details help to make the story all the richer!

ABOUT THE AUTHOR

Award-winning author Jayne Castel writes epic Historical and Fantasy Romance. Her vibrant characters, richly researched historical settings, and action-packed adventure romance transport readers to forgotten times and imaginary worlds.

Jayne is the author of a number of best-selling series. In love with all things Scottish, she writes romances set in both Dark Ages and Medieval Scotland.

When she's not writing, Jayne is reading (and re-reading) her favorite authors, cooking Italian feasts, and going on long walks with her husband. She lives in New Zealand's beautiful South Island.

Connect with Jayne online:
www.jaynecastel.com
www.facebook.com/JayneCastelRomance
https://www.instagram.com/jaynecastelauthor/
Email: contact@jaynecastel.com

www.ingramcontent.com/pod-product-compliance
Lightning Source LLC
Chambersburg PA
CBHW021113110726
47900CB00007B/2171